Those Who Fight Monsters

Tales of Occult Detectives

Edited by Justin Gustainis

EDGE SCIENCE FICTION AND FANTASY PUBLISHING
AN IMPRINT OF HADES PUBLICATIONS, INC.

CALGARY

EDGE

Edge Science Fiction and Fantasy Publishing
An Imprint of Hades Publications Inc.
P.O. Box 1714, Calgary, Alberta, T2P 2L7, Canada

Edited by Justin Gustainis
Interior design by Janice Blaine
Cover Illustration by Robert Nixon
ISBN: 978-1-894063-48-7

EDGE Science Fiction and Fantasy Publishing and Hades Publications, Inc. ac-
knowledges the ongoing support of the Alberta Foundation for the Arts and the
Canada Council for the Arts for our publishing programme.

Library and Archives Canada Cataloguing in Publication

Those who fight monsters : tales of occult detectives / edited by Justin
Gustainis.

Issued also in electronic format.
ISBN 978-1-894063-48-7
1. Detective and mystery stories, American.
2. Occult fiction, American. I. Gustainis, Justin

PS648.D4T46 2011   813'.087208   C2010-907824-1

FIRST EDITION
(l-20110113)
Printed in Canada
www.edgewebsite.com

"From ghoulies, and ghosties, and
long-leggedity beasties, and things
that go bump in the night, Good Lord
deliver us."

Old Scottish prayer

"There *are* things that go bump in the
night... And we are the ones who bump *back*."

Professor Trevor Bruttenholm

Table of Contents

THOSE WHO FIGHT MONSTERS

MONSTERS

Tales of Occult Detectives

INTRODUCTION

"Down These Mean Crypts a (Wo)Man Must Walk"

by Justin Gustainis

As the subtitle tells you, this book is devoted to stories of occult detectives, a term that I define fairly broadly—to include any fictional character who contends regularly with the supernatural. Thus, although not all occult detectives are monster fighters, all monster fighters are clearly occult detectives.

We decided to go with the present main title because *Those Who Detect the Occult* just didn't have the same "zing" to it.

The character of the occult detective has been part of our popular culture for more than a century. The most comprehensive listing of supernatural sleuths can be found at G. W. Thomas' "Ghostbreakers" website (occultdetective.tripod.com/all.htm), although it needs updating. Thomas lists 164 occult detective characters—in books, films, comics and television—appearing between the mid-Nineteenth Century and 1999.

From the beginning, (probably J. Sheridan Le Fanu's Martin Hessilius, in 1872), the occult detective often wasn't—a detective, that is. He was often a doctor, sometimes a scientist, occasionally (as in the person of Abraham Van Helsing) both.

In modern fiction, the occult detective may be, among other things, a private eye, a police officer (in a universe that recognizes the supernatural), a reporter, a bounty hunter, a priest, a wizard/ witch for hire, an antiquarian, an assassin—even a waitress.

As this collection shows, the contemporary occult detective takes many forms, and may be male (John Taylor) or female (Jill Kismet), human (Pete Caldicott) or nonhuman (Dan Hendrickson), professional (Marla Mason) or amateur (Kate Connor), a saint (Piers Knight, sort of) or a sinner (Jezebel), gay (Tony Foster) or straight (Quincey Morris), cop (Jessi Hardin) or criminal (Tony Giodone). But each shares at least two traits with the others: specialized knowledge, and the courage to use it. Thus, they have more in common with the hard-boiled private eye than the classical sleuth. The occult detective is closer to Philip Marlowe than Hercule Poirot, and today usually appears in stories that are more "hard-boiled" than "cozy."

Classical detective stories were all about the puzzle, usually (if ungrammatically) expressed as "who done it?" Once the cerebral investigator solved the mystery, action was usually left up to the authorities ("Inspector, arrest that man!").

But the private eye goes beyond mere deduction. He (or she) may investigate, certainly—examining evidence, interviewing witnesses, consulting experts to interpret what has been uncovered. But, having put the pieces of the puzzle together to form a unified whole, the private eye *does* something about it. The title of Mickey Spillane's first Mike Hammer novel expresses this point clearly: *I, the Jury.* And although most fictional private eyes are not brutal vigilantes like Mike Hammer, they usually share his desire to act against the bad guys, once the latter have been uncovered; it is no coincidence that in *The Big Sleep* Philip Marlowe compares himself to "a knight in dark armor."

This willingness to confront evil on its own terms is also characteristic of the occult detective, who knows that wooden stakes have other uses besides holding up tents, and wolfsbane is not just a pretty flower.

However, the occult detective is more than just a supernatural private eye. In fact, I would argue that he or she embodies some of the central roles found in any society.

The occult detective serves as a *doctor*, who brings specialized knowledge and skill to bear upon some affliction—someone who can diagnose the illness, treat it effectively, and propose effective preventative measures for the future.

The occult detective takes the role of a *shaman*, who understands the supernatural world and those who dwell within it.

The shaman serves as a communication channel between the two worlds—and sometimes, even travels between them.

The occult detective is a *hero*, in the classical sense—an extraordinary individual who, with strength, skill, and courage, protects the community from those who would do it harm.

Small wonder, then, that the contemporary occult detective has found a home within the fiction genre (or sub-genre) known as "urban fantasy"—a term that usually refers to stories set in a world much like our own, but with the addition of a supernatural element.

Occult detectives predate the category "urban fantasy," but then so does urban fantasy itself. The literature came first, the label sometime later. Applying the generally accepted definition, Stoker's *Dracula* was urban fantasy—at the time it was published. The story depicts the actual Victorian world its readers lived in—with the interesting addition, however, of the undead.

The movie *Ghostbusters* (1984) also appeared before the common use of "urban fantasy," but clearly falls within that category. The film takes place in a New York City much like the real one, except that ghosts and other supernatural creatures exist, posing varying degrees of danger to the populace—from slimy annoyance to the potential End of the World as We Know It.

The film's opening theme asks, "Who you gonna call? And by the time the marshmallow man is toast, we all know the answer.

More than twenty-five years have passed since Venkman and the boys first strapped on their gear, but the essential question remains unchanged. Even in the 21st century, whenever demons walk the earth, werewolves prowl the countryside, or vampires ride the night winds in search of innocents' blood...

Who you gonna call?

In the pages that follow, courtesy of some of today's best writers of urban fantasy, you will find fourteen delightful, disturbing, and downright creepy answers to that question.

I hope you enjoy them.

—J. G.

LITTLE BETTER THAN A BEAST

— A Marla Mason Story —

by T. A. Pratt

"This is for you, Miss Mason." Granger, the idiot hereditary magician of Fludd Park, handed a crumpled envelope across her desk.

Marla took the envelope, which was smudged from Granger's mud-streaked hands, and hefted it. It was age-browned and soft, made of some heavy paper with a lot of cloth mixed into the fibers. "And what's this?"

"It's been in our house underneath the trees," Granger said, smiling affably, face as broad and unsubtle as a snowplow blade. "In the safe, with a note, that said, give to the chief sorcerer of Felport on such and such a date."

Marla frowned. There was nothing written on the envelope, and it was sealed with several blobby hunks of wax. She could make out the barest shape of an impression in the central blob, maybe some kind of bird, a hawk or a crow, as if a signet ring had been pressed into the wax when it was soft, a million years ago. "This has been in your family, like for safekeeping? For how long?"

Granger looked at the ceiling and hummed and drummed his blunt fingers on the desk, which was how you could tell he was thinking. Marla didn't have much use for nature magicians in general, and inbred nature magicians with an inviolate hereditary line of succession and a seat on her highest councils were even worse. "A long time. As many springs as there are days in a year, maybe much more."

Three-hundred-sixty-five *years* or so, then? That would date this letter from the earliest days of Felport's founding in the 17th century, back when it was nothing but a few settlers clinging to life. In those days Granger's great-great-great-great-whatever-grandfather was just the sorcerer in charge of keeping the town commons and farmland healthy and green, long before the village became a thriving shipping and industrial center, and even longer before its recent rusty decline, an economic slowdown Marla was doing her best to reverse in her capacity as chief sorcerer and protector of the city. None of the city's population of ordinaries, oblivious to the magic in their midst, would know the new biotech companies and urban renewal projects were Marla's doing, but that was okay; she wasn't in this job for the glory. She just loved her city, and wanted it to thrive.

"Any idea what the letter says?" Marla didn't particularly want to open the thing. She'd had a bad winter, combating a plague of nightmares, along with the interdimensional invaders old Tom O'Bedbug still insisted were fairies from Faeryland, and she'd been hoping for a quiet spring. She didn't think a letter from the early days of the city would be likely to contain good news.

"No ma'am, we were told to hold it, not read it, just keep it until such and such a date." His beaming face suddenly closed down, smile gone like the sun slipping behind a mountain. "But I got distracted, spring is coming and times are so busy in the park, so such and such a date accidentally passed, some days ago, only as many days as I have fingers, about, not so many as could be, not too late, right?"

Marla picked up a letter opener shaped like the grim reaper's scythe. "So I was supposed to get this a week or ten days ago?"

"Thereabouts," Granger said, head bobbing, happy they were in agreement.

If I could fire him, or have him committed... But Granger was a powerful magician, in his way, and even if he wasn't much use to the city's secret shadow government of sorcerers, he mostly stayed out of the way in the park, and his elementals had been formidable warriors in last winter's battle against the nightmare-things. She considered reprimanding him for not bringing the letter on time, but it would be like hitting a puppy fifteen minutes after it pissed on the carpet—the poor thing wouldn't even understand what it was being disciplined for.

Marla used the letter opener to pry up the wax blobs, then unfolded the envelope, which wasn't an envelope at all, but just a sheet of paper folded in on itself. The message wasn't very long, but it said everything it needed to.

She came around the desk, shouting "Rondeau! I need you!" and clutching her dagger of office. This was going to be a bloody afternoon.

"Is everything okay?" Granger said, bewildered by her sudden action.

"Everything's just beastly," Marla said.

"The mother-effing beast of *Felport*," Rondeau said, long strides matching Marla's own as they hurried along the sidewalk toward the center of the old city, north of the river. This was a neighborhood of cobblestone streets and quaint crammed-together shops (many spelled "shoppe" on the signs, with the odd "ye olde" as a modifier), a touristy district where you could buy hunks of fudge as big as pillows and stay in a bed-and-breakfast where an early president had slept, once, allegedly.

"That's what the letter says." Marla frowned at the compass-charm in her hand, ducking into an alleyway that led, she hoped, to the tiny square that was the site of Felport's founding. There was a fancier, more obvious Founder's Square a few blocks away, with a monument, but she was dealing with magical rather than the municipal history. She wanted the spot where Felport's first chief sorcerer, Everett Malkin, spoke the spells of binding that tied each successive chief sorcerer to the city, ritually entangling the strengths, weaknesses, and interests of Felport itself with its protectors.

"So, uh, what exactly is the beast of Felport? Werewolf, demon, undead mutant water buffalo? My grasp of local history is a little shaky." Rondeau shifted the heavy shoulder bag Marla'd given him to carry, and things inside clinked together.

"Probably because you never went to school," Marla said. Rondeau was her closest friend and business associate—he owned the nightclub where she kept her office, and they'd saved one another's lives far more often than they'd endangered them—but he'd had a non-traditional childhood and never saw the inside of a classroom. "Nobody seems to know exactly what the beast was. In the early 17th century, Felport was just a trading post with a nice bit of coastline, good for loading up and emptying boats. People kept trying to settle here in greater numbers...and something kept killing them, even worse than the usual New World problems of murderous natives and disease and bad winters and starvation. Bodies would be found chewed up, missing certain necessary organs, like that, killed by something worse than bears, nobody knew what—some kind of beast. People started calling the place 'the fell port'— 'fell' as in dangerous, bad, scary—which is where the city got its name. Eventually a sorcerer named Everett Malkin came along, really liked the location, and convinced some settlers to join him, despite the region's nasty reputation. He said he'd keep the beast of Felport, whatever it was, away. And he did. He was the city's first chief sorcerer."

Rondeau yawned. "I'm glad I missed school. That story was boring, except for the bit about dead bodies. So if Everett whatever killed the beast hundreds of years ago, how is it supposed to bother us today?"

"I didn't say he killed it—he drove it off." Marla stopped walking, looked at her compass charm, which was spinning wildly, and nodded. "This is the spot." They were in a tiny cobblestoned courtyard, a pocket of forgotten space with only one alley leading in and out, surrounded by the windowless portions of various old brick buildings. A droopy tree grew in an unfenced square of grayish dirt, and a storm drain waited patiently to collect the next spring thunderstorm's rain, but otherwise the courtyard was bare.

"So what now?" Rondeau said, flipping open his butterfly knife.

Marla shaded her eyes and looked at the square of sky above. Very nearly noon. "Well, if I'd gotten the letter a week ago like I was supposed to, I'd have this place surrounded with containment teams and every contingency plan imaginable, and I'd feel pretty well prepared after spending a few days reading Malkin's old enciphered journals, and researching every conceivable theory on the beast of Felport. But, since Granger is an idiot and I had no advance notice, we wait for midday, and if something appears, we beat the shit out of it."

Rondeau put down the shoulder bag and Marla sorted through it, taking out charmed stones, knives crackling with imbued energies, and even an aluminum baseball bat ensorcelled with inertial magic to give it an extra bone-shattering wallop. Finally, she removed her white cloak lined inside with purple, her most potent and dangerous magic, which exacted a terrible price every time she used it. She put on the cloak, fastening it at the throat with a silver pin in the shape of a stag beetle, telling herself she probably wouldn't need its power. After all, how bad could the beast be? It was a *beast*. Sure, the stories said it was all kinds of unstoppable, but tales tended to grow in the telling, and four hundred years offered lots of time for embellishment.

After hefting the bat, Rondeau flipped his knife closed and put it away, choosing the blunt object over the razor's edge. "Okay, you got a letter from Everett whatever saying he sent the beast of Felport umpty-hundred years into the future, and you might want to keep your eyes out for it. This raises a couple of questions for me."

"Oh, good. I love your questions. They're always so insightful." Marla did a few stretches, her joints popping, then checked the knives up her sleeves.

"Number one: I thought time travel was impossible?"

"Traveling backwards in time is. Or, at least, no sorcerer I've heard of has ever cracked it. Some adepts say they figured out how to move forward in time, though it's more like putting yourself off to the side in an extra-dimensional stasis, set to re-enter normal space-time at a later date, unaffected by the passing time. But not many try to do it, since there's no way you can go *back* again after seeing the wondrous future." She took a leather pouch over to the alleyway and emptied it, dumping a dozen thumbtacks and pushpins—all augmented with charms of snaring and paralysis—across the courtyard's only exit, just in case.

"Seems like it could be a good trick for waiting out the statute of limitations," Rondeau said, in the tone of voice that meant he was contemplating casino robberies.

Marla snorted. "Any sorcerer capable of going forward in time would have more elegant ways to avoid being arrested for something, Rondeau. It's bigtime mojo. I couldn't do it, and I can do damn near anything I set my mind to."

"Too bad. It'd be nice to skip the occasional boring weekend. Okay, so my second question: isn't sending the beast of Felport to the future kind of a dick move? Getting rid of your current problems and leaving it for your descendants to deal with?"

"Yep," Marla said. "Everett Malkin was, by most accounts, a nasty piece of work. A badass sorcerer with a knack for violence and the interpersonal warmth of a komodo dragon—"

"Doesn't sound like anybody I know," Rondeau murmured.

"—but, to be fair, the guy was in kind of a bind. The story goes he used charms and protective circles and various kinds of exorcism and banishment and eventually even tried appeasement, by which I mean human sacrifice, to keep the beast of Felport at bay, but it was all just temporary. The thing kept coming back. He couldn't kill it, couldn't drive it away, just failed and failed, and his little settlement was on the verge of permanent disintegration. So one day he sucked it up, gave his dagger of office to his apprentice and chosen successor, and went out into the woods to finish things once and for all. And, apparently, he left this letter explaining his plan to send the beast into the future, to be delivered to whatever poor sucker happened to be in charge four centuries later." Marla shrugged. "Malkin never came back, but the beast never troubled anyone again, and now we're waiting for...whatever."

"Maybe he didn't send the beast into the future at all," Rondeau said. "Maybe they just, like, killed each other."

"We can hope," Marla said, but the words had barely been uttered when the courtyard suddenly got a lot more crowded.

A hard wind blew, making Marla squint, and a brown hairy thing the size of two gorillas fighting over a tractor tire appeared about three feet in the air, then slammed to the ground hard enough to crack the stones. There was an impression of tusks, snout, and hard black eyes, but it was hunched and crouched and twisting and moving too fast for her mind to encompass it. It stank like the sewers under a slaughterhouse. Marla began speaking words of binding and tossed a handful of charmed stones, but the rocks just bounced off the thing's matted hide— disappointing, since they should have respectively burned, frozen, and turned it to stone—and then an arm swung out, long as an extension ladder, and smashed Marla against a brick wall. Rondeau went in manfully, baseball bat cocked, but the thing swatted him aside like an annoying fly.

Marla stood up, about to reverse her cloak, to make the soothing white exterior switch places with the bruise-purple lining and unleash her most deadly battle magic—when the beast flung something slightly larger than Marla herself through the air, straight at her.

That's a person, Marla realized, and then about two hundred pounds of human body—dead or alive, she wasn't sure yet— hit her square in the chest and knocked her flat. She grunted, shoved the guy off her body, and struggled to her feet, all the wind knocked out of her.

The beast of Felport took a moment to consider its handi-work, and Marla thought, *Run for the alley, fucker, get caught in my bear traps*, and then the beast crouched, leapt about fifteen feet in the air, grabbed a jutting chunk of brick wall, and went up the side of a building and over the rooftop, like a gecko climbing a garden wall.

"That's bad," Rondeau said, picking himself up and taking out his cell phone. "Guess I should call the Chamberlain."

"It's her neighborhood," Marla said, "and I sent her a message before we left telling her there might be some shit hitting her fan this afternoon. Damn it."

Rondeau looked toward the roof where the beast had escaped. "Yeah. Who knew anything so big could jump like that?"

"I did," said the body the beast had thrown at Marla, sitting up and rubbing his head. He was a big, broad-shouldered man with a nose like a cowcatcher and bushy eyebrows, dressed in the filthy ragged remains of what might once have been nice old-fashioned clothes. He rose and stalked toward Rondeau. "And so would *you* if you had read the journals I left behind, detailing everything I knew about the beast! You came here utterly unpre-pared. What kind of chief sorcerer *are* you?"

"He's no kind of chief sorcerer at all," Marla said, already seeing where this was going. "I'm the chief sorcerer here."

The man whirled to face her, frowning. "You?" He gestured to Rondeau. "This one is a swarthy immigrant of some kind, that is troubling enough, but you—you are a *woman*."

"Yes," Marla said. "Very perceptive. And you're Everett Malkin, I presume."

"Incredible," Malkin said, staring at the cars going past.

"Yup," Marla said. "I guess it would be." The three of them sat on a bus stop bench, waiting for the Chamberlain's limo to arrive.

"The city itself, though I'm pleased to see its growth, has changed but little. I have spent time in the capitals of Europe, after all."

Wait until you see the skyscrapers in the Financial District, Marla thought. *Or the clubs and quickie check-cashing joints and bars in my neighborhood*. They were still in the old city, where an attempt was made to keep a certain vintage feel, but culture shock would hit him eventually.

"You plan to call together the whole council?" Malkin asked. He gnawed at an apple Marla'd bought for him. Rondeau's joke about how he must be hungry, seeing as how he hadn't eaten in 400 years, had fallen flat, though, and Rondeau had been quiet and sulky ever since.

"Just the Chamberlain for now. This is her neighborhood, and from what you said, the beast won't go too far. If it's in her baili-wick, the Chamberlain will find it."

Malkin grunted. "Another 'her.' You are the chief sorcerer, or so you tell me—should not the heart of the city be your 'neigh-borhood,' as you say?"

Marla snorted. "This? This is toy-town. A tourist trap. Old-fashioned stuff for history buffs and tourists scared to stay in the *real* city. The heart of the city nowadays, where the action is, that's south of the river. That's where I live."

Malkin mulled that over, and finally said, "You have told me of the Chamberlain, and the current Granger—sad it is to hear his lineage has decayed. I would not have entrusted him with the letter had I known his offspring would be ruined—but who are the other sorcerers of note? In my day it was only myself, Granger, and my apprentice, Corbin."

"There's a chaos magician named Nicolette, she looks after the financial district. The Bay Witch watches the water and the port. A sympathetic magician named Hamil over by the university. Viscarro, who lives in catacombs beneath the city. A junkyard wizard named Ernesto out in the industrial section. That's about it for the council, but there are lots of talented apprentices and freelancers in town, too—a mad-scientist technomancer type named Langford, an order-magician named Mr. Beadle—not to mention the usual wannabes and alley wizards."

"I will need to meet all of them as soon as they can be gath-ered," Malkin said.

"Oh, yeah?" It was rare for all the sorcerers to get together—they usually only had councils when some dire threat menaced the city, something Marla couldn't handle herself, and she wasn't sure yet the beast of Felport qualified. "Why's that?"

"They must meet their new chief sorcerer," Malkin said. "I will assume your position, of course."

Before Marla could respond to *that* bit of apocalyptic non-sense, a long black limousine slid along the curb before them, its back door swinging open. The Chamberlain, dressed in her usual impeccable evening-wear finery, beckoned with an elegant hand. "Come on, then. Let's hear about the latest disaster."

Malkin leaned forward, squinting. "Is this woman...a Spaniard?"

"I'm black, dear," she said. "Of West African descent, though my people are from Felport for many generations."

"This future is a peculiar place," Malkin said, but he climbed into the limousine after Rondeau, settling himself down on the dark leather seats across from the Chamberlain and Marla. Despite his ragged appearance—and the fact that this was his first time in a car—he looked at ease. "Your carriage is...most pleasant."

"I understand you brought a monster to my community," the Chamberlain said, smiling a smile that was not friendly at all.

Malkin frowned. "I expected sorcerous techniques to improve in the intervening centuries, so that the current rulers could defeat the beast with ease."

"Kind of like people who die of brain cancer and have their heads frozen so they can be thawed out in the future when there's a cure for tumors and decapitation," Rondeau said, apparently trying to be helpful.

Malkin just looked at him blankly and continued. "Instead I find an unprepared...*woman* playing at sorcery, who did let the beast escape."

"You might want to watch it with the sexist shit," Marla said. "You're kind of outnumbered here."

"Women can excel at erotic magic, and herbwifery, and certain nature magics, but the more intellectual rigors of advanced sorceries are not suitable for the weaker sex." Malkin shrugged. "I mean no offense. These are merely facts."

"Are you *sure* we can't send him back in time?" the Chamberlain said.

"I don't even know what he's doing *forward* in time," Marla said. "Your letter said you were setting a time-trap for the beast. Why the hell did you hitch a ride?"

"The beast seized me," Malkin said, shifting uncomfortably. "We struggled. Then the beast stepped into the circle of power. We were transported. I...did not intend to join him."

"Well, now you're here, and so's the beast, so tell us what we're dealing with," Marla said.

Malkin nodded. "The natives said the beast was a dark god that had roamed the land since the beginning of time. It cannot be harmed by iron, or fire, or blades, or charms. Even my dagger of office, which can cut through all things, only scratched the beast, and the wound closed instantly."

Marla touched the dagger at her waist—it had been Malkin's dagger, passed down from chief sorcerer to chief sorcerer over the centuries, and it was one of her most potent weapons, capable of slicing through everything from steel cables to ghosts.

"Some magics worked," Malkin said. "A spell to make it sleep for a thousand years succeeded in making it slumber, for but half a dozen seasons. Spells of disorientation caused it to wander, lost, for another year. But it *learns*, and once it overcomes a particular spell, the spell loses all efficacy. I do not know if it is a demon, a sorcerer from long ago who attained immortality, or, indeed, an ancient god."

"Okay, but what does it *want*?" Marla said.

"Want? It is a *beast*. It wants to kill all who encroach on its territory. It wants to rend flesh. It prefers to sleep in the day, and emerge at night, wandering and howling. Its motives are no more comprehensible than those of any other beasts. I am sure it is disoriented by the changes here, and it will go to ground somewhere, hiding, and wait until dark to emerge. And then ..." He shook his head. "The beast will not stop until the city is scoured to dirt. It is clever. It will set fires, build traps. Your people will die."

Setting arson and building booby traps didn't sound very beast-like to Marla, but then, Malkin was from another time—he considered Marla and the Chamberlain and even Rondeau, who was Hispanic, basically beasts, too, didn't he?

"Call together a council," Malkin said to the Chamberlain. "I will announce my return to the position of chief sorcerer, and formulate a strategy."

The Chamberlain looked at Marla, raising an eyebrow, and Marla sighed. "I'm not stepping down, Captain Retro. I'm still in charge here. We honor your past service and all that jazz, but you can't just come back and—"

"Silence, woman. Give me my dagger of office, and let me begin my work. Sorcery is no business for you. Despite your mannish affect you are not unattractive, so perhaps you can serve me in some other—"

Marla punched him in the throat. Malkin gagged, grabbing at his windpipe—Marla hadn't hit him hard enough to do permanent damage, but he wouldn't be speaking any spells for a while—and fished a sachet of sleep potion out of her pocket. The Chamberlain and Rondeau both grabbed their noses as Marla slapped the cloth pouch of lavender and stranger herbs into

Malkin's open mouth. He gagged, gasped, and then dropped into a deep, supernatural slumber.

"This guy," Marla said. "This guy is going to be trouble. I don't think I'll be able to sucker-charm him again, either."

"He does need to confront certain new realities," the Chamberlain said. "But, Marla, that's *Everett Malkin*. He's legendary." The Chamberlain had a certain reverence for the past —much of her power came from her relationship with the ghosts of Felport's founding families, including the persistent spirits of many former sorcerers from the early days.

"I liked him better when he was just a legend," Marla said. "He'll be asleep for a while, you mind watching him for me?"

"I—I suppose. And if he wakes up, he can speak with the ghosts—his apprentice, Corbin, is among the residents on my estate. But, Marla, what of the beast?"

"Yeah," Marla said. "The beast is another problem. I'm gonna have to go see a guy about that."

Marla wore black, loose-fitting pants and a snug top that kept her arms free, the better to aim the specially modified sniper rifle she cradled. Rondeau was dressed like an extra in a movie about a special forces operation, all black padded vest and a helmet and night-vision goggles (which he found more fun than Marla's more practical magical night vision). He persistently referred to their operation as "playing dress-up," which was annoying, but Marla knew she could rely on him in a pinch—and he had a backup rifle, albeit less fancy than the weapon Marla held. They were on the dark balcony of a charming little pied-a-terre a few blocks from the place where the beast and Malkin had appeared. The apartment's rightful residents were off in Aspen or something, wherever rich ordinaries spent early spring.

"What if the dart doesn't work?" Rondeau said. "We got a plan B?"

"I throw you to the beast, and while he's dismembering you, I sneak around and hit him on the head with the rifle butt."

"That's *always* your plan B."

The Chamberlain's diviners had tracked the beast to an uninhabited apartment across the quiet upscale residential street, where their best remote-viewer said it was sleeping heavily on a mound of blankets and the shredded remains of a mattress. The beast hadn't torn the door off its hinges to get inside—it had unobtrusively jimmied a side door with its claws. Smart beast, laying low. Marla wondered if it would be possible to communicate with it...but communication wasn't part of the plan.

"Something moved there," Rondeau said, pointing to the front window, where a shadow had shifted. "Poor thing must be scared to death. One minute you're fighting your mortal enemy in the woods, and the next, poof, you're in the future and there's not a tree in sight."

"Let's hope it's still disoriented," Marla said. She watched through the scope as the side door opened and the beast slouched out, its physiognomy still a mysterious jumble of ape-like and boarlike and manlike and, well, *beastlike*.

She squeezed the trigger three times, and three darts flew through the air to bury themselves in the beast's flesh. The darts were each charmed with a different armor-piercing and true-aim spell, and she hoped at least one of them would hit—worst case, all three would hit, and the beast would overdose and die, and wait, that was kind of the best case, too.

The beast lifted its shaggy head, looked straight at Marla, then charged toward the balcony where she and Rondeau stood, loping and leaping and snarling.

"Oh this is fucked," Rondeau said, and lifted his air rifle, firing another dart at the approaching furry projectile. The beast jumped for the balcony...and bounced off the railing, landing on the street, sprawled on its back, unconscious. Maybe it was immune to Malkin's sleep spells, but times had changed, and Marla had mixed up a potent cocktail of chemical and magical tranq-juice, concentrated enough to make a blue whale yawn. Still, who knew how much time they had to finish the plan?

Marla stood looking down at the beast while Rondeau was on his cell calling in Langford and the rest of the team. Comprehending its form was difficult, as if it had joints and limbs that weren't entirely in this dimension. Whatever it was, demon or god or refugee from another plane of existence, it didn't belong here. Maybe it had once, when Felport was just trees and dirt and hills, but this was a human place, now. The beast couldn't stay, even if it had a prior claim on this land as a home.

"Let's get it on the truck," Marla said. "And then go see Malkin."

"You *fool*," Malkin said, stalking into one of the Chamberlain's many parlors. He was dressed in period finery doubtless dug out of mothballs in some deep basement in the Chamberlain's estate, and he smelled faintly dusty. "You dare to attack me, and leave the city vulnerable to the beast's—"

"Gods, shut *up*, the beast is taken care of," Marla said. "Come on, I'll show you. Coming, Chamberlain?"

"Oh, indeed," she said brightly. "I haven't begun to tire of Mr. Malkin's company at *all*."

Malkin didn't shut up. "You will be flogged in the town square," he said, following Marla, Rondeau, and the Chamberlain out of the mansion, toward the truck parked in the driveway. "You will be stripped of whatever authority you think you have, and banished. I am the *chief sorcerer* here, and I will not be—"

Marla pulled open the back of the truck, and Malkin shut up when he saw the beast bound with 'chanted chains in the back, watched over by the technomancer Langford, who had a tranquilizer pistol in one hand and a complicated-looking cell phone in the other.

"So you rendered it unconscious," Malkin said. "Very well, but what happens when it wakes?"

"I don't imagine it will wish to wake," Langford said mildly. He beckoned, and the others climbed into the back of the truck. "Though I do wish I could be allowed to vivisect it. I'm not fond of mysteries, and this creature is unprecedented in my experience."

"I've got nothing against scientific curiosity," Marla said, "But I'm a pragmatist, and studying it is too dangerous."

"Standing here while it *slumbers* is too dangerous," Malkin snapped. "You are unfit to lead, and your folly is too great to be borne—"

"The beast is harmless," Langford said. He pointed to a silvery mesh net that covered the beast's lumpy skull. "This device controls the electrical impulses within the beast's brain. It's a beautiful place, in there. If you're a monster."

"I do not understand," Malkin said. "This...hat...does what?"

"We couldn't beat the thing," Marla said. "You told us yourself, it's immune to everything, and what it's not immune to, it *gets* immune to. So, if we can't defeat it, I figured, why not give it what it wants?"

"Think of it as an illusion," the Chamberlain said, having been briefed on the plan—the *whole* plan—in a phone call earlier. "The beast believes it is back in Felport in the early days, before there were settlers, alone in the woods."

"The simulation was easy enough to create," Langford said. "There are geographical surveys, so reconstructing the landscape wasn't difficult. Likewise the weather. Woodland creatures are simple to emulate, too, and there are hardly any humans, just the occasional native for the beast to dismember."

"The beast has been enchanted to believe it dwells in the past?" Malkin blinked, clearly wrongfooted by the whole situation.

"Well, at least a third of it is technology," Langford said. "Creating false experiences by manipulating electrical impulses in the brain is within the grasp of science, though outside the bounds of most ethical systems. I did use magic to bridge the impossible bits, admittedly."

"But the beast *fights* enchantments," Malkin said. "And when it wakes—"

"Why would it fight?" Marla said. "It's got what it wants. If this thing is capable of being happy, it's going to be happy. But don't worry. We're taking it to a little place outside the city, called the Blackwing Institute. It's where we keep sorcerers who go crazy and pose a danger to themselves, and others, and the substance of reality."

"And the sorcerer who runs it, Dr. Husch, is totally hot," Rondeau said.

Marla rolled her eyes. "We'll keep the beast in a cell deep in the basement, with every kind of technological and magical countermeasure we can think of, in case it ever wakes up. Don't worry. It's a secure site."

"We're sure you'll like it there," Langford said, and shot Malkin with the tranquilizer pistol.

"We could have given Malkin a perfect fantasy life, too," Langford said. "It would have to be far more complex than the one I created for the beast, but it's certainly possible."

"Fuck that," Marla said. "Why would I want to make him happy? He called me the weaker sex."

"Carry on, then," Langford said, and waved as Rondeau drove the truck off into the night.

"His real name is Barry Schmidt," Marla said, sitting with Dr. Husch before the security monitors. Malkin was on screen, sleeping on a bed in a pleasantly-appointed—but escape-proof —apartment in the Institute's east wing. "An apprentice from out west. Poor bastard actually thinks he's Everett Malkin, the first sorcerer of Felport, you believe that? He came to the city and started talking about how he was the rightful ruler, demanding I give him my dagger, crazy stuff like that."

"Hmm," Husch said, a vertical worry line marring her smooth pale forehead.

"And then he summoned the beast of Felport from, you know, the primordial whatever," Rondeau chimed in. "So he's got some magical chops, no doubt about that. Better to keep him in maximum super-isolation, we figure, with every magic-nullifying countermeasure you've got."

"Heck, keep him sedated forever," Marla said. "That'd be fine with me."

"You know I believe in therapy, not mere containment," Husch said. She looked at the Chamberlain. "Tell me, Chamberlain—do you think there's any chance he *is* Everett Malkin? The beast of Felport is bound, dreaming peacefully, in my basement, and if one creature can come from the past, can't another?"

Marla tried not to tense up. The Chamberlain was the key here. Rondeau was trustworthy, and Langford was both trustworthy and uninterested, but the Chamberlain could change her mind. She had a potent connection to the early days of Felport through her relationship with the ghosts, and she didn't really like Marla all that much. But, on the other hand, Malkin had ordered her around like a servant, and the Chamberlain said the ghosts who'd known Malkin—especially his apprentice Corbin—had really hated the guy, so maybe she'd stick to the plan.

"Oh, no," the Chamberlain said, smooth as her own silk gown. "That man is not Everett Malkin. I checked with the ghosts, and they say he's nothing like Malkin was. He is merely a madman, I'm afraid, a troubled soul who read too many histories. But his delusion is very fixed. He's clever, too—he might pretend to be cured, even if he isn't. Be careful."

"The poor dear. It's good you brought him to me. At the very least, I'll make him comfortable." Husch raised one perfect eyebrow. "He really demanded you relinquish your dagger of office, Marla, and said he was going to take over the city?"

"He did."

"I suppose he's lucky you left his head attached, then."

"Hey," Marla said. "Don't ever let anybody tell you I'm not a benevolent and enlightened ruler."

T. A. Pratt's stories have won a Hugo (and lost a Nebula and World Fantasy Award), and have appeared in The *Best American Short Stories, The Year's Best Fantasy and Horror,* and other nice places. He lives in Oakland CA and has a website at **www.tim-pratt.org**

Despite lacking much in the way of tact and having a tendency to solve all her problems with violence, **Marla Mason** has been chief sorcerer and protector of the city of Felport for a few years now, and no one's succeeded in assassinating her yet.

DUSTED

— A Cosa Nostradamus Story —

by Laura Anne Gilman

"Sylvan Investigations. Daniel Hendrickson speaking."

People tend to be surprised when they hear the name of my agency. I guess it's not what they expect from a big city PI. They don't expect the investigator to pick up the phone, either. In all the movies the PI has a cute secretary/gal Friday answering his phones and trying to block the bad guys from rushing into his office.

I handle the cute myself, and I answer my own damn phone. Overhead's bad enough without having to pay someone else's salary, too, and I prefer to work alone.

The caller didn't care about my dimple or my boyish grin. He wanted to sell me a subscription to the *Post*.

"Not if you paid me," I told him, and hung up. Some day they'd invent call discarding. Like call forwarding, only it would hang up preemptively on telemarketers.

I really needed a job. Not for the money—my pension from the NYPD took care of the basics, and I lived a pretty simple life. But I was bored. Bored was bad. Bored was boring.

"Mr. Hendrickson?"

I looked up to see a man standing in my doorway. Fifty-ish, solidly built, with graying brown hair and worried eyes.

"I was told you...you find missing people?"

I pushed back my chair and considered him. "That I do."

Parent, I pegged him. Runaway. Boy. Maybe. Maybe girl. And where's...ahh.

Behind him, the mother. Petite without being tiny, with brown curls and doe eyes that were red-rimmed, now. Daughter. Definitely daughter.

"Come in, please." I stood up and gestured to them, indicating the chairs by my desk. They came in, looking around. I let them take time to size up the place. Whatever brought them here, it wasn't easy, and they needed to be reassured. It also gave me the chance to size them up.

I had the basic two-room suite set-up, but I kept all the action up front. The furniture was basic brown wood, the chairs comfortable but not elegant, and the sofa was leather, but scruffed just enough that people felt comfortable sitting on it. The wall behind my desk was covered with photos and citations from my PD career and a few since then, for show. The letters from clients went on the wall to my right, so I could see them, on bad days. I'm not much for modesty—if you're selling your skills, put 'em front and center.

His name was Jack, and she was Ellen, and their absent daughter, age fourteen, was Susan. All-American family: mom and pop and loving daughter, like a picture book, except someone had ripped Miss Susan out of the picture.

Or she had cut herself out, neatly and quietly, leaving behind two very worried, self-blaming parents.

I actually preferred it when they blamed themselves. It was easier to get information out of them.

The first thing I knew was that they were Null. Talent—the humans who can use magic—always enter my office like they're about to apologize. At least until they see that I don't have any electronics in sight for them to fry, either accidentally or on purpose. Talent feed off current, the hip term for magic, and current, like its name, runs cheek and jowl with electricity. Imagine the fun when they tangle. Yeah. There's a reason I keep the computer in the back room.

No, this couple were Null, and they didn't know about the *Cosa Nostradamus*, either. You can always tell if they do. For one thing, they notice things about me.

Like the fact that I'm not entirely human.

A missing kid could go anywhere. It all depended on who she was, and what she wanted. I started with her last sighting: the lobby of her high school, up on East 74th. She'd been there on Tuesday afternoon, hanging with her homegirls, or whatever the slang was around the 14-year-old set these days, and then, an hour later...she wasn't. The police had already questioned her friends and boyfriend, and I had—through my ex-partner— gotten copies of those reports. They were all unsurprisingly unhelpful. Normal day, normal traumas, normal schedule. The kids broke to go their separate ways, and nobody knew anything until Susan's parents started calling and texting her peer group that night, looking for their wayward daughter.

Talking to the friends didn't get me much further, either. They seemed like good kids, all worried about Miss Susan. Nothing they said sounded suspicious or questionable, and none of them were suspects. Just...normal kids, as much as that sort of thing was possible.

So Miss Susan became an official Missing Person. My former *compadres* in the NYPD did their usual sweep of the obvious places; the bus station creepers and ladies' room Lotharios who like to sweet-talk young girls into unsavory arrangements. No luck. They were still looking, but if you knew how many kids go missing every year, you'd know why they weren't busting their humps over a girl who might or might not have gone under her own power.

But now I was on the job. The fact that I'd been a cop wasn't in my favor among the *dirtirati*, but the fact that I was part of the *Cosa Nostradamus* won some of those points back. One outcast recognized another. If there had been gossip around about Miss Susan, I would have gotten wind of it.

No such luck. Human or fatae, nobody was talking. To all intents and purposes, Susan had walked out of her high school, and disappeared.

To a human, that might mean anything. To me, it suggested something entirely different.

I walked out into the street, blinking a little at the sunlight, since the baseball cap I'd jammed over my curls didn't do quite enough to shield my eyes. My father's species wasn't much for sunlight, except maybe to nap in while recovering from their hangovers, and I'm willing to admit I'd inherited significant night-owl tendencies. That, and the pair of thumb-sized horns that my thick curls didn't quite cover, were about all I'd gotten from him, thankfully.

All right, that and a way with the ladies. The fact that my father had been a charmer was supported by the fact that my human mother, on discovering that her weekend of passion with a faun during Fleet Week had resulted in a pregnancy, decided to keep the result of said pregnancy: me.

I wondered sometimes if she'd made the right decision.

"Hey."

The piercing whisper was all too familiar. I looked up, squinting and cursing again at the sunlight, to see a small creature perched in the overhang of the building to my left, like some kind of furry gargoyle. A piskie. I stepped back, leaning against the wall as though contemplating the midday traffic passing by on Broadway.

"Hey Boo. You got something I should listen to?"

"Your skidoodle."

"I'm listening." Boo had brought me scoops before. If there was something useful, I'd reward the little pisher, and he knew it. If it was useless I'd kick his ass to Pretoria for wasting my time. He knew that, too.

"She got dusted" Boo told me.

I dragged the toe of my boot against the cement. "Aw, fuck."

I'd been afraid of that. Dusted, from a fatae, doesn't mean what it does in human slang. It's worse. It's what happens when a Null teenager—usually a girl, but not always—discovers that the fatae are real. They want nothing more than to traipse off with their newfound discovery, to go play with the fairies. Unfortunately, most of my fatae cousins are just as tricky and unreliable, if pretty, as human fairy takes suggest, and the playing...rarely ends well.

If my Miss Susan had taken up with Manhattan's answer to Trooping Fairies, I might as well hand her parents back their check and call it a night. The fatae rarely give back what they take, especially not if they thought someone else wanted it.

"Who with?" I asked my informant, who shrugged his furry shoulders, and scampered off.

Great. Well, that was why there was an "I" in "Investigator—I was the one who actually had to work.

The thing about the *Cosa Nostradamus* is that it's pretty polarized. You have the human Talent on one side, and the non-human fatae on the other, and they don't often mingle. Not socially, anyway. Lucky for me, horns and hooves made me fatae enough to be able to ask the questions that would get a human hurt. That didn't mean I could go in like an Appalachian cave dragon on a bender, though. You had to know the players. That was what had made me useful on the force, and was a lot of what made me successful now: I could work both sides of that street. And I knew that there was one fatae breed that not only gossiped like a knitting circle, but was amenable to some gentle bribery.

"For me?"

The salamander looked longingly at the glowstick, but didn't take it out of my hand. We were on the West side of the Park, just below the Rambles, at dawn. I'd hauled my ass out here to make sure I caught one of the firebrands before they were really up and moving. Sure enough, one of them had been having breakfast along the stone wall, catching the early morning rays and hotfooting the occasional jogger for laughs.

"A gift for you," I agreed, placing it on the top of the stone wall. The salamander considered it without touching it, then looked up at me, its lidless eyes surprisingly expressive. It wanted it, oh so very badly, but it wasn't sure why I was just handing it over. It assumed I wanted something.

It was right.

"I'm looking for someone who has gone missing. A young girl. Her parents miss her."

It picked up the glowstick in its front leg, the tiny claws snapping it so that the chemicals started to glow. "Pretty," it said. They could burn without scorching, but the concept of a cool light fascinated them. I guess you always want what you can't have—or do.

It cocked its slender head at me, the foot-long body still stretched out along the wall, managing to be both relaxed, and ready to scamper at the slightest threat. "How young the girl?"

"Fifteen. Rumor says she's been dusted."

"Blond or redhead?"

"Blondish."

That's where the 'smart one' myth comes from, by the way. Brunettes. Less likely to get dusted. Other trouble, yeah, but not by following the pretty little man into the greenways. Don't ask me why, it just is.

"How long?"

"Five days. Five. Four days too long for a girl to be dusted. Once it takes, it's tough to ever get out of your system. Seven days, seven years—seven is the magical number. I had a very real deadline.

The salamander nodded. "Maybe. Maybe. We hear talk. You need to go low down to talk to someone. Down into the metal caves."

Gnomes. Wonderful. This case just kept getting better and better.

Fortunately, I knew where to go for help.

The door was opened by one of the least attractive women I've ever met.

"Heya doll," I said, swooping in to steal a kiss. She let me, rolling her eyes and taking my hat.

"What trouble are you bringing this time, Danny-boy?"

Unlike her face, her voice was lovely, a gentle alto that would have put any of my full-blooded cousins into unstoppable heat. I admitted to myself that I wasn't totally immune.

"No trouble, doll, I swear. Not for you, anyway.

"And for my husband, who doesn't know how to say no?"

"I just want to ask his advice. He won't even leave his studio." I hoped.

Lee was a Talent who had an unbelievable gift that wasn't magical at all, at least not as Talent went. He was a sculptor, working with metal to create figures that totally baffled me, but sold for large amounts of money. His studio, on the top floor of their narrow townhouse, had huge windows, and a floor half-covered in an electrostatic carpet.

Lee used current to meld his metal, not fire. One bad day, if he forgot to discharge after working, he could take out his entire grid. The fact that he never had told you a lot about the man.

He was working on something when I came in, so I took one of the cushioned chairs at the far end of the room and waited. About ten minutes later the sparks stopped flying, and he stepped over to a thick black mat to ground himself.

"What's up, Danny?"

"I need your advice on how to approach gnomes."

Lee stopped short, clearly not sure if I was joking or not.

"They're metal. You work metal. I figured you'd know something that could help me out, some spell or something that would make them, I don't know, malleable?"

Lee shook his head sorrowfully. "Your ignorance of magic is terrifying."

Tough to argue with that, especially since I do it intentionally. My kind—fatae in general—don't use magic, as such; we *are*
magic. As a human, I'm basic Null—can see magic, sort of, but
can't use it at all. Some Nulls can't even see it, can't even see the
fatae strap-hanging beside 'em on the subway. It's a sliding scale.

"Seriously, Lee. I have to go down and deal with the gnomes.
They have something I need back."

"And you think that I have an answer. Man, they're fatae—
you should have a better grasp of them than I ever could."

I shrugged, craning my neck to look up at him. I'm not short,
but Lee was one damn long drink of water. "They don't much
like the flesh-folk."

He winced. "They're not really made of metal. You know that,
right?"

"We know that. I'm not sure they do."

"Yeah." He leaned against the wall and thought. I let him.

"All right. There's one tribe, I've done some trading with
them."

"Hah!" I crowed, making a subtle fist-pump gesture. "I knew
it."

"Shut up. I've done some trading with them, I said. Not
enough to figure out how their brains work and I'd sure as hell
never use current on them; it would be bad manners, and I'd
never get supplies from them again, anyway."

"So you can tell me who to talk to?"

"No. But I can talk to them for you."

Oh hell. "Your wife is going to kill me."

Lee just laughed. I think he's used to that reaction.

The metal tunnels were actually long, large metal pipes that
had been fitted in shafts decades ago, for some MTA project or
another, and then abandoned. No wonder we always ran a deficit,
the way they lost materials. You went in through the waterways,
everyone knew that, if they knew about gnomes at all, but that's
where things got hazy. For me, anyway. Lee sloshed along in his
galoshes like he was going to market. I guess for him, he was.

"Who is that?" The voice came out of the gloom without
warning, cranky and suspicious.

"Who the hell do you think it is? Lee held up a hand, and
sparks flickered at his fingertips, illuminating the small circle in
front of him. A gnome sat on a metal shelf that had been grafted
into the tunnel, blinking in the current-light. "Who else has to

bend over double in these damn tunnels, and sounds like a fuck-ing moose slogging through this damned sewage?"

It took a minute and then my brain kicked back in. Lee, calm-tempered, soft-spoken Lee, was in trading mode. Was that how gnomes spoke to each other, or how they expected humans to speak, overall?

"Ah. You. Wasn't expecting you." The gnome was about knee-high to me, which meant that Lee could have stepped on him and barely noticed.

"Well, I'm here. You have any redweight?"

"You want redweight, you gotta call ahead. Not grow on trees down here." The gnome giggled like it had said some-thing unbearably witty. My eyes had adjusted enough to take in details: I'd known that gnomes were small, but I hadn't realized how much they looked like Beaux Arts fairies. Pretty little bas-tards. No wonder they were able to enrapt stupid Null children into following them underground into the sewers.

"How about black ash?" Lee asked.

"Maaaaaaaaybe. What you got in trade?"

Lee reached into his pocket and pulled something out. I craned my neck to see what gnomes considered fair trade for their handiwork, but his hand was tilted so I couldn't see into his palm. Secret of the trade, I guess. Talent were just as secretive in their way as the fatae.

"Too much," the gnome said in alarm. "Too much for black ash."

"Hrm. So it is." Lee started to put whatever it was back in his pocket, and then stopped. "But maybe we could deal, anyway. You answer a question, a small question, and I call it fair trade."

"Hrmmmm. Small question. And black ash?"

"I call it fair."

"Then not small question."

"Small question, important answer. If not truth, then all deals end."

Oh, the gnome did not like that, not at all. It hopped from one foot to the other, tilting its head as though it was listening to something far away. Maybe it was: I bet these tunnels car-ried sound unspeakably well, and I doubted there was only one guard along this stretch of sewer.

"Ask," the gnome said, finally.

"Did you dust a young human girl, near-grown, blonde, in the past sevenday. Is she here?"

"That two question." But it considered again, and this time I was damn sure I heard the high-pitched echo of other voices, up and down the metal tunnel.

"Blonde girl come freely," it said finally, and with finality. "Honored guest."

I snorted at that. For honored guest read 'slave'... The fatae liked to have someone else to do the housework. I didn't think they'd hurt her, but there were other things living in the underground city, and gnomes were notoriously careless of their guests. Metals, they protected. Humans—disposable.

"Give. We bring you black ash. Now go."

Lee made the exchange, and they shook hands on it, the gnome's hand absurdly lost in his.

"Come on. Let's go." Lee said to me.

Waitaminute. "I need to—"

"We need to go. Now. Lee looked over his shoulder, clearly worried.

I'd asked him for help because he knew the underground kingdom. We went.

"You can't go back there."

"I have to."

"Danny. Daniel."

Nobody calls me Daniel, not even my Mom. Only my old lieutenant ever called me that, and only when he was about to ream me out something spectacular, so I'd know to loosen up my sphincter.

"I have to go back," I told him, against his disapproving look. "The girl is down there."

Lee sighed. "Of her own free will. Mostly."

Yeah. The "mostly" was the kicker. She had chosen to leave home and go live in the underground kingdom; gnomes didn't have glamour, not really, just a lot of exotic allure and pretty skin. On the "however" side, she was a legal minor, and no human should spend any length of time down there, not unless they were fixing to come down with asthma and Vitamin D deficiency. And her parents had paid me to get her back.

Humans didn't belong down there.

Lee paced back and forth in his studio, five paces in either direction, turn-and-glare. "You're going back down there no matter what I say, aren't you?"

"Yeah. But you're not going back with me," I told him. "It could get ugly and that's not your thing."

Lee looked mulish, but didn't argue. He was much more of a 'make art not war' sort, and he was okay with that. No heroics in that boy.

"If caught, I'll swear I tortured you to hand over the map."

He scowled at me. "Very funny. They won't torture you, anyway, they'll just eat you. Goat's a rarity down there, and you've put on a nice layer of fat since you left the force."

"The hell I have." I'd noted the surprisingly sharp teeth on that gnome, but not thought to wonder about it. "And they don't eat people." I'd never heard that they did, anyway...

Lee gave up trying to scare me. "If they did, they'd have been burned out of there by now. No. Just rats and stray pets. Look, if you insist on this, there's not a damn thing I can do against them. My magic doesn't work that way. But I might be able to help you find the girl, once you're down there..."

Twenty-four hours later I was back in the tunnel, carrying a small metal sphere in the cup of my left hand and a rubber-tipped metal wand in the other. I felt like a proper idiot, and was prepared at any second to drop the damn wand in order to grab for my gun. Some kinds of cold steel made me feel more secure than others.

The wand carried a current-charge that would stun anything that came out at me, although I wasn't sure if it would be a fatal shock or a jump-back-Jack. Lee'd handed it to me without comment, and I'd taken it instinctively, the cool metal fitting perfectly into my grip. "I thought you said you didn't have anything that would work against gnomes?"

"This isn't for gnomes. It's for the ROUS."

It took me a minute, then I got the joke. "Very funny."

"Danny, I've been down there more than you have. I'm not kidding. Bullets won't do the job. If you see anything with a tail, shock it and apologize later."

Comforting. So I was moving through the tunnel, my gun holstered and my wand at the ready, keeping one eye on the shadows shifting against the walls and the other on the globe in my palm. That was the important bit of magic: it would lead me in the direction of my girl. Or a girl, anyway. A human. Lee had spelled it to seek out an upright bipedal without the metallic-gritty blood of a gnome. So, assuming they didn't have half a dozen captive or pet humans down here...

Something moved, off to my left. I stopped, my heart racing a little more than I enjoyed, and waited. A skittering noise, and the swish of what might have been a long tail attached to a giant rat-ass. Or it could have been my over-pumped imagination. I took a better hold on the wand, and started forward again.

The quality of light was starting to increase, which means I was entering the gnomes' domain. Joy. On the plus side, whatever had been skittering in my shadow decided to stay back. I guess the gnomes had rat-proofed or something. Or it didn't like the taste of their flesh. Either way, it was a good thing. But I kept the wand out, anyway. I really didn't want to have to shoot anyone. Even down here, there would be paperwork.

"You. Lost?"

I swear, the gnome hadn't been there half a second ago. But it was now, a foot high and all of it filled with the finest street corner 'tude you could muster. Dress it in colors and it'd pass for a gangbanger.

"Nope. Visiting. Here to see a shut-in friend."

I can't blame my genetic donor for my smart mouth—that came down straight from the maternal line.

The gnome didn't seem to have much of a sense of humor. But he didn't call for backup, either. Just stared at me with those oversized eyes, the ones that you just know can find you in the middle of the night in a pitch-black room, and nodded, then let me pass by.

That creeped me out, way more than anything else had. Why wasn't he worried. What were the little metal-skins planning?

"Huuuuman..." A taunting whisper, a mocking call, the tingle of fairy-dust on my skin, like a shiver in the middle of the night, coming from ahead of me.

"Huuuuuman."

That one came from somewhere off to my left. The shiver became an itch, the urge to follow, to find the treasure such a creature undoubtedly hid here, below ground, in its mines.

"I don't think so, boys." I was a little old and jaded to be dusted that easily. I had no desire to be found, seven years from now, starved to death in a metal hole.

"And don't bother with the rats, either," I said, more loudly. "I'll just turn them into stew."

Bravado—if they actually did have rodents of unusual size down here, there's no way I'd be able to hold off more than one, two max. But the whispering faded away, and they let me continue on unmolested.

No idea how much longer I walked, waiting any moment for giant teeth to dig into my arm or leg, getting more and more unnerved each moment, when I came to a four-pronged branch in the tunnels. One way was the correct choice, the others would leave me stranded somewhere I didn't want to be. Maybe with rats. That's why the little bastard wasn't worried; it knew odds were good I'd end up lost.

"All right, Lee, now'd be a good time for your toy to work."

As though it were listening, the globe in my hand flashed red when I moved it past the leftmost option, so I turned that way.

In the distance now I could hear noises, the rumble of machinery and voices blending into grey noise. A while in, and doorways broke the smooth walls, the sheet-steel doors boasting tiny latches just perfect for gnome hands. There weren't any markings on the doors that I could see, but remembering the bush-baby peepers on that gnome, I didn't assume that meant there weren't huge signs everywhere my crap day-timer sight was missing.

Another multi-pronged split in the hallway, and I waved the globe back and forth slowly, letting it tell me where to go. If I hadn't had the globe, I'd have been lost ten ways from Monday. Hopefully it would work on the way out, too. Or my bones would wash out into the East river's low tide seven days from now, gnawed bare.

"Stop freaking yourself out, Hendrickson."

This time the globe suggested the right side, and about five doors down that hallway, it flared so bright I almost dropped it.

"Here, then?" The sphere declined to answer. Either it was worn out, or it didn't feel my stupid-ass question deserved an answer.

I tried the door handle but, as expected, couldn't quite get my hand to work the latch properly. Thinking quick, I took the wand and bent the non-grounded end slightly. The metal was soft enough to do it without much effort, although I hated to ruin the thing. Not just because I didn't know what effect it might have on it as a weapon but because it was a beautiful piece. Lee couldn't make anything simply utilitarian. It wasn't his nature.

The bend slid under the handle, and I could apply the right pressure to make the lock click open. Go me. I pushed gently, and the door swung open. Alert to anything from screams to gunshots to a vase coming down on my head, I stepped inside.

The room was about as far from the bleak exterior hallway as you could get. The walls were gray rock, framed at ceiling and floor with a dark, patina'd metal, and the floor was mostly covered in a thick fleecy rug, white and soft to the touch. There wasn't any art on the walls, but the bed had a bright blue coverlet, and there were pillows that looked comfortable. A white wood vanity with a mirror above it, and enough geegaws scattered around to make any 14-year-old girl happy, I guessed.

No photos of her loving parents, I noted. No photos at all. No artwork, nothing representational. The fatae loved beauty, but mostly their own. Not so much about looking at pretties someone else made. That seemed to be a human thing...something Miss Susan was already losing.

"Who are you?"

I had been so busy looking around, I hadn't secured all the entrances. I turned slowly to face the girl who'd come in through a side door, cursing myself upside and down. Thankfully, she was carrying a towel, not something that could be thrown or otherwise used as a weapon, and seemed disinclined to scream.

"Hello, Susan. I'm Danny. Your folks asked me to stop by and check on you. They've been worried, you know."

Susan didn't even blink, although she did shrug. Draping the towel across her neck, she walked into the room and sat down at the vanity, peering into the mirror as though checking for wrinkles. Her posture and pose was that of a mature woman, but her body was still skinny-gawky teenager, and her pose was just that—a pose.

"You should at least have left them a note, told them that you were all right."

"They'll forget about me, get a new kid," she said, oh so casually. "That's how it works, right?"

Oh we were going to play that game, were we.

"Sometimes. But mostly, no. Mostly the parents worry and stress and hire people to go looking, and sometimes they even risk their own lives—their souls—to bring back their loved one."

I wasn't getting through, I'd known I wouldn't the moment I saw her. She was completely dusted. To her, this wasn't a dreary hole in a dreary tunnel: it was fairyland, and she was the shiny new queen. Why did nobody read *Thomas the Rhymer* any more?

"You're here to try and talk me back into going Above. I'm not interested. Tell my parents I'm fine."

"You really think they're going to believe that. Come tell them yourself."

"No. If I leave, I'll never find my way back. Ageo told me so. I'm not going to risk all this just to reassure them."

Well, she had the Snow Queen cold down already. I very much did not like Miss Susan at all.

"Look. She stopped and looked at me. She had her father's eyes, and her mother's mouth. Nowhere near as pretty as she wanted to be, but not bad, overall. Give her another ten years and she might even break a few hearts. But not if she stayed down here.

"You have no right to tell me what to do."

"True. I don't." And telling her anything would be useless, even if she hadn't been dusted—she was a teenager. Short of dragging her out of here by her hair, there wasn't much I could do.

The hair thing was tempting. But I had one card I hadn't played. I hadn't even thought to, honest, but seeing her sitting there trying so desperately to be what she thought was adult and sophisticated and...fatae-acceptable...

She had been missing for six days now. One day left, before she was lost to the above world forever.

I made my decision before I let myself think about it. If I thought about it, we'd lose her.

Miss Susan thought I was human. Most people do. I think human, I live human, I pass for human even among people who are looking for non-human; at least until the NYPD decided to change unofficial policy and I had to get out or be asked some uncomfortable questions at my next physical.

But I'm not human. Not entirely.

I ran my hands through my hair, intentionally flattening the brown curls so that my horns showed through, impossible even for a Null to overlook. They're not elegant or impressive or even any use as a weapon, but they're there, if I choose to shown them: short, curved nubs rising out of my scalp like...okay, like a baby goat's, yeah. I could have taken my boots off to show the hoof-like growth that protects my toes, but it was too damn much effort to pull off cowboy boots, and I didn't need it anyway. The horns would catch her attention, and then my genetics—and her brain chemistry—would handle the rest.

"Susan."

She had gone back to the mirror, painting up her eyes to look wider, more helpless...more gnome-like. What a waste. Although I suppose she should be thankful the angeli didn't catch her eye. Those sadistic bastards would encourage her to do body mods, just for their own entertainment.

"Susan."

I moved across the room and stood behind her. My reflection in her mirror was from hip to shoulder, and I paused a moment to consider how that would look to her. I'm in damn good shape, in the prime of my life, and if you don't mind some pelt I'm told I'm pretty damn cute. Didn't matter. This wasn't about sex or even physical attraction, but seduction. The gnomes lured her down; I had to lure her back.

My dusting had to be stronger than theirs.

I placed a hand on her shoulder, lightly enough to be a caress, firmly enough to be thrilling to a young girl who didn't know the first thing about men but was old enough to be intrigued. Carefully, carefully. I relaxed the tight hold I normally kept on my instincts, leaned forward so that my face came into view in the mirror, close to her ear, and whispered again, "Susan."

Susan's gaze flicked up, instinctively, against her will, and met my gaze in the mirror. My narrow face seemed leaner, my cheekbones more prominent, my eyes more gold than brown, and the horns almost shimmered white in the silvered mirror.

There was no way I could have passed for human, not in any crowd.

Susan's pink-painted mouth fell open a little, showing teeth that had been a gift from the orthodontist, and her gaze lifted and zeroed right in on my horns. Typical.

"You think that you know what's fantastic in this world?" I asked her, still keeping my voice low, my touch gentle. "You think it's down here, in these caves and stone and steel?"

She swallowed hard, but didn't move, the eye pencil still in her hand.

"Up above, my sweet. Up above, in the green grass and the flowering trees. The sun warms our bones and we dance until we are exhausted and then we sprawl in the shade and feast until we sleep, and then we rise and do it again."

Her breathing sped up, just a bit, and I moved my hand down from her shoulder to her upper arm. "We eat fresh fruit and cheese, and wash it down with wine, and shout into the winds... We are free. None of this enclosed space, this lack of fresh air or blue sky. Gnomes look down, they see only the dirt. Nothing grows here. Come with me, sweet Susan. Come see the world in all its glory. See the magic that surrounds us, every day."

Everything I was telling her was true. Full-blooded fauns were hedonistic, careless, loving sorts. Useless in any practical manner, but a lot of fun to hang out with, and they simply adored every tingle of magic they could get their hooves on.

Pity they were also callous bastards.

"I am promised here..." she managed. Her eyes were very wide now, like she'd ingested a full dose of belladonna, and she hadn't blinked once while I was talking, then her lids fluttered three, four, six times in a row, trying to recover.

"Promises are made to be broken," I told her. "Otherwise there wouldn't be half as much art or music in the world."

That went over her head a bit—ah, the teen years, when you think everything's forever, and their hearts will never be broken.

I was about to educate her.

I knelt down and rested my chin lightly on her shoulder, still keeping my touch gentle. Spooking her now would be catastrophic. "You've only seen one side of fairyland," I told her. My voice was brown sugar and warm breezes, soft grass and the smell of apple blossoms and honey. "Come see more of it. Griffins and dryads are in Central Park, my sweet, and dragons live in the hills of Pennsylvania. Piskies flitter in the Botanical Gardens, and kelpies swim off the Seaport's piers..."

All true. Of course, the dryads didn't mingle much, and the dragons didn't mingle at all, kelpies were nasty-tempered, smelly beasts...and the less said about piskies the better.

"So much to see...so many creatures to dance with. How can you let yourself waste away here, living in this single room like a drudge when you should be a princess..."

Her eyes sparkled at that, and I almost had her. My hand rose up her arm again, stroking her hair. "Sunlight suits you, my sweet," I said, leaning in for the kill. "Come with me, and I will show you the true wonders of the fairy world."

I sounded like a B-grade Hollywood movie, but it was working. Her eyes started to glaze over, and her mouth curved up in a dreamy smile, even as I threaded my fingers in her hair, and tugged her head back just a little, as though to deliver a first kiss.

Her head lolled to the side, her body utterly relaxed as my dusting took effect, and I scooped her into my arms without hesitation.

It was a crap way to rescue a princess, but I wasn't exactly prince charming.

By the time Miss Susan recovered from the hormonal overload enough to protest, she was back in her parents' care, and I was on my way back to the office. They had been all sorts of overjoyed not only to see her, but to have assurances that she was unmolested. I didn't have the heart to tell them that she wasn't entirely untouched. All I did was remove her from the scene—and I'd dusted her myself to do it.

Yeah, I had good intentions and good results, but she had the taste now—sexual, the rush magic could bring, and odds were pretty damn good that she'd disappear again, chasing after another hit. They'd lost her already; they just didn't know it yet.

All I could hope was that the images I'd used in my dusting would keep her above ground this time. There were other humans who associated with those breeds...they'd be able to keep an eye out for her, teach her the ropes. Keep her out of too much trouble. And maybe by then, she'd have grown up enough to handle it.

The fatae weren't bad company, as it went. It was just better to accept what *you* were, before you went chasing something else.

That thought kept me company as I walked up the steps to my office, and let myself in the door, looking around the space with a sense of relief. Home. Wood furniture, plants, light...they were all a steady, solid reminder. I was human.

But my little stunt reminded me that I was also faun. My father's son, the product of my magical genes. A real charming sonofabitch when it came to women.

I didn't like it, I didn't let it out very often...but it was me, as much as current—and art—was Lee. Me, who I am. What I am.

I sat down in my chair, and reached for the bottle in my desk. Not to forget; I never drank to forget. I drank to remember. I drank so that the pleasant warmth of the booze, the heady shot of inebriation, would remind me that I wasn't entirely fatae. My human half was stronger. I wasn't my father.

Some days, I needed the reminder.

Laura Anne Gilman is the author of the "Cosa Nostradamus" urban fantasy novels (most recently *Hard Magic*), as well as the mainstream fantasy *Weight of Stone: Book 2 of The Vineart War*. She lives in New York City, where she also runs d.y.m.k. productions, an editorial consulting company. Her website may be found at **www.lauraannegilman.net**

Danny Hendrickson is a former NYPD officer, currently working as a private investigator in New York City. He likes to keep his half-faun genetics under his hat, so to speak.

THE DEMON YOU KNOW...

— A Demon-Hunting Soccer Mom Story —

by Julie Kenner

Kate

My name is Kate Connor, and I'm a suburban mom with a husband, a teenager, and a toddler. I'm also a demon hunter. And no, I don't mean that metaphorically. I really do hunt demons from Hell, although I thankfully don't have to go to Hell to do that. Instead, the demons come to me, and more often than I'd like, actually.

Demons, you might know, walk among us all the time. The air is, literally, filled with demonic essence living in the ether, a little fact that, frankly, can creep you out if you think about it too long. What's even creepier is that a demon's essence can also inhabit the body of a human. Sometimes the demon possesses the human, in which case you have a whole spinning-head, Linda Blair thing going on. That's not my area; for that, you call a priest.

More often (because what demon wants to walk around looking like the thing in *The Exorcist?*), a demon will move into a body at the moment of death, just as the human's soul is leaving. You've heard of those situations where someone is thought to be dead—a fall, a drowning—but then the victim is "miraculously" brought back to life. Most of the time, that's no miracle. It's a demon. And one who brings with it strength beyond which the human had in life, and a body that's pretty dang hard to kill. You want to off a demon, you have to stab it in the eye. Not as easy as it sounds, trust me on that, but pretty much any jab that punctures the sclera and reaches the vitreous humor will do. I've used knives, ice picks, barrettes and even Happy Meal toys.

Manage to inflict that injury, and the demonic essence is sucked right back out into the ether.

Of course, demons can't pop into any old body. The souls of the faithful *fight*, and the window of opportunity passes pretty quickly. So it's not as if the world is overrun with demons walking around in human shells. But there are enough to keep me busy, and my fellow demon hunters, too. I work for *Forza Scura*, a super-secret arm of the Vatican, although I have to confess I haven't kept the secret quite as hush-hush as I should. My husband knows. My fourteen-year-old daughter Allie knows. My best friend Laura knows.

And it's quite possible my toddler knows, too, but he isn't saying.

Not that I'm completely incapable of keeping a secret. I haven't told the postman or the guy who runs the 7-11 on the corner. And although I know my martial arts instructor is curious about why a thirty-something mother of two can best him on the mat, so far I haven't succumbed to a whim and told him. Why? Because I am, more or less, capable of controlling my whims. Because I don't fly off the handle and do stupid things simply because my friends (or husband, or kids) want me to.

Responsibility.

Now there's a buzzword. And 'prudence'. And 'common sense.'

All qualities that a demon hunter needs to possess. Especially *prudence*. And clear, level-headed thinking. The ability to act fast in a crisis and not jump into a situation without first doing at least a basic assessment. All those are tools in a Hunter's toolbox, and as much as certain fourteen-year-olds might wish it were so, that particular skill set isn't acquired overnight. Which is why my particular fourteen-year-old, despite making serious strides on the knife-throwing and ass-kicking side of the equation, isn't yet going on regular patrols with her designated trainer. Namely, me.

A fact that has definitely raised the Teenage Sulk and Whine Meter in our house to Def Con One. And which, in a lovely bit of circular logic, completely justifies my refusal. Because if she was being clear-headed and prudent, she'd know that I was right—and there would be no whining, no angst, no moping about. Of course, when I tried *that* bit of logic on her, I was immediately assaulted with her standard reply of *Mother*, in a tone meant to express all sorts of unpleasant things, none of which it's prudent to say outright to your mom.

So maybe she's learned a little prudence after all...

I hoped so. Because right then she was in a situation that required the utmost common sense and prudence. And, possibly, a few ass-kicking skills, too.

Right then, my daughter Allie was on a date, or what I considered a date, although Allie swore it was nothing more than a group of friends going to the movies.

The entire lot had piled into my minivan earlier, and I'd driven them to the mall, the plan being to meet some other friends for dinner and a movie before the girls headed off to a sleepover, where another mom would get to deal with a gaggle of hormonally charged girls. The boys, presumably, would go home frustrated.

I remembered the way Jeremy's fingers had grazed Allie's back as they'd walked toward the mall entrance, the way Allie had smiled up at him, her lips soft and shiny from liberal applications of lip gloss (probably to make up for the fact that I'd refused to allow any other make-up).

She could call it a friendly movie outing all she wanted to, but I knew it was a date. My childhood might have been atypical, what with growing up in the *Forza* dorms and spending my Friday nights chasing preternatural vermin through the catacombs of Rome, but I was still a girl, and I'd been around the block more than once.

There are a lot of things that make moms nervous. The first time you leave your baby with a sitter. The first day of kindergarten. And, of course, the first time your daughter battles a demon right in her own backyard.

All those pale in comparison to an unchaperoned date, even one that technically isn't a date.

I took a sip of coffee and sighed. For the first time in ages I had the house to myself. My daughter was on a date. My husband had taken our toddler to see his parents. But I couldn't even enjoy the solitude.

Instead, all I could think as I sat in my kitchen, trying hard not to think at all, was that I hoped those talks about prudence and responsibility had gotten through my daughter's thick skull.

Allie

"This is stupid," I shouted, trying to be heard over the music that filled the room and the bass beat that shook the floor. I held tight to the punch that Jeremy had brought me before sliding back into the throng of Coronado High students that filled the huge mansion's foyer. "We're going to get into so much trouble!"

"It's just a party, Al," Mindy said, leaning close so she didn't have to yell as loud. "It's not like we're doing anything *bad*." She said "bad" in the kind of voice that suggested backseats and kissing and the kind of stuff I'd never done before. And, honestly, didn't want to do yet, even though I could talk a good game in the girls' locker room. It wasn't like I was a prude or anything, but I wasn't sure I wanted that kind of hormonal rush yet. Besides, I didn't have the best of luck with boys. The first time I went out with a guy, he turned out to be a demon. The second time he was only a minion, but from my perspective, that was just as bad. Maybe worse. So pardon me if in my almost fifteen years of wisdom, I'm now thinking that maybe I should have my knife-fighting skills honed before I get in the backseat with a boy.

Not that I can explain any of that to Mindy. She doesn't know my mom's secret. And she sure doesn't know that I'm training to be a demon hunter, too.

I took a sip of my punch and almost spit it out. Whatever it had been spiked with tasted nasty. Not that the taste was slowing Mindy down.

"My mom would ground me for a year if she knew I was here, and you know your mom would, too."

She lifted a shoulder. "So?"

I love Mindy, don't get me wrong, but she's been kind of a pain lately. Her parents are getting divorced, so Mom says I'm supposed to be patient with her. But I wasn't entirely sure that meant that I was supposed to let her drag me to forbidden parties.

"You're not going to have fun if you don't relax a little," Mindy said. "Honestly, Allie. It's not like we're picking up guys on the beach or hitchhiking on the Coast Highway. It's a party. And everybody we know is here."

I took another sip of my drink, felt my head do a spinning thing, and saw Jeremy smiling at me from across the room. I wasn't sure I entirely agreed with Mindy's assessment, but I had to admit that at the moment the perks were pretty good. Party.

Friends. A boy who liked me. And, yeah, I know I had the whole justification thing going about *so* not needing a boyfriend, and *so* not wanting to deal with the stress of kisses and bodies and all that hormonal stuff, but at the same time, it's not like I could just flip a switch and not be fourteen anymore. I *was* a hormonal mess. I knew it, because not only did my mom spend half her life saying so, but also because I got the only A on our health quiz this semester. Trust me. *All* fourteen year olds are hormonal messes.

Jeremy made a beeline for me, his smile just shy enough to make my stomach do flip-flops. "Did you miss me?" he said. Like Mindy, he had to lean in close, and his breath tickled my ear. I caught Mindy's eye as Carson drew her away toward the make-shift dance floor. She wasn't saying anything, but was making embarrassing "go for it" expressions—embarrassing enough to make me think that already she'd hit the punch bowl once too often.

Right as I was thinking that I needed to cut my best friend off, she stumbled over her own feet, a sure sign she was trashed. Instinctively, I took a step forward, but stopped right away, because someone caught her—and he wasn't Carson. Instead, he was an absolutely dreamy guy who couldn't have been more than sixteen years old. The kind of guy you see in magazines advertising deodorant soap, the idea being that if you don't stink, you can land a guy like that.

"Marlin Wheatley," Jeremy said, leaning close.

I didn't turn around. How could I, since that would mean I had to stop staring?

"No way is he in his twenties," I whispered, remembering what I'd been told about our host. "He's got to still be in high school."

Jeremy moved slightly, and I imagined he was shrugging. "Dunno. Guess he's just one of those guys."

I guessed so. One of those gorgeous, model-perfect, Greek-God-on-a-mountaintop kind of guys with a fabulous mansion overlooking the ocean, who throws awesome parties with cutting-edge music and tables and tables topped with amazing food and mindblowing drinks. Yeah. One of those guys.

Now, that guy was holding Mindy tight while she regained her balance. But he wasn't looking at her. Instead, he was looking right at me. There was something so familiar about his eyes. If I wanted to, I really thought I could float away in them.

Except part of me didn't want to. Part of me thought that would be a very bad idea. There was something about him... something deep in his eyes...

"Allie!"

I started, the movement breaking eye contact. I'd been thinking something...worrying about something, and I glanced back at Mindy, but she was upright and holding hands with Carson and everything seemed hunky-dory.

I turned to Jeremy, confused.

"Hey," he said. "Are you okay?"

"I..."

"You got this look. All worried and...I don't know." His brow furrowed. "You don't want to leave, do you?"

That knocked me back to reality. "I thought about it," I admitted. "My mom wouldn't exactly approve."

As far as Mom knew, the plan had been a movie followed by a sleepover at Parker's house. (Parker is a girl, so that's not as risqué as it sounds.) The boys, of course, were not invited to that part of the evening.

"Forget this crap," Carson had said once we were safe inside the mall. "Tonight's Marlin Wheatley's party."

"Who?" I'd asked, and they'd all looked at me like I was from Mars. Turns out, Wheatley's some rich twenty-something computer bazillionaire who'd moved to the area a few months ago and has been talking up this party for ages.

"Why?"

Jeremy and Parker had looked at each other and shrugged. "Don't know. Guess he wants to make sure people come."

"But why throw it in the first place?"

"He's a college drop-out geek. This is probably his way of meeting girls. Who cares, anyway? It's a party."

I probably could have said something, but I didn't, and after about thirty minutes, we pulled up in front of the biggest house I'd ever seen. I had no idea where we were, other than that we were on one of the cliffs overlooking the Pacific in a mega-ritzy neighborhood I'd never seen before. Walking to the front door, I could smell the ocean, and the lights of the house seemed magical against the black night sky.

At that one moment, I had absolutely no hesitation about blowing off the movie and sneaking off to a party.

Inside, when I'd smelled the alcohol in the punch and saw the guy I share a lab table with in biology barf into a potted plant, the second thoughts set in.

Still, there was nothing inherently bad about a barfing lab partner, right? Just because he drank too much didn't mean I would. And I couldn't deny the biggest, most glaring fact of all—I really liked the way Jeremy was looking at me. If I was a widdle girl who made a phone call to her mommy, would he ever look at me that way again?

"Earth to Allie," he said. "Come on. Don't do that to me. Tell me you don't want to leave."

"No," I said, not realizing until that moment that I was certain. "I don't want to leave."

He pressed his hands over his heart and pretended to swoon. "Saved," he said. "I was expecting a mortal blow."

I laughed, and thought that felt pretty darn nice.

Mom might not think I was ready to make decisions in the field, but we weren't talking demons here. This was a party. And just because she was a demon hunter didn't mean she could go in and hijack all of my decisions from me. I was fourteen years old! I was *supposed* to be going to parties with friends. I'm pretty sure that's in the rule book somewhere.

"I'm staying," I said again, just because I liked the way it sounded. Then I smiled up at Jeremy. "In fact, I think I want more punch."

"You're Allie, right?"

I dropped the dipper back into the bowl, splattering the pink liquid onto my shirt, as I looked up to find Marlin smiling at me from the kitchen doorway.

"Sorry," he said silkily. "I didn't mean to startle you."

"No, you..." I trailed off because, hey, he had startled me. What was the point of denying it?

He nodded toward the bowl. "You like the punch."

"Yes," I lied. Actually, I'd come into the kitchen hoping to find something in the refrigerator to drink instead. I'd lucked out, too. The punch was apparently a mixture of pink lemonade, Sprite, and some unidentifiable alcohol of the wow-is-that-strong variety. I didn't like it. And so I'd filled my cup to the brim with plain old pink lemonade, and then had gone to the punch bowl to do a color comparison.

Yes, I know I should simply be able to say, "No, I don't like the punch," or, "Gee, the alcohol in the punch is making my head swim." Instead, I was going to silently lie by carrying around a big cup of my own version of punch. Cowardly, maybe, but it would keep me sober. I might be defying Mom by staying at the party, but getting drunk on top of that? If she found out, I'd be grounded until my wedding night. Which I wouldn't have, because she'd never let me near a guy again.

A slow grin spread across Marlin's face, and those odd eyes twinkled as he peered at the clear plastic tumbler filled with pink lemonade that I now held—a tumbler that was about the size of four of the cups that were piled high in the foyer next to the punch bowl. "I think I have a bigger glass if you'd like."

I lifted my chin and hoped I looked like a high school student defending her right to drink spiked punch. "No thanks. I've already had a lot. This is just about perfect."

He moved closer, although his voice seemed to stay very far away. His hand touched my back, and I had the oddest sensation that his fingers were going right through me. I tried to stifle a shiver but didn't quite manage.

"Problem?" he asked, his voice slick and oily, his breath so minty I had to assume he wasn't drinking the punch.

"Cold punch," I said. "Brain freeze."

"Ah." He put pressure on my back, and like a dutiful puppy, I moved forward. "I was looking for you. Mindy and Carson and Jeremy joined me in the study along with a few more of your friends. Will you join us? It's less boisterous than the foyer and ballroom, but easier to talk."

"Sure," I said. In some part of my mind, I recognized that he spoke strangely, his words overly formal or something. But I couldn't really think about it. I tried a bit, but the thoughts wouldn't stick, and by the time we reached the study, I'd forgotten all about it.

The room was oak-paneled and fancy, like something out of an old movie, and I looked around, taking in the paintings in gilt frames, the ornate furniture on which my friends and a bunch of other kids were sitting, and the massive wooden desk.

I saw Carson and Jeremy on a sofa, just sitting and talking. Mindy was on an overstuffed loveseat nursing another cup of punch. She looked up at me, her eyes glassy and her smile crooked, and I started toward her, determined to cut her off.

I'd taken one step when it happened—the room changed. The formal-looking study disappeared in a snap and suddenly I was in a room filled with nothing but red and black. Blood, I realized, and it coated the walls, the scent of it filling my nose and making me want to gag.

Something squished under my feet, and I looked down to find myself tromping on maggots, their fat little bodies bursting beneath my shoes.

And right in front of me, the big wooden desk was now a giant stone slab, like the kind ancient tribes used to make sacrifices to the gods.

Oh God, oh God, oh God...

I closed my eyes and tried to breathe normally, and when I opened them again—slowly and tentatively—the room was completely back in order.

What the heck?

I glanced at the lemonade in my hand. Maybe I should have cut myself off sooner.

On the couch, Mindy was peering at me, her forehead crinkled. I must have looked freaked, because she pushed herself up and started toward me. She, at least looked normal. At least that's what I thought at first. Then I saw the weird tentacle things that were wrapped around her ankles and wrists. She, however, didn't seem aware of them at all. And I sure as heck didn't understand why I was seeing them.

I blinked again, and the tentacles disappeared, but the blood was back. Then the tentacles were, and I stood there hyperventilating as I realized that the long, gray squid-like arms were attached to all the kids, and that they extended back to Marlin, who'd taken a seat behind the blood-soaked sacrificial stone. I mean the desk. The slab. *The desk.*

I had no idea why I was seeing two versions of the same room, one very decidedly coming at me straight from the Horror Channel. But I did know with absolute certainty that Marlin was a demon. I mean, that was the only explanation, right? And his minty-fresh breath was a big, minty clue. Too minty. I should have realized; hadn't mom trained me to notice breath? And didn't demons have the nastiest breath imaginable? The kind of breath that they would mask with liberal doses of mouthwash and tons and tons of minty candies.

Oh, shit.

The room was changing with every glance, as if I was looking at one of those holographic bubblegum cards that change slightly depending on the angle.

"Allie?" Mindy asked. "Are you okay?"

"I...no. My head feels weird." What was I supposed to say? Did you know there's a squid creature attached to you, and it's Marlin? "I think it must be the drink."

I think it must be the drink...

That was it! I was absolutely, positively certain of it. Everyone in that room except me was drunk on punch, and none of the kids in that room saw what I was seeing—and what I was seeing was reality mixed in with a little bit of a mirage. Only it was the *blood* that was the reality, along with the tentacles and the maggots. And the stone table.

The oak paneled study was the fantasy—and the punch induced it. It was spiked with more than alcohol, that was for sure.

But I'd stopped drinking the punch, so I wasn't drunk, even though Marlin had invited me in because he assumed I was. I only had a little bit of demon juice in me, and so I could see what the room really looked like...and I was scared to death.

Once more, I'd gone on a date, and been sucked into demonville. I mean, that's all great and fabulous once I'm a demon hunter, but right now, I'm a high school student, and it's not like I've got my knife in my itty bitty purse.

In fact, all I had in my purse that could even remotely pass for a weapon was nail clippers.

I drew in a breath for courage, and decided that one tiny pair of clippers would just have to do.

Then I saw two more tentacles sliding across the floor heading straight toward me, and I knew that nail clippers weren't the answer. I wasn't ready for this. How could I fight this?

Mom.

The tentacles were only a few feet away now, and I clapped my hand over my mouth, mumbled something about needing to throw up, and turned and raced out the door.

I didn't know where I was or what I was going to do, but I knew I had to find someplace safe, then hole up and call my mom, so I pulled open the first door I found and lunged into a dingy, dust-covered bedroom filled with moldy, decaying furniture and a stench that made me want to really throw up.

I ignored it and pulled out my cell phone and my nail clippers. I jabbed the speed dial number for home, then opened the clippers and extended the metal file, giving me a weapon that extended about one and a half inches. In other words, completely freaking useless for self-defense against most creatures, but deadly to a demon if I could put that point through his eye. The trick, of course, was not getting dead first.

On the other end of the line, the phone rang.

"Come on, come on..."

One ring, then another and another until finally, "Hello?"

"Mom!"

That was all I said. Because right then Marlin burst through the door, yanked the phone out of my hand, and hurled it through the window. Glass shattered under the force, but I barely heard the noise. Instead, all I heard were my own screams.

"So you know," Marlin said, his mouth moving, but a deeper voice coming out. *"It matters not. This year's sacrifices have been chosen. Your failure to drink fully of the elixir is of no consequence. What you have seen does not matter. The dead tell no tales, Alison, and you cannot stop us. Judemore will rise. He will feed. And he will bestow his bounty upon me for yet another year."*

He said all of that, and then he smiled. And before I even had time to think that I really didn't like the look of that smile, he lunged.

And guess what? I was right. My nail clippers with their tiny metal file were no match against Marlin. I needed a knife. A gun. A Civil War replica sword. Something—*anything*—to fight with.

I had nada though, so I hauled out every martial arts trick I'd learned, and I few that I made up right there on the fly—but he was one hell of a lot tougher than me, and I wasn't even slowing him down.

I wanted to cry with frustration. More, I wanted to cry with anger—at myself for being such a complete and total idiot. For coming here. For doing everything wrong. And for getting myself, my best friend, and a bunch of kids killed.

Because that was what was going to happen. I knew it the moment Marlin hauled me off the floor and carried me kicking and screaming and beating and fighting into the study. I knew when he tied me to a blood-soaked chair.

I knew when he didn't pry my fingers open and take my tiny nail clippers, leaving them instead as a symbol of what I couldn't accomplish no matter how hard I tried.

Tears streamed down my cheeks, and I tried to listen to what Marlin was saying, but I couldn't hear through the rush of my fear.

Right then, I wanted my mom, and not in a way most kids want a parent when they were in trouble.

I wanted my mom to burst through those doors and kick some demon ass.

But I knew she couldn't. I'd barely said a word. She probably didn't even realize I was in trouble.

I'd messed up. Big time.

And I wasn't even going to be around to get grounded for it.

Something hard and tight locked around my heart and my breath felt fluttery and hot. *Fear.*

I didn't want to die.

But right then, I really didn't think that I had a choice.

Kate

Not good, I thought as I desperately tried to call Allie back. *Frantic calls from your daughter that end abruptly are never a good thing.*

No answer. For that matter, no ring. The phone went straight to voice mail.

My stomach twisted with worry. I should *never* have let her go to the mall. What was I thinking? Malls were dangerous. Hell, the world was dangerous. Who knew that better than me?

As my mind churned, my fingers were busy looking up Parker's phone number, then dialing, then tapping out a rhythm on the counter as I waited for a ring, then an answer.

Finally, a sleepy voice came on the line.

"Is Allie okay?" I asked without preamble.

A pause, during which every dark fear I'd ever known bubbled up inside me.

"Who?"

"Allie!" I shouted. "My daughter. She's there with Parker and Mindy."

"Kate?" I heard the confusion in Rhonda Downing's voice. "What are you talking about? Parker and the girls are sleeping over at Tanya's house." In the silence that followed, I heard her understanding. "Aren't they?"

"Call," I said sharply. "Call and find out."

I slammed the phone down, because I already knew what the answer was. The girls weren't at Tanya's anymore than they were at Parker's. They'd planned and plotted to go somewhere, though, and now they were in trouble, and I didn't have any way to find them.

Think, dammit, think.

I didn't even know if the trouble was of the human or the demon variety. Not that it mattered. I was going to find them, I was going to save them, and then I was going to ground my daughter until college.

First, I had to find her.

How? They could be anywhere. All I knew was that she had her phone, or at least was near it. Maybe I could triangulate the phone signal? They did that in the movies, right? So maybe if I called Rome, someone at *Forza* could—

Mindy.

I didn't need *Forza*—for that matter I wasn't even sure if my Hollywood triangulation plan would work. But I knew that I could track Mindy.

But were they together? Dear God, please let them be together.

I raced toward the back door, then sprinted across the back yard to Laura's house. My best friend is also Mindy's mom, and they live in the house directly behind us, which makes it convenient for moments like these. Not that my heart could stand many moments like these.

"Does Mindy have her iPhone?" I asked after pushing my way inside, past Laura who stood blinking and sleepy in a bathrobe. The phone had been a guilt-loaded present designed to lessen the emotional trauma of the divorce. Mindy had been thrilled, and Laura had justified the purchase by pointing out the cool feature that let you go onto the Internet to find a lost phone—or, presumably, track down the missing child who was holding it. "I need to know where she is!"

Horror crossed her face and I realized belatedly that I could have approached the whole "our daughters are in danger" thing a little more gently. To Laura's credit, however, she didn't interrogate me until she was already at the computer.

I barely had time to tell her what happened when a map appeared on screen showing the location of the phone. "I'm off," I said. I'd grabbed my favorite jacket on my way out the door, so I had my stiletto in the sleeve and another knife in my purse, along with a bottle of holy water. I also keep supplies under the front seat of my minivan, but I didn't want to waste time going back to my house.

"Take my car," Laura said, when I'd told her as much. "And bring my baby back." She sounded brave, but I could see the worry on her face and knew it reflected my own.

"I will," I said, and I meant it. I only hoped I could do it. More than that, I hoped that Allie was still with Mindy.

That, however, wasn't something I could worry about. This was the only lead I had. Allie *had* to be there, and I raced west toward the cliffs that overlooked the coast, maneuvering my way up into one of San Diablo's ritzier neighborhoods until I finally found the address where Mindy's phone now was.

Immediately, I knew I had the right place. There were cars everywhere, and teenagers littering the lawn and massive front porch. The fear that had gripped me loosened a little. Maybe this wasn't life-or-death after all. Maybe she'd gone to a frat party. Maybe she'd dropped the phone.

Maybe I needed to get inside that house and find out for myself.

Inside, I found more kids, more eating, more music, more drinking.

But I didn't find Allie or Mindy.

I glanced around, frantic, not sure where to even start looking. The place was huge.

As if in answer, a scream ripped through the room, cutting through even the din of the party. I couldn't have been the only one who heard it, and yet I was the only one who reacted, and I was sprinting up the stairs, heading for the source, before the echo of the sound had died out.

What I found turned me cold.

A baby-faced man standing in the center of an oak-paneled study, arms outstretched, his body bathed in red, his skin bulging and popping as something within him rose and grew. And, yeah, I knew what that something was: a demon.

He was surrounded by about a dozen kids sitting casually around the room, not freaking out or even reacting despite the writhing, changing thing in the middle. All the kids, including Mindy, who had a goofy smile on her face. Everyone, that is, except Allie—she was tied to a chair, and my heart twisted when I saw her. I, however, forced myself to concentrate on my goal: killing the demon.

This was not your run-of-the-mill body-inhabiting demon, and yet I'd heard of this kind of thing. Young men who gave themselves body and soul to a demon in order to gain power and never-ending youth. To keep it up, though, they had to make constant sacrifices.

The human/demon hadn't even noticed me as far as I could tell. The rising had thrust it into a trance, but I guessed that wouldn't last long. Soon the awakening would be complete, and it would want to feed. And that, I thought, was where all the kids came in.

I needed to take advantage of the trance. I needed to kill the thing right then, and I raced forward to do just that.

"Mom!" Allie screamed. "Be careful! You can't see it, but he's a demon, and he's—"

"I can see him," I said, tackling the beast and knocking him to the floor. This was going to be too easy.

"Really?" She was so incredulous she almost sounded normal. "What about the room? The tentacles?"

"Tentacles?" I'd been poised to jab my stiletto through his eye. Now I hesitated.

"He's holding onto the kids. All of us. Me, too," she said, glancing down at her ankles as if in support of her statement. "There was punch, but I only drank a little, and I could see what was real and they couldn't and—"

"I get it," I said, though I didn't completely. I got enough. The kids who'd drunk the punch must see the demon as I saw him, they just weren't afraid. Because they were part of it now. Part of the ceremony, part of the world. Kill the demon, and they'd step up to fight. Either that, or they'd die, too.

To ensure the kids stayed alive (and to make sure they didn't become demonic fighting minions), we had to cut the tentacles before we killed the beast. And since I couldn't see them...

I jumped off the demon and raced toward Allie, who was screaming questions at me. I sliced the ropes that bound her, then handed her the larger knife. "Cut them," I said. "Cut all the tentacles. I can't kill him until the kids are free."

Her eyes went wide, but she didn't hesitate. Didn't question, and despite the fact that I was beyond furious with her for sneaking off to a party, right then, I was pretty damn proud.

Quickly, she reached down and sliced through the tentacles that bound her. When she did, the demon I'd left on the floor shook with life.

Damn. I'd been afraid of that.

"I'll keep you safe," I said, racing back to the demon. "Hurry!"

She'd sliced through another tentacle by the time I got back to the demon. I landed a solid punch to its bulbous, writhing face. I risked a sideways look and saw a boy who'd been sitting calmly in a chair sink to the floor in a dead faint. *Good.* I'd rather a roomful of kids not see this.

Another set of tentacles cut, and this time the force of the break brought the demon to life. He leaped up, knocking me off him, then turning to attack Allie. I tackled him, buying her time to slice through another, as the demon twisted and kicked, and I blocked and parried.

I had my stiletto and damned if I didn't want to use it. Fighting was easier when you were going for the kill. Trying to slow things down was hard. And painful, I thought, when he picked me up and hurled me toward the desk. I landed hard on my back, my breath going out of me, but I didn't have time to think about the pain. Allie had reached the last kid—the last set of tentacles.

Mindy.

But the demon was on his way there, too.

No way.

I lunged, knocking him down before he could get to Mindy. I screamed for Allie to hurry, fighting to position myself as she hacked at the last two tentacles.

"Now!" she yelled, and I lashed down with my stiletto—and as I did, the demon thrust out his arm, knocking the blade from my hand and sending it skittering across the room. *Shit!*

I clutched his wrist, my knees clamped tight as I straddled him, but I couldn't hold him for long. I needed a weapon, something I could slide into his eye—something sharp and pointy that could kill a demon.

"Mom!" Allie said, and as she spoke, she tossed me something small and silver. Instinctively, the demon tilted his head up and opened his eyes wide.

And that was all it took.

I snatched the clippers from the air, held them with the pointy file sticking out, and plunged the metal deep into the demon's eye.

Immediately, I heard the hiss of the demon leaving the body. Beneath me, all that was left was a shell.

A dead body.

And there I was in a roomful of kids, all of whom would surely awake from their faints soon enough.

I sighed. A dead body wasn't going to go over well with them.

Lamenting the fact that demons don't disappear in a puff of ash and smoke, I grabbed the body under the arms and started dragging it. "Open it," I said to Allie, motioning with my head to a door at the back of the room.

She ran ahead, and I shoved the body into the small, dark closet. For now, that would have to be enough, especially since there was no time to do more.

Around us, all the kids were stirring. I saw Jeremy's eyes go wide, then saw him look around frantically, relaxing when his eyes found Allie.

"What happened?" he mumbled.

"You should go home, Jeremy," I said. Then looked around at the entire group, "All of you."

Faced with a disapproving adult, they all slunk out guiltily. All except Mindy, who was looking at me with no small amount of trepidation. "Hi, Aunt Kate," she said. She cleared her throat, then turned her attention to Allie. "We're in a lot of trouble, aren't we?"

Allie cocked her head to the side and looked at me, her eyebrows raised in question, as if the fact that she'd done herself proud in the demonic ass-kicking department would erase all the other wrongs of the night.

I didn't answer. After a minute, that was answer enough.

Allie sighed. But not her usual exasperated sigh. This one was a sigh of resignation and acceptance, and I knew then that although the lesson had been hard fought, she'd learned a bit more about prudence and responsibility tonight.

"We're definitely in trouble," her words said, and I know that's what Mindy heard. But what I heard was, "I love you, Mom."

"I love you, too, kid," I whispered. "Now let's go home."

Chronologically, this story falls between Deja Demon *and* Demon Ex Machina. —Julie Kenner

Julie Kenner does not hunt demons, but she does spend her days wrangling two small children and an equal number of cats, not to mention a husband. She's also the author of numerous novels, including the "Kate Connor: Demon Hunting Soccer Mom" series and the newly released "Blood Lily Chronicles." Visit Julie online at **www.juliekenner.com**

Soccer mom **Kate Connor** spends her days driving carpool, organizing Gymboree playdates, and hunting demons. Just another day in suburbia...

THE SPIRIT OF THE THING

— A Nightside Story —

by Simon R. Green

In the Nightside, that secret hidden heart of London, where it's always the darkest part of the night and the dawn never comes, you can find some of the best and worst bars in the world. There are places that will serve you liquid moonlight in a tall glass, or angel's tears, or a wine that was old when Rome was young.

And then there's the *Jolly Cripple*. You get to one of the worst bars in the world by walking down the kind of alley you'd normally have the sense to stay out of. The *Cripple* is tucked away behind more respectable establishments, and light from the street doesn't penetrate far. It's always half full of junk and garbage, and the only reason there aren't any bodies to step over is because the rats have eaten them all. You have to watch out for rats in the Nightside; some people say they're evolving. In fact, some people claim to have seen the damn things using knives and forks.

I wouldn't normally be seen dead in a dive like the *Jolly Cripple*, but I was working. At the time, I was in between clients and in need of some fast walking around money, so when the bar's owner got word to me that there was quick and easy money to be made, I swallowed my pride. I'm John Taylor, private investigator. I have a gift for finding things, and people. I always find the truth for my clients; even if it means having to walk into places where even angels would wince and turn their heads aside.

The *Jolly Cripple* was a drinker's bar. Not a place for conversation, or companionship. More the kind of place you go when the world has kicked you out, your credit's no good, and your stomach couldn't handle the good stuff any more, even if you could afford it. In the *Jolly Cripple* the floor was sticky, the air was thick with half a dozen kinds of smoke, and the only thing you could be sure of was vomit in the corners and piss and blood in the toilets. The owner kept the lights down low, partly so you couldn't see how bad the place really was, but mostly because the patrons preferred it that way.

The owner and bartender was one Maxie Eliopoulos. A sleazy soul in an unwashed body, dark and hairy, always smiling. Maxie wore a grimy T shirt with the legend IT'S ALL GREEK TO ME, and showed off its various bloodstains like badges of honour. No one ever gave Maxie any trouble in his bar. Or at least, not twice. He was short and squat with broad shoulders, and a square brutal face under a shock of black hair. More dark hair covered his bare arms, hands, and knuckles. He never stopped smiling, but it never once reached his eyes. Maxie was always ready to sell you anything you could afford. Especially if it was bad for you.

Some people said he only served people drink so he could watch them die by inches.

Maxie had hired me to find out who'd been diluting his drinks and driving his customers away. (And that's about the only thing that could.) Didn't take me long to find out who. I sat down at the bar, raised my gift, and concentrated on the sample bottle of what should have been gin; but was now so watered down you could have kept goldfish in it. My mind leapt up and out, following the connection between the water and its source, right back to where it came from. My Sight shot down through the barroom floor, down and down, into the sewers below.

Long stone tunnels with curving walls, illuminated by phosphorescent moss and fungi, channeling thick dark water with things floating in it. All kinds of things. In the Nightside's sewers even trained workers tread carefully, and often carry flamethrowers, just in case. I looked around me, my Sight searching for the presence I'd felt; and something looked back. Something knew I was there, even if only in spirit. The murky waters

churned and heaved, and then a great head rose up out of the
dark water, followed by a body. It only took me a moment to
realize both head and body were made up of water, and nothing
else.

The face was broad and unlovely, the body obscenely female,
like one of those ancient fertility goddess statues. Thick rivulets
of water ran down her face like slow tears, and ripples bulged
constantly around her body. A water elemental. I'd heard the
Nightside had been using them to clean up the sewers; taking
in all the bad stuff and purifying it inside themselves. The
Nightside always finds cheap and practical ways to solve its
problems, even if they aren't always very nice solutions.

"Who disturbs me?" said the sewer elemental, in a thick, glu-
tinous voice.

"John Taylor," I said. Back in the bar my lips were moving,
but my words could only be heard down in the sewer. "You've
been interfering with one of the bars above. Using your power
to infuse the bottles with your water. You know you're not supposed to get involved with the world above."

"I am old," said the elemental of the sewers. "So old, even I
don't remember how old I am. I was worshipped, once. But the
world changed and I could not, so even the once worshipped
and adored must work for a living. I have fallen very far from
what I was; but then, that's the Nightside for you. Now I deal
in shit and piss and other things, and make them pure again.
Because someone has to. It's a living. But, fallen as I am...*no one*
insults me, defies me, cheats me! I serve all the bars in this area,
and the owners and I have come to an understanding...all but
Maxie Eliopoulos! He refuses my reasonable demands!"

"Oh hell," I said. "It's a labour dispute. What are you asking
for, better working conditions?"

"I just want him to clean up his act," said the elemental of the
sewers. "And if he won't, I'll do it for him. I can do a lot worse to
him than just dilute his filthy drinks..."

"That is between you and him," I said firmly. "I don't do arbi-
tration." And then I got the hell out of there.

Back in the bar and in my body, I confronted Maxie. "You
didn't tell me this was a dispute between contractors, Maxie."

He laughed, and slapped one great palm hard against his
grimy bartop. "I knew it! I knew it was that water bitch, down in
her sewers! I just needed you to confirm it, Taylor."

"So why's she mad at you? Apart from the fact that you're a
loathsome, disgusting individual."

He laughed again, and poured me a drink of what, in his bar, passed for the good stuff. "She wants me to serve better booze; says the impurities in the stuff I sell is polluting her system, and leaving a nasty taste in her mouth. I could leave a nasty taste in her mouth, heh heh heh... She pressured all the other bars and they gave in, but not me. Not me! No one tells Maxie Eliopoulos what to do in his own bar! Silly cow... Cheap and nasty is what my customers want, so cheap and nasty is what they get."

"So...for a while there, your patrons were drinking booze mixed with sewer water," I said. "I'm surprised so many stayed."

"I'm surprised so many of them noticed," said Maxie. "Good thing I never drink the tap water... All right, Taylor, you've confirmed what I needed to know. I'll take it from here. I can handle her. Thinks I can't get to her, down in the sewers, but I'll show that bitch. No one messes with me and gets away with it. Now —here's what we agreed on."

He pushed a thin stack of grubby bank notes across the bar, and I counted them quickly before making them disappear about my person. You don't want to attract attention in a bar like the *Jolly Cripple*, and nothing will do that faster than a display of cash, grubby or not. Maxie grinned at me in what he thought was an ingratiating way.

"No need to rush away, Taylor. Have another drink. Drinks are on the house for you; make yourself at home."

I should have left. I should have known better...but it was one of the few places my creditors wouldn't look for me, and besides ...the drinks were on the house.

I sat at a table in the corner, working my way through a bottle of the kind of tequila that doesn't have a worm in it, because the tequila's strong enough to dissolve the worm. A woman in a long white dress walked up to my table. I didn't pay her much attention at first, except to wonder what someone so normal-looking was doing in a dive like this...and then she walked right through the table next to me, and the people sitting around it. She drifted through them as though they weren't even there, and each of them in turn shuddered briefly, and paid closer attention to their drinks. Their attitude said it all; they'd seen the woman in white before, and they didn't want to know. She stopped before me, looking at me with cool, quiet, desperate eyes.

"You have to help me. I've been murdered. I need you to find out who killed me."

That's what comes from hanging around in strange bars. I gestured for her to sit down opposite me, and she did so perfectly easily. She still remembered what it felt like to have a body, which meant she hadn't been dead long. I looked her over carefully. I couldn't see any obvious death wounds, not even a ligature round her neck. Most murdered ghosts appear the way they did when they died. The trauma overrides everything else.

"What makes you think you were murdered?" I said bluntly.

"Because there's a hole in my memory," she said. "I don't remember coming here, don't remember dying here; but now I'm a ghost and I can't leave this bar. Something prevents me. Something must be put right; I can feel it. Help me, please. Don't leave me like this."

I always was a sucker for a sob story. Comes with the job, and the territory. She had no way of paying me, and I normally avoid charity work... But I'd just been paid, and I had nothing else to do, so I nodded briefly and considered the problem. It's a wonder there aren't more ghosts in the Nightside, when you think about it. We've got every other kind of supernatural phenomenon you can think of, and there's never any shortage of the suddenly deceased. Anyone with the Sight can see ghosts, from stone tape recordings, where moments from the Past imprint themselves on their surroundings, endlessly repeating, like insects trapped in amber...to lost souls, damned to wander the world through tragic misdeeds or unfinished business.

There are very few hauntings in the Nightside, as such. The atmosphere here is so saturated with magic and super-science and general weird business that it swamps and drowns out all the lesser signals. Though there are always a few stubborn souls who just won't be told. Like Long John Baldwin, who drank himself to death in my usual bar, *Strangefellows*. Dropped stone dead while raising one last glass of Valhalla Venom to his lips, and hit the floor with the smile still on his face. The bar's owner, Alex Morrisey, had the body removed, but even before the funeral was over Long John was back in his familiar place at the bar, calling for a fresh bottle. Half a dozen unsuccessful exorcisms later, Alex gave up and hired Long John as his replacement bartender and security guard. Long John drinks the memories of old booze from empty bottles, and enjoys the company of his fellow drinkers, just as he always did (they're a hardened bunch, in *Strangefellows*). And as Alex says, a ghost is more intelligent than a watch dog or a security system, and a lot cheaper to maintain.

I could feel a subtle tension on the air, a wrongness; as though there was a reason why the ghost shouldn't be there. She was an unusually strong manifestation; no transparency, no fraying around the edges. That usually meant a strong character, when she was alive. She didn't flinch as I looked her over thoughtfully. She was a tall, slender brunette, with neatly-styled hair and under-stated makeup, in a long white dress of such ostentatious simplicity that it had to have cost a bundle.

"Do you know your name?" I said finally.

"Holly De Lint."

"And what's a nice girl like you doing in a dive like this?"

"I don't know. Normally, I wouldn't be seen dead in a place like this."

We both smiled slightly. "Could someone have brought you here, Holly? Could that person have..."

"Murdered me? Perhaps. But who would I know, in a place like this?"

She had a point. A woman like her didn't belong here. So I left her sitting at my table, and made my rounds of the bar, politely interrogating the regulars. Most of them didn't feel like talking, but I'm John Taylor. I have a reputation. Not a very nice one, but it means people will talk to me when they wouldn't talk to anyone else. They didn't know Holly. They didn't know anything. They hadn't seen anything, because they didn't come to a bar like this to take an interest in other people's problems. And they genuinely might not have noticed a ghost. One of the side effects of too much booze is that it shuts down the Sight; though you can still end up seeing things that aren't there.

I went back to Holly, still sitting patiently at the table. I sat down opposite her, and used my gift to find out what had happened in her recent past. Faint pastel images of Holly appeared all around the bar, blinking on and off, from where she'd tried to talk to people, or begged for help, or tried to leave and been thrown back. I concentrated, sorting through the various images until I found the memory of the last thing she'd done while still alive. I got up from the table and followed the last trace of the living Holly all the way to the back of the bar, to the toilets. She went into the Ladies, and I went in after her. Luckily, there was no one else there, then or now; so I could watch uninterrupted as Holly De Lint opened a cubicle, sat down, and then washed down a big handful of pills with most of a bottle of whisky. She went about it quite methodically, with no tears or hysterics, her face cold and even indifferent, though her eyes still seemed terribly sad. She killed herself, with pills and booze. The last image showed her slumping slowly sideways, the bottle slipping from her numbed fingers, as the last of the light went out of her eyes.

I went back into the bar, and sat down again opposite Holly. She looked at me inquiringly, trustingly. So what could I do, except tell her the truth?

"There was no murderer, Holly. You took your own life. Can you tell me why..."

But she was gone. Disappeared in a moment, blinking out of existence like a punctured soap bubble. No sign to show that anyone had ever been sitting there.

So I went back to the bar and told Maxie what had happened, and he laughed in my face.

"You should have talked to me first, Taylor! I could have told you all about her. You aren't the first stranger she's approached. Look, you know the old urban legend, where the guy's just driving along, minding his own business, and then sees a woman in white signaling desperately from the side of the road? He's a good guy, so he stops and asks what's up. She says she needs a lift home, so he takes her where she wants to go. But the woman doesn't say a word, all through the drive, and when he finally gets there; she's disappeared. The guy at the address tells the driver the woman was killed out there on the road long ago; but she keeps stopping drivers, asking them to take her home. Old story, right? It's the same here, except our woman in white keeps telling people that she's been murdered, but doesn't remember how. And when our good Samaritans find out the truth, and tell her; she disappears. Until the next sucker comes along. You ready for another drink?"

"Can't you do something?" I said.

"I've tried all the usual shit," said Maxie. "But she's a hard one to shift. You think you could do something? That little bitch is seriously bad for business."

I went back to my table in the corner, to do some hard thinking. Most people would just walk away, on discovering the ghost was nothing more than a repeating cycle... But I'm not most people. I couldn't bear to think of Holly trapped in this place, maybe forever.

Why would a woman, with apparently everything to live for, kill herself in a dive like this? I raised my gift, and once again pastel-tinted semi-transparent images of the living Holly darted back and forth through the dimly-lit bar, lighting briefly at this table and that, like a flower fairy at midnight. It didn't take me long to realize there was one table she visited more than most.

So I went over to the people sitting there, and made them tell me everything they knew.

Professor Hartnell was a grey-haired old gentlemen in a battered city suit. He used to be somebody, but he couldn't remember who. Igor was a shaven-headed kobold with more piercings than most, who'd run away from the German mines of his people to see the world. He didn't think much of the world, but he couldn't go back, so he settled in the Nightside. Where no one gave a damn he was gay. The third drinker was a battered old Russian, betrayed by the Revolution but appalled at what his country had become. No one mentioned the ice-pick sticking out the back of his head.

They didn't know Holly, as such, but they knew who she'd come here after. She came to the *Jolly Cripple* to save someone. Someone who didn't want to be saved—her brother, Craig De Lint. He drank himself to death, right here in the bar, right at their table. Sometimes in their company, more often not, because the only company he was interested in came in a bottle. I used my gift again, and managed to pull up a few ghost images from the Past, of the living Craig. Stick thin, shabby clothes, the bones standing out in his grey face. Dead, dead eyes.

"You're wasting your time, sis," Craig De Lint said patiently. "You know I don't have any reason to drink. No great trauma, no terrible loss...I just like to drink, and I don't care about anything else. Started out in all the best places, and worked my way down to this. Where someone like me belongs. Go home, sis. You don't belong here. Go home, before something bad happens to you."

"I can't just leave you here! There must be something I can do!"

"And that's the difference between us, sis, right there. You always think there's something that can be done. But I know a lost cause when I am one."

The scene shifted abruptly, and there was Holly at the bar, arguing furiously with Maxie. He still smiled, even as he said things that cut her like knives.

"Of course I encouraged your brother to drink, sweetie. That's my job. That's what he was here for. And no, I don't give a damn that he's dead. He was dying when he walked in here, by his own choice; I just helped him on his way. Now either buy a drink or get out of my face. I've got work to do."

"I'll have you shut down!" said Holly, her voice fierce now, her small hands clenched into fists.

He laughed in her face. "Like to see you try, sweetie. This is the Nightside, where everyone's free to go to Hell in their own way."

"I know people! Important people! Money talks, Maxie; and I've got far more of it than you have."

He smiled easily. "You've got balls, sweetie. Okay, let's talk. Over a drink."

"I don't drink."

"My bar, my rules. You want to talk with me, you drink with me."

Holly shrugged, and looked away. Staring at the table where her brother died. Maxie poured two drinks from a bottle, and then slipped a little something into Holly's glass. He watched, smiling, as Holly turned back and gulped the stuff down, just to get rid of it; and then he smiled even more widely as all the expression went out of her face.

"There, that's better," said Maxie. "Little miss rich bitch. Come into my bar, throwing your weight about, telling me what to do? I don't think so. Feeling a little more...suggestible, are you? Good, good... Such a shame about your brother. You must be sad, very sad. So sad, you want to end it all. So here's a big handful of help-ful pills, and a bottle of booze. So you can put an end to yourself, out back, in the toilets. Bye-bye, sweetie. Don't make a mess."

The ghost images snapped off as the memory ended. I was so choked with rage I could hardly breathe. I got up from the table and stormed over to the bar. Maxie leaned forward to say something, and I grabbed two handfuls of his grubby T-shirt and hauled him right over his bar, so I could stick my face right into his. He had enough sense not to struggle.

"You knew," I said. "You knew all along! You made her kill herself!"

"I had no choice!" said Maxie, still smiling. "It was self-defense! She was going to shut me down. And yeah, I knew all along. That's why I hired you! I knew you'd solve the elemental business right away, and then stick around for the free drinks. I knew the ghost would approach you, and you'd get involved. I needed someone to get rid of her; and you always were a soft touch, Taylor."

I let him go. I didn't want to touch him any more. He backed cautiously away, and sneered at me from a safe distance.

"You feel sorry for the bitch, help her on her way to the great Hereafter! You'll be doing her a favour, and me too. I told you she was bad for business."

I turned my back on him, and went back to the drinkers who'd known him best. And before any of them could even say anything, I focused my gift through them, through their memories of Craig, and reached out to him in a direction I knew but could not name. A door opened, that hadn't been there before, and a great light spilled out into the bar. A fierce and unrelenting light, too bright for the living to look at directly. The drinkers in the bar should have winced away from it, used as they were to the permanent gloom; but something in the light touched them despite themselves, waking old memories, of what might have been.

And out of that light came Craig De Lint, walking free and easy. He reached out a hand, smiling kindly, and out of the gloom came the ghost of Holly De Lint, also walking free and easy. She took his hand, and they smiled at each other, and then Craig led her through the doorway and into the light; and the door shut behind them and was gone.

In the renewed gloom of the bar, Maxie hooted and howled with glee, slapping his heavy hand on the bartop in triumph. "Finally, free of the bitch! Free at last! Knew you had it in you, Taylor! Drinks on the house, people! On the house!"

And they all came stumbling up to the bar, already forgetting what they might have seen in the light. Maxie busied himself serving them, and I considered him thoughtfully, from a distance. Maxie had murdered Holly, and got away with it, and used me to clean up after him, removing the only part of the business that still haunted him. So I raised my gift one last time, and made contact with the elemental of the sewers, deep under the bar.

"Maxie will never agree to the deal you want," I said. "He likes things just the way they are. But you might have better luck with a new owner. You put your sewer water into Maxie's bottles. There are other places you could put it."

"I take your meaning, John Taylor," said the elemental. "You're everything they say you are."

Maxie lurched suddenly behind his bar, flailing desperately about him as his lungs filled up with water. I turned my back on the drowning man, and walked away. Though, being me, I couldn't resist having the last word.

"Have one on me, Maxie."

Simon R. Green has worked as a shop assistant, bicycle repair mechanic, actor, journalist, and mail order bride. And every day he's glad he doesn't have to do any of that any more. His best known series are the "Deathstalker" books, (like "Star Wars," only with a plot that makes sense,) the "Nightside" books, and the "Secret Histories," featuring Shaman Bond, the world's most secret agent. Although he does not have a website as such, there is a tribute site, to which he sometimes contributes information, at **www.bluemoonrising.nl**

John Taylor is a private eye who operates in the Twilight Zone, solving cases of the weird and uncanny. His beat is the Nightside, that sour secret heart of London, where the sun has never shone and it's always three o'clock in the morning, the hour that tries men's souls. Gods and monsters can be found there, often attending the same self-help groups. John Taylor is your last chance for justice, the truth, and other disturbing things.

HOLDING THE LINE

— A Jill Kismet Story —

by Lilith Saintcrow

I landed *hard*, ribs snapping and a wash of red agony pouring through me. High tittering laughter from the hellbreed with the primrose-colored eyes, screams of approval from the clustered Traders. Five against one, and here I was on the floor.

This is not going well.

"Oh, Kismet." The tittering hellbreed actually had the gall to play to his Trader gallery. "Did you fall *down*?"

Hot salt blood dribbled on my chin. The scar—the mark of a hellbreed's lips—chuckled wetly on my wrist, a burst of razor-wire power jolting up the bones and cresting over my shoulder, my ribs popping out and hastily fusing back together. My left hand closed around a gun butt, and I found out that the prim-rose-eyed bastard had thrown me over near my whip.

Well. Better late than never. My right hand shot out, grabbed the bullwhip's handle, and the sonofabitch was still laughing when I rolled up off the floor and the leather flashed out, a high hard crack that was the jingling silver flechettes at the end of the whip breaking the sound barrier. The hip leads in whip-work, a slight advantage women have. When added to speed and cussedness and the etheric force humming through the scar and jacking me up into superhuman, it was all I was going to get.

It was going to have to be enough.

Naked light bulbs swung at the end of cords, crazy-dappling shadows over the warehouse's interior. The whip lashed, and flayed the primrose-eyed hellbreed's face. It cut him off mid-chuckle, and if I wanted him dead now would have been the time to shoot him.

But I didn't. Instead, I shot the Trader springing at me in midair, and to my right, the one who had somehow cottoned on that I wasn't down and out yet. He'd swapped some of his humanity for superstrength and superspeed, but my aim was true and half his hell-trading head evaporated. That took the pep out of him, bigtime.

Lucky shot. I was just lucky all over tonight.

The screaming started, and from there it was straightforward. My next shot took out one of the hellbreed ringmaster's bending-backward little knees. He had folded down and was screaming, the black ichor that passes for their blood bubbling out past the thin fingers clasping his face. Said face was now a mess of ham-burger and there were three more Traders to deal with.

I hadn't thought they'd be stupid enough to stay at their last known hangout. Not when they knew I was after them. I hadn't precisely made a mistake—I'd just thought about questioning them before I started killing.

Mikhail would have told me not to bother. But he wasn't here. Twenty-nine days since the Weres lit his pyre and his soul rode the smoke to Valhalla.

I was on my own.

Four minutes later the last Trader died gibbering at the end of a long smear of black-tinted blood, the corruption eating up his tissues and making the body do a St. Vitus's dance. The pacts Traders make claim more than the soul, and maybe they would think twice about mortgaging themselves if they could see what happens when one of them bites it.

I don't know. All I see are the ones who chance it.

I turned back to the hellbreed. He wasn't so pretty now, and I hoped I'd gotten one of his eyes, popped it like a bubble. The whip coiled neatly and stowed itself, habitual movements while I kept the blubbering hellbreed covered. I ached all over and my ribs twitched, bone resetting itself. The scar pulse-burned on my right wrist, sawing against the nerves of my arm.

Slow and easy here, Jill.

My smart eye was hot and dry, watching the plucking under the fabric of the surface of the world. He could really be that hurt, burbling and moaning into his hands. But the tension in his shoulders—clad in once-elegant navy Brooks Brothers, now spattered with blood and other fluids—told me otherwise. His suit coat flopped around a little, low on his right side where the first bullet had taken a chunk out of him. Black ichor dripped and the noises he was making were straight out of a nightmare.

"Cut it out." My voice sliced through his. The silver charms tied in my hair rattled and buzzed, blessed metal reacting against the contamination in the air. "You're not *that* hurt."

"Bitch," he blubbered into his hands. "Oh you *bitch*."

You'd think they'd find something more original to call a female hunter. I kept the gun on him, every muscle quivering-alert. The scar burned, working into my flesh. "You can guess what I'm after." Each word very carefully weighted. "Slade. A hunter. Taller than me. Black hair, silver charms. Disappeared about twelve hours ago."

"Bitch," he moaned again.

I didn't have time. So I blew away his other knee. The report boomed and caromed through the warehouse's interior, and he crawfished on the floor, whisper-screaming because he'd run out of air.

"You have arms, too," I reminded him. "Shoulders. Ribs. Genitalia. *Start talking*."

In the end it took one of his elbows, too. By then the Traders were smears of bubbling black, corruption eating at their tissues, and the primrose-eyed 'breed screamed until I put him out of his misery. Silence descended through the foul reek.

I swallowed hard, set my jaw, and took just enough time to clean the contamination of hellbreed away with whispering blue banefire, shaken off my fingers like oil, before I got going. I didn't even stop to wash the blood off my face.

When another hunter calls, you go. It's that simple. We who hold back the tide of Hell don't ask for help lightly. I had irons in the fire back home, but Slade had called. A short message—*Trouble brewing. Something big. Need backup.* And I was on a plane and out of my town before the sun rose, ending up in his territory over a thousand miles away. Where the skies were always gray and there was a coffee shop on every single corner. The whole city smelled like concrete and old, moldy java.

I didn't have a chance to ask why he'd called me, since he'd disappeared before I could get here.

We'd done hunter residencies together in New Orleans with Katja Lefevre, and that had been one sliptilting screamfest after another. I still had scars twitching from those six months. But you don't ask questions. A hunter won't call another away from her territory without a damn good reason.

His house on its quiet tree-lined street was empty, the front door smashed to flinders and Slade himself gone. The local Weres, Slade's backup, knew nothing. The hellbreed weren't opening their mouths much. All I had was a name—*Narcisa*. And another one: the Dutch.

I didn't know what Narcisa meant. But the Dutch was a hellbreed club downtown, near the open air market where they threw fish around during the day.

I was glad to miss that. I mean, come on. Flinging *fish?*

The skyline here was alien territory. Santa Luz is desert, but Slade's city lives under a perpetual gray drizzle. You wouldn't think it would make much difference to a nocturnal creature. Dark is dark, and it gets cold in the desert too.

I crouched on the rooftop, dripping hair, dripping from my nose and fingertips, my leather trench shedding water thanks to the waterproofing. Weather means very little to a full-fledged hunter, but the chill in this place reached right into my bones.

It wasn't physical.

Across the street, the neon sign for the Dutch—a flying ship, of all things, with both oars and sail, lovingly rendered in glowing tubes—cast sickly green and red glow down into the wet street. Music pulsed in bass-thumping ribbons inside, the double doors flung wide in invitation. There was a line going down the block, but nobody seemed to have umbrellas. Just standing there in the wet.

No Traders in the line—they walked right in past the Trader bouncers. No visible hellbreed, but they would be inside.

They usually are. Ready and waiting, like spiders in a web.

Back in Santa Luz it was an hour ahead but a world away. Dark falls quickly out in the desert, like a guillotine blade. I would have hit the streets as dusk did, and probably already been in one or two short sharp fights. Since Mikhail was dead, plenty of them thought I'd be easy to get past or roll over.

Don't think about that, Jill. Focus.

I eased my weight back and forth, watching. A hunter learns early to draw a cloak of silence over the waiting, an uncanny stillness. Within that circle of quiet, though, you have to move a little bit. Shifting and adjusting to keep the muscles primed for action.

And as usual while I was waiting, the memories came back. My teacher's final gurgle as the scarlet gush of his life left him, his body stiffening then slumping in my arms, becoming dead-weight. The bitch who killed him was gone, good luck finding her now. And here I was a thousand miles from my city on a wild goose chase, and God only knew what was going on at home—

Stop. Intuition tingled. *Look, Jill. Something's there.*

Indeed, something was. A long glossy-black limousine pulled up to the curb, and the bouncers tensed. A Trader—blond, male, long legs, in a sharp dark suit—strolled out of the club's wide-flung mahogany doors.

The scar puckered, a hurtful throb. The mark of a hellbreed's lips against the tender inner flesh of my right wrist tasted the predatory glee on the air.

I was harder to kill now. Much harder.

Was it worth the price I'd paid? Especially since I hadn't been fast enough or strong enough when it counted.

Stop it. Look at what's happening.

Premonition tingled along every inch of me. A hunter becomes a full-blown psychic before long. Sorcery will do that for you.

And when you spend your life dealing with the nightside it's more of a survival mechanism than a perk.

So I kept still, blinking the rain out of my eyes. Watched the Trader open the limo's door, watched the long lean white leg slide out of the interior and the black stiletto heel touch wet cement. She rose out of the back of the car like a bad dream, dead-white curves poured into something slinky-black and sequined, slit up the sides. A mass of tumbled jet-black curls, and even at this distance the set of the slim shoulders was wrong.

A hunter can see below the carapace of beauty they wear. We can see the *twisting* in them.

This was a full hellbreed, waltzing in the front door. And if the Trader bowed and scraped any more, he would be licking the sidewalk.

It had to be the mysterious Narcisa.

A glitter caught my eye. There, around her wasp-waist, a belt of threads and jingling silver, the surface of the metal flowing with blue light, not quite popping free as sparks. I let out a soundless sigh. It's just like an arrogant fuck of a hellbreed to flout and taunt with a substance they're deadly-allergic to. If the silver rubbed her skin it would leave a bubbling, blistering burn.

They were charms. The same kind of charms as those tied into my hair with red thread. They didn't jingle as I moved again, my tented fingers against the lip-roof, bootsoles gripping. Steel-toed and steel-heeled, but flexible enough to grab under the ball of the foot, and silent as I touched the wet roughness of rooftop and cursed inwardly.

Now why would you be wearing those, bitch?

I had an idea, and it wasn't a nice one. So I reached for the copper cuff covering the scar. As soon as I stripped it off, my sensory acuity jacked up into the red and the flashing diamonds of small raindrops hit like an army's feet drumming.

My legs straightened. If any of those charms were Slade's, another hunter showing up might spook her. And if I went in guns blazin', the way I prefer to, she had a better chance at getting away in the resultant chaos.

So, I would have to be sneaky.

Moments later, the rooftop was empty.

The Trader sat in the driver's seat, window open and a cigarette fuming in the chill air. The alley enclosed the limo, wet trash drifted in the corners. The Dutch's back entrance—or one of them, I would bet there were more—didn't look like anything special. Just an alley.

Except for the rain, it could have been a corner of my city. They don't all look the same. But they're a crowd. You have to cut them out, take them one by one, before you can tell them apart.

I weighed my options. I could wait all night, but if she was wearing Slade's charms, I might not have that long.

He could be dead already, Jill.

The machine in my head, the one trained into me from the very beginning, clicked away. For me the machine's birth was in the instant Mikhail plucked me from that snowbank, the .22 vanishing into his pocket. *Not tonight, little one,* he'd said. I'd decided that very moment, calculating my chances of being good enough for him.

Except at the end, I hadn't been.

I tensed. But the Trader below just flicked his ash. That's how I could tell it was a he—the shape of the hand, the blunt fingers. He wasn't smoking much, just lighting cigarette after cigarette and letting it burn. If it was a superstition, it was an odd one. If, however, it was a nervous tic, then he had reason to be nervous.

Squiring around a hellbreed who had hunter charms jingling on her belt.

The machine inside my head was still jotting up percentages. What were the chances that Slade was still alive? They got smaller every minute I sat here and waited. If the 'breed thought she was being followed, this stop could be a decoy, but my intuition was tingling so hard I was almost jittery. Like too much coffee from the stands on every corner, jolts going through me. Training clamped down on my nervous system, damping the flood of adrenaline and the nervousness.

It might be too late to save Slade. But it wouldn't be too late to avenge him.

Avenging isn't good enough. You know that.

I leaned forward a little, cold water threading its fingers through my hair and kissing the metal of the charms. Kept still and silent, waiting. *Just a few minutes more.*

You don't stay—or even become—a hunter without knowing when to buck those percentages. Something told me Slade was still alive. And maybe hoping I'd come get him. If there was enough of him left to hope.

The limo's engine roused, softly. I tensed, muscle by muscle, heartrate picking up just a little.

Keep your pulse down, milaya. Mikhail's voice. A fresh jab of pain, spurring me toward action. *Quiet and quick, little snake under rock. But not with thunder following you around.*

My heart hurt. But when the slice of door appeared in the back of the club and the hellbreed stepped out, silver twinkling around her seashell hips and a black umbrella opening like a poisonous flower over her carefully-mussed curls, I moved without hesitation. I hung in midair for a bare moment, etheric energy burning in a sphere and rain flashing crystalline all around me, before the drop swallowed me and there was no more time for brooding.

Even if your heart is breaking, you've got to get the job done.

I didn't feel too good about dragging the hellbreed into Slade's house by her curling black hair, but I didn't have any other place that would serve. She splashed black ichor and rainwater over the worn blue carpet in his front hall. By the time I had her tied in a high chair from the breakfast bar separating the dining room from the kitchen, my left arm was aching high-up from where the humerus had snapped and there was a trail of guck from the battered-in front door to the dining room.

Slade apparently practiced in here, it was hardwood and weapons hung on the wall, not a table in sight. But then, I didn't have a dining-room table either. Cooking was a low priority. I poured down takeout and liquid courage when I remembered to. Or when my body insisted point-blank.

I tested the silver-coated handcuffs again. Secure. I had extra handcuffs, around her matchstick ankles. Slade had some blessed silver-threaded rope hanging up in neat loops near his AK-47 and a rapier on the wall, and I'd hooked it down while I dragged the bitch in. I took my time tying her up—elbows, knees, everything. She was trying to chew through the gag.

It's not every day you kidnap a 'breed. I wanted no mistakes.

I stepped back, looked at my work. More blood on my face, drying on my torn T-shirt, one leg of my leather pants shredded and flopping and soaked with more blood.

Killing her would have been cleaner than what I was about to do. Disgust bit in under my breastbone, hot and acid. I swallowed it.

Once in New Orleans I'd been up against a mass of Traders, working the disappearance of a teenage girl. Dropped right into a snake's nest. The scar on my arm was still fresh, I was new to the jacked-up sensory acuity and power it provided, and I'd had my doubts about the whole damn thing, including my survival. Then Slade kicked the door in and from there it was nothing but work. The same kind of work it is every night, for every hunter in the world.

I'd thanked him, but he shrugged it off. For Slade, not looking for me just wasn't an option. Not diving into the fight, where we were outnumbered twelve to one, wasn't an option.

I will hold you the line, milaya. Mikhail's voice, again. The first time I ever went *between*, the decent into Hell that makes a hunter what he or she is. The thing that strips away the shell so we can see the twisting. *I stay right here, and I hold you the line.*

I pushed the thought away. Pulled out my second-biggest knife, and the hellbreed stilled. Her eyes were black. No iris, no white, just *black* from lid to lid. Like tar, swallowing a struggling animal whole.

I lifted the knife a little, and those black eyes widened. But behind the fear—it was just a screen, really—was the calculation. The cold ratlike look. *How can I make this work for me? What do I do to get out of this?*

"Slade," I said. "Hunter. Taller than me, black hair, silver charms." I let my eyes drop to her waist, where the black dress hadn't torn and the charms glinted. One flour-pale breast sagged out of the tight top, and sequins dripped when she heaved against the ropes. Her pale leg tensed, slipping out from under the torn skirt like a waxen maggot. "You have one chance." I sounded flat, tired. Almost bored. My blue eye was hot, watching the space around her for any shimmer of bad intent. "After that, I start cutting."

The last thing I did was cut the silver charms away and stuff them, jangling and spitting with blue sparks, into one of my pockets. The hellbreed's body, what was left of it, slumped, held up only by the ropes, corruption racing through its tissues.

They rot fast, when they go. Bile fought for release in the back of my throat. What I'd just done was in no way clean combat. I swallowed hard, telling myself that at least I'd granted her a quick death once I knew she had no more to tell me.

Her victims hadn't gotten the same deal. Oh no. They never do.

It was faint comfort. The kind that wasn't really comfort at all. I looked around at Slade's weaponry and took what I needed. That's one thing about a hunter's house—the weaponry is always logically arranged.

Outside, the rain had turned into a persistent curtain of sleet. How did people live here? Jesus. But it did wash the stink of fear and hellbreed ichor off me.

By the time I reached the Dutch again, faint pearly light was staining the eastern horizon. Dawn would come reluctantly, peering through a thick veil of gray cloud. Urgency beat behind my breastbone, but I had no car and no way to get one. No time to stop to call for Were backup—and Weres don't go up against hellbreed, anyway. They aren't built for it.

No time even to meet up with Slade's police liaison. What could they do, the cops? Other than get killed going in where I was about to.

Near dawn, and the line at the door hadn't gone down. It would have been depressing, if I hadn't been moving too fast for it to matter.

I streaked across the street like a missile, using every erg of inhuman speed I possessed. Took the first bouncer with a short upward strike, bone breaking and the nasal promontory driven into the brain. Even though most Traders go for bizarre body mods married to a scrim of hellish beauty, the underlying anatomy is basically the same as the rest of us.

Underneath, we can't get away from what we are.

I had the second one down and shot twice before the scream-ing started and the Trader who had minced out to open Narcisa's limo door burst through the doorway. He looked surprised, didn't even have time to snarl before the whip cracked across his face and I filled him with silverjacket lead. He dropped like a poleaxed steer; I stretched out in a leap across his body and darted through the open doors.

Each hellbreed hole is slightly different. The breed-only ones are mostly underground, the maggots hiding from the sun. The mixed Trader-and-breed ones are usually run by a mover and shaker in the local breed community, and decorated according to that breed's particular obsessions. I don't know if "obsessions" is the right word. There's a 'breed in my city who has her place filled with stuffed cats of every size and description—actual taxidermist-stuffed corpses of felines.

This particular hole was painted, velvet-swathed, and curli-cued like a baroque French bordello. Crimson and glaring yellow, the dance floor white and black squares like a chessboard. The bar was a huge twisted thing of metal and old dark-stained oak, bottles ranked glowing behind it against a mirrored wall.

And it was crawling with Traders. Not too many full 'breed. The beautiful damned were startled, gem-bright eyes opening wide and dark velvet mouths opening. Moving fast, boots thud-ding the floor, I shot a Trader between the eyes as he snarled at me, and cut a path straight for the iron door set near the back.

There's always a door, and it's always made of that dark, dark iron. There's always a red velvet rope in front of it, like it's some sort of VIP lounge, but there's never a line. Two guards, dumb slabs of muscle with submachine guns. I was on them before the one on the right could even raise his, killed him first, took the one on the left with a leaping dropkick, knocking the barrel aside so he sprayed the oncoming Traders with hot lead. That worked so nicely I put him down hard and grabbed the sub-machine gun, recoil jolting all the way up my arms as I fired controlled, two-shot bursts into the crowd of Traders. Kicked the door, the scar chuckling on my wrist as barbwire heat poured up my arm, swept down my chest. The iron made a hollow boom and sagged, I kicked it again and I slid in crabwise, still shooting until the gun ran out of ammo. I chucked it at one of the Traders, it clocked him right on the forehead with a sound that would have been funny if it had been in another situation.

Wow, these things do a lot of damage. Won't help with the breed, though. Speed it up, Jill.

The long hall stretched in front of me. Doors on either side, each as anonymous as the next. But thanks to Narcisa, I knew which one I was aiming for.

The one at the end.

The one standing ajar, slowly opening as I pelted down the hall, whip jangling and right hand flashing down to my belt, grabbing what I wanted with a swift jerk and snapping it away.

Everything now depended on speed.

I hit the slowly-opening door going full throttle, it snapped away from the hinges and I rode it like a surfboard, my boots gripping its surface. The shock of landing was broken by something kind-of-soft; I still used it to push off and landed on the table. It was a long dinner-affair with wrought-iron candelabra at even intervals, I kicked one off as I pounded down the table. Hellbreed scattered—the movers and shakers of the local community, gathered here to carve up a helpless city like a big fat roast.

Narcisa had told me enough to guess what they were aiming at. With the city's hunter out of commission, they would have free rein until another hunter could be found. We are so few.

At the far end, something white hung from the ceiling, a shape against the black wall. Two arms, stretched up and clasped in leather cuffs, and a pale body topped with a shock of black hair. Stripes of blood, dried and fresh, marred the paleness. Bruises glared.

The squealing behind me ratcheted down into a growl. I didn't stop, just tossed the grenade back over my shoulder and leapt off the end of the table, over the empty twisted monstrosity of an iron chair at the head. Hit the wall, fingers digging into leather restraints and my knees slamming into concrete. My other hand swept with the knife, leather parting like water. We swung, and the metal pins driven into the ceiling gave with a shriek.

That's the price of hellbreed-enhanced muscle and bone. A heavier ass. I didn't need to cut the leather he was hanging from anyway—my weight would have torn it free—but I'm glad I did.

It pays to be *sure*. Almost-sure can get you killed.

BOOM.

The impact would have crushed me against him if we hadn't already been falling. I *twisted*, hoped I wasn't going to break any of *his* bones, took the shock of the landing on my right side. Silver nails driven in through my ears, a warm gush from my nose, a rib snapped but my arm wasn't broken. I knew this because I was already hauling him up. Smoking silver-laced shrapnel peppered the walls, and every single hellbreed in here had taken a full shot.

Move fast, Jill. Move now.

He was limp laundry. Deadweight hefted up over my shoulder, and now I had to get us both out. I couldn't stop to check his pulse, but if he was dead I could at least make sure he got a burial or a pyre—the Weres would know what he preferred. And afterward I could serve vengeance on every single hellbreed in this room. They don't heal quick after their hard shell is breached with silver, and I'd marked everyone in here with that handy little grenade. I had two more of them, too.

Now it was just time to get *out* of here.

I found out I was yelling. "Holding the line, Slade!" My voice sounding oddly muffled because I was half-deaf from the shock of the grenade. *"Holding the fucking line!"*

And I guess it was my night for miracles. Because as I headed for the hall, my right hand flashing down to get another grenade and my legs pumping, the scar burning as it burrowed in toward bone, he stopped flopping bonelessly against my shoulder. He twitched, and kept moving a little, helping as much as he could while in a fireman's carry. I also heard, through the ringing deadness in my ears, that he was yelling.

Goddamn.

Slade's house was full of Weres. They were repairing his door, cleaning up the mess I'd made in his sparring room, and just generally setting things to rights. One of them, a lithe tawny werecougar, was in the kitchen humming while he cooked something that smelled really good. That's Weres for you—there's no event on earth they won't serve munchies for.

I hadn't even asked any of their names.

Slade coughed. I eased him back down on the bed and lowered the glass of water. Even healing sorcery takes a toll on the body, and he'd been in bad shape. But internal bleeding was stopped and as long as he had a day or so of rest and quiet, he'd be all right. I ran my smart eye over him again, critically, seeing the thin fine lines of blue sorcery humming in his flesh.

"Jesus," he whispered when he finished hacking. "I got to quit smoking."

I snorted. He didn't smoke, but the bravado was necessary. When you get torn down and carried out of a hellbreed hole during a firefight, completely naked and yelling, the humor becomes a need instead of a luxury.

"Narcisa." His face screwed up under its mask of bruising. Two of the lioness Weres had helped me sponge-bathe him, rumbling the deep throbbing noise they use when one of their own is badly hurt. It's their own peculiar kind of healing sorcery, and he'd needed all he could get. "Female, hellbreed, black hair—"

"I got her." *In your dining room, as a matter of fact.* "She's not going to hunt any hunters again."

"Good deal." He thought for a couple of seconds. "Moroc, too? Head hellspawn...brown and green, likes to...wear velvet... like fucking Lord Fauntleroy? Was by the door...when you busted in..."

I considered telling him to take it easy. Knew he wouldn't anyway. "I don't know. I think the door landed on him. Grenade might've got him."

"Grenade." A shadow of a smile on his tired, bruised face. "Knew you'd..." Trailed off.

"Of course you did." My face felt like stone. *I'm a hunter, Slade. Of course I came when you called. And if you'd been dead, I would have cleaned out that hole and done my best before I had to go back to my city.* "I'm holding the line, Slade. Rest."

"They were going...going to...with *my* city—"

With him out of the way, the hellbreed could do what they liked. Hunters are stretched thin, for all the Church and the authorities do their best to help. It's not everyone who can do this sort of thing. It's not the kind of job you can apply for or put on a business card.

Because really, there's such a thin line between them and us. We have to be like what we hunt in some ways.

But we hold that thin fine line. I don't know if it makes us truly better. I do think it makes us different.

At least, I hope it does. If it doesn't, it means every hunter commits murder every night for nothing. I refuse to believe that. For every one we kill, a victim lives. Maybe even more than one.

Does one balance out the other?

It has to. I have to believe it does. We all have to believe it does.

"Your city's safe." It had been a long time since I even tried to sound soothing. "You're back on the job. The Weres will stay here. You should be ready to get ornery tomorrow night at the latest."

On the outside, helped with sorcery, yes. I didn't want to ask what he'd suffered after Narcisa got hold of him. To be stripped of your weapons and at the mercy of the hellbreed we hunt, to know your city and the innocents that depend on you are vulnerable and unprotected...Jesus.

He nodded. Sagged back into the pillows. I smoothed the coverlet down over his chest. The scar was flushed and full under its copper carapace.

"You look good, Kiss."

I made a face. *Don't call me that.* "Mayhem suits me."

His face changed a little, and I thought he was going to thank me. To stop him, I dug in one of my pockets. "Oh, hey." I tried to sound casual. "These are yours. Some of them, probably."

The charms dripped from my fingers onto his nightstand, chiming sweetly. They didn't run with blue light or sparks—there was no contamination in the air for their blessings to react to. The scar was covered, but I was still careful when I dug the second handful of them out. I didn't know what blessed silver would do to a hellbreed mark.

"Yeah." He coughed again, a little, but it was an embarrassed noise instead of a hacking. "Can't believe I got trapped. Won't happen again."

I shrugged. There was nothing I could say. "You have a line on who..." *Who betrayed you?* I didn't need to finish the question.

"Yeah. Ebersole. One of my contacts. Goddamn hellbreed. Seduced a good cop."

This time I didn't need to shrug. Not such a good cop, if it ended up with a hunter hanging like a side of beef. The 'breed hadn't killed him right away because they wanted to *play.*

"You need me to hang around?" I fished out the last lone charm—a silver wheel, red thread and a strand of blond hair clinging to it. I wondered what other hunter had been betrayed into Narcisa's clutches, and if he or she knew that they were avenged.

It probably wasn't any comfort.

"Nah. From here...it's all mop-up." He closed his eyes. His throat worked as he swallowed. "You probably got stuff boiling ...at home."

"As always." But I lingered for a few more moments. "Slade..."
Are you really going to be all right?

But that was a fool's question. None of us were all right. If we were, we wouldn't be working this job.

"Huh?" He was struggling to stay awake. Which meant the crisis was over. He'd wrap up the leftovers tomorrow night. I would have to wash the blood off me before I got back on a plane, though my coat and pants would flop around, torn. And at home in Santa Luz there were things to attend to.

Who knew? I might be the one calling, next time.

"Nothing." I waited until his breathing evened out and he fell into unconsciousness. The bruising was shrinking visibly, healing sorcery humming to itself as it worked. I don't use it much myself nowadays, the scar takes care of most of that.

Mikhail told me striking a bargain with that hellbreed was a good idea. I hoped like hell it was true. I hoped there was a difference between me and a Trader. Even if I'd just done...what I'd done, looking for Slade.

We all have to believe we're different.

Hunters don't say goodbye. Superstition, maybe, but when you live on the nightside it's foolish to disregard it. Besides, it hurts too much if the farewell ends up being final. Best to leave things unsaid, as insurance. A talisman.

My pager buzzed in its padded pocket. My city, calling me back. I'd probably get a late-morning flight if I put my hustle on now, or had one of the Weres call to book me one.

I smoothed the pale-blue down coverlet one more time. The day was well and truly up, and Slade's bedroom window filled with gold.

It had stopped raining. Blue sky peeped through shredding white clouds. Go figure.

"I'm holding the line, Slade," I said. The words were quiet in the dimness.

I picked up the wheel charm with its strand of blond hair. Looked at Slade's face, felt the ache of loneliness rise in my chest.

I missed my teacher. God, how I missed him.

I had red thread in another pocket, and while I was in the cab to the airport, the wheels shushing on wet pavement and the cabbie carrying on a one-way conversation with some AM talk radio, I tied the silver wheel into my own dark curls. The other charms chimed as I shook my head a little, settling them together.

Then I settled down to wait for the next stage of the journey home.

Lilith Saintcrow is the author of several paranormal romance, urban fantasy, and young adult series, including the "Jill Kismet" and "Strange Angels" series. She lives in Vancouver, Washington, with her children, several cats, and other strays. Her website may be found at **www.lilithsaintcrow.com/journal**

Jill Kismet is the resident hunter of Santa Luz, a city somewhere in the American Southwest. She likes bullwhips, .45s, and breakfast burritos. Oh, and holding back the tides of Hell. She's a big fan of that.

DEFINING SHADOWS

— A Detective Jessi Hardin Story —

by Carrie Vaughn

The windowless outbuilding near the property's back fence wasn't big enough to be a garage or even a shed. Painted the same pale green as the house twenty feet away, the mere closet was a place for garden tools and snow shovels, one of a thousand just like it in a neighborhood north of downtown Denver. But among the rakes and pruning shears, this one had a body.

Half a body, rather. Detective Jessi Hardin stood at the open door, regarding the macabre remains. The victim had been cut off at the waist, and the legs were propped up vertically, as if she'd been standing there when she'd been sliced in half and forgotten to fall down. Even stranger, there didn't seem to be any blood. The gaping wound in the trunk—vertebrae and a few stray organs were visible in a hollow body cavity from which the intestines had been scooped out—seemed almost cauterized, scorched, the edges of the flesh burned and bubbled. The thing stank of rotting meat, and flies buzzed everywhere. She could imagine the swarm that must have poured out when the closet door was first opened. By the tailored trousers and black pumps still in place, Hardin guessed the victim was female. No identification had been found. They were still checking ownership of the house.

"Told you you've never seen anything like it," Detective Patton said. He seemed downright giddy at stumping her.

Well, she had seen something like it, once. A transient had fallen asleep on some train tracks, and the train came by and cut the poor bastard in half. But he hadn't been propped up in a closet later. No one had seen anything like *this*, and that was why Patton called her. She got the weird ones these days. Frankly, if it meant she wasn't on call for cases where the body was an infant with a dozen broken bones, with lowlife parents insisting they never laid a hand on the kid, she was fine with that.

"Those aren't supported, are they?" she said. "They're just standing upright." She took a pair of latex gloves from the pocket of her suit jacket and pulled them on. Pressing on the body's right hip, she gave a little push—the legs swayed, but didn't fall over.

"That's creepy," Patton said, all humor gone. He'd turned a little green.

"We have a time of death?" Hardin said.

"We don't have shit," Patton answered. "A patrol officer found the body when a neighbor called in about the smell. It's probably been here for days."

A pair of CSI techs were crawling all over the lawn, snapping photos and placing numbered yellow markers where they found evidence around the shed. There weren't many of the markers, unfortunately. The coroner would be here soon to haul away the body. Maybe the ME would be able to figure out who the victim was and how she ended up like this.

"Was there a padlock on the door?" Hardin said. "Did you have to cut it off to get inside?"

"No, it's kind of weird," Patton said. "It had already been cut off, we found it right next to the door." He pointed to one of the evidence markers and the generic padlock lying next to it.

"So someone had to cut off the lock in order to stow the body in here?"

"Looks like it. We're looking for the bolt cutters. Not to mention the top half of the body."

"Any sign of it at all?" Hardin asked.

"None. It's not in the house. We've got people checking dumpsters around the neighborhood."

Hardin stepped away from the closet, caught her breath, and tried to set the scene for herself. She couldn't assume right away that the victim lived in the house. But maybe she had. She was almost certain the murder had happened somewhere else, and the body moved to the utility closet later. The closet didn't have enough room for someone to cut a body through the middle, did it? The murderer would have needed a saw. Maybe even a sword.

Unless it had been done by magic.

Her rational self shied away from that explanation. It was too easy. She had to remain skeptical or she'd start attributing everything to magic and miss the real evidence. This wasn't necessarily magical, it was just odd and gruesome. She needed the ME to take a crack at the body. Once they figured out exactly what had killed the victim—and found the rest of the body—they'd be able to start looking for a murder weapon, a murder location, and a murderer.

The half body looked slightly ridiculous laid out on a table at the morgue. The legs had been stripped, and a sheet laid over them. But that meant the whole body was under the sheet, leaving only the waist and wound visible. Half the stainless steel table remained empty and gleaming. The whole thing seemed way too clean. The morgue had a chill to it, and Hardin repressed a shiver.

"I don't know what made the cut," Alice Dominguez, the ME on the case, said. "Even with the burning and corrosion on the wound, I should find some evidence of slicing, cutting movements, or even metal shards. But there's nothing. The wound is symmetrical and even. I'd have said it was done by a guillotine, but there aren't any metal traces. Maybe it was a laser?" She shrugged, to signal that she was reaching.

"A laser—would that have cauterized the wound like that?" Hardin said.

"Maybe. Except that it wasn't cauterized. Those aren't heat burns."

Now Hardin was really confused. "This isn't helping me at all."

"Sorry. It gets worse. You want to sit down?"

"No. What is it?"

"It looks like acid burns," Dominguez said. "But the analysis says salt. Plain old table salt."

"Salt can't do that to an open wound, can it?"

"In large enough quantities, salt can be corrosive on an open wound. But we're talking a lot of salt, and I didn't find that much."

That didn't answer any of Hardin's questions. She needed a cigarette. After thanking the ME, she went outside.

She kept meaning to quit smoking. She really ought to quit. But she valued these quiet moments. Standing outside, pacing a few feet back and forth with a cigarette in her hand and nothing to do but think, let her solve problems.

In her reading and research—which had been pretty scant up to this point, granted—salt showed up over and over again in superstitions, in magical practices. In defensive magic. And there it was. Maybe someone *thought* the victim was magically dangerous. Someone *thought* the victim was going to come back from the dead and used the salt to prevent that.

That information didn't solve the murder, but it might provide a motive.

Patton was waiting at her desk back at the station, just so he could present the folder to her in person. "The house belongs to Tom and Betty Arcuna. They were renting it out to a Dora Manuel. There's your victim."

Hardin opened the folder. The photo on the first page looked like it had been blown up from a passport. The woman was brown-skinned, with black hair and tasteful makeup on a round face. Middle-aged, she guessed, but healthy. Frowning and unhappy for whatever reason. She might very well be the victim, but without a face or even fingerprints they'd probably have to resort to DNA testing. Unless they found the missing half. Still no luck with that.

Ms. Manuel had immigrated from the Philippines three years ago. Tom and Betty Arcuna, her cousins, had sponsored her, but they hadn't seemed to have much contact with her. They rented her the house, Manuel paid on time, and they didn't even get together for holidays. The Arcunas lived in Phoenix, Arizona, and this house was one of several they owned in Denver and rented out, mostly to Filipinos. Patton had talked to them on the phone; they had expressed shock at Manuel's demise, but had no other information to offer. "She kept to herself. We never got any complaints, and we know all the neighbors."

Hardin fired up the Internet browser on her computer and searched under "Philippines" and "magic." And got a lot of hits that had nothing to do with what she was looking for. Magic shows, as in watch me pull a rabbit out of my hat, and Magic tournaments, as in the geek card game. She added "spell" and did a little better, spending a few minutes flipping through various pages discussing black magic and hexes and the like, in both dry academic rhetoric and the sensationalist tones of superstitious evangelists. She learned that many so-called spells were actually curses involving gastrointestinal distress and skin blemishes. But she could also buy a love spell online for a hundred pesos. She didn't find anything about any magic that would slice a body clean through the middle.

Official public acknowledgement—that meant government recognition—of the existence of magic and the supernatural was recent enough that no one had developed policies about how to deal with cases involving such matters. The medical examiner didn't have a way to determine if the salt she found on the body had had a magical effect. There wasn't an official process detailing how to investigate a magical crime. The Denver PD Paranatural Unit was one of the first in the country, and Hardin—the only officer currently assigned to the unit, because she was the only one with any experience—suspected she was going to end up writing the book on some of this stuff. She still spent a lot of her time trying to convince people that any of it was real.

When she was saddled with the unit, she'd gotten a piece of advice: the real stuff stayed hidden, and had stayed hidden for a long time. Most of the information that was easy to find was a smoke screen. To find the truth, you had to keep digging. She went old school and searched the online catalog for the Denver Public Library, but didn't find a whole lot on Filipino folklore.

"What is it this time? Alligators in the sewer?"

Hardin rolled her eyes without turning her chair to look at the comedian leaning on the end of her cubicle. It was Bailey, the senior homicide detective, and he'd given her shit ever since she first walked into the bureau and said the word "werewolf" with a straight face. It didn't matter that she'd turned out to be right, and that she'd dug up a dozen previous deaths in Denver that had been attributed to dog and coyote maulings and gotten them reclassified as unsolved homicides, with werewolves as the suspected perpetrators—which ruined the bureau's solve rate. She'd done battle with vampires, and Bailey didn't have to believe her for it to be true. Hardin could at least hope that even if she couldn't solve the bizarre crimes she faced, she'd at least get brownie points for taking the jobs no one else wanted.

"How are you, Detective?" she said in monotone.

"I hear you got a live one. So to speak. Patton says he was actually happy to hand this one over to you."

"It's different, all right." She turned away from the computer to face the gray-haired, softly overweight man. Three hundred and forty-nine days to retirement, he was, and kept telling them.

He craned around a little further to look at her computer screen. "A tough-nut case and what are you doing, shopping for shoes?"

She'd cultivated a smile just for situations like this. It got her through the Academy, it got her through every marksmanship test with a smart-ass instructor, it had gotten her through eight years as a cop. But one of these days, she was going to snap and take someone's head off.

"It's the twenty-first century, Bailey," she said. "Half the crooks these days knock over a liquor store and then brag about it on MySpace an hour later. You gotta keep on top of it."

He looked at her blankly. She wasn't about to explain MySpace to him. Not that he'd even dare admit to her that he didn't know or understand something. He was the big dick on campus, and she was just the girl detective.

At least she had a pretty good chance of outliving the bastards.

Donning a smile, he said, "Hey, maybe it's a vampire!" He walked away, chuckling.

If that was the worst ribbing she got today, she'd count herself lucky.

Canvassing the neighborhood could be both her most and least favorite part of an investigation. She usually learned way more than she wanted to and came away not thinking very highly of people. She'd have to stand there not saying anything while listening to people tell her over and over again that no, they never suspected anything, the suspect was always very quiet, and no, they never saw anything, they didn't know anything. All the while they wouldn't meet her gaze. They didn't want to get involved. She bet if she'd interviewed the Arcunas in person, they wouldn't have looked her in the eyes.

But this was often the very best way to track down leads, and a good witness could crack a whole case.

Patton had already talked to the neighbor who called in the smell, a Hispanic woman who lived in the house behind Manuel's. She hadn't had any more useful information, so Hardin wanted to try the more immediate neighbors.

She went out early in the evening, after work and around dinnertime, when people were more likely to be home. The neighborhood was older, a grid of narrow streets, eighty-year-old houses in various states of repair jammed in together. Towering ash and maple trees pushed up the slabs of the sidewalks with their roots. Narrow drives led to carports, or simply to the sides of the houses. Most cars parked along the curbs. A mix of lower-class residents lived here: kids living five or six to a house to save rent while they worked minimum-wage jobs; ethnic families, recent immigrants getting their starts; blue collar families struggling at the poverty line.

Dora Manuel's house still had yellow tape around the property. When she couldn't find parking on the street, Hardin broke the tape away and pulled into the narrow driveway, stopping in front of the fence to the back lot. She put the tape back up behind her car.

Across the street, a guy was on his front porch taking pictures of the house, the police tape, her. Fine, she'd start with him.

She crossed the street and walked to his porch with an easy, nonthreatening stride. His eyes went wide and a little panicked anyway.

"I'm sorry, I wasn't hurting anything, I'll stop," he said, hiding the camera behind his back.

Hardin gave him a wry, annoyed smile and held up her badge. "My name's Detective Hardin, Denver PD, and I just want to ask you a few questions. That okay?"

He only relaxed a little. He was maybe in his early twenties. The house was obviously a rental, needing a good scrubbing and a coat of paint. Through the front windows she could see band posters on the living room walls. "Yeah...okay."

"What's your name?"

"Pete. Uh...Pete Teller."

"Did you know Dora Manuel?"

"That Mexican lady across the street? The one who got killed?"

"Filipino, but yes."

"No, didn't know the lady at all. Saw her sometimes."

"When was the last time you saw her?"

"Maybe a few days ago. Yeah, like four days ago, going inside the house at dinnertime."

Patton's background file said that Manuel didn't own a car. She rode the bus to her job at a dry cleaners. Pete would have seen her walking home.

"Did you see anyone else? Maybe anyone who looked like they didn't belong?"

"No, no one. Not ever. Lady kept to herself, you know?"

Yeah, she did. She asked a few more standard witness questions, and he gave the standard answers. She gave him her card and asked him to call if he remembered anything, or if he heard anything. Asked him to tell his roommates to do the same.

The family two doors south of Manuel was also Filipino. Hardin was guessing the tired woman who opened the door was the mother of a good-sized family. Kids were screaming in a back room. The woman was shorter than Hardin by a foot, brown-skinned, and her black hair was tied in a ponytail. She wore a blue T-shirt and faded jeans.

Hardin flashed her badge. "I'm Detective Hardin, Denver PD. Could I ask you a few questions?"

"Is this about Dora Manuel?"

This encouraged Hardin. At least someone around here had actually known the woman. "Yes. I'm assuming you heard what happened?"

"It was in the news," she said.

"How well did you know her?"

"Oh, I didn't, not really."

So much for the encouragement. "Did you ever speak with her? Can you tell me the last time you saw her?"

"I don't think I ever talked to her. I'm friends with Betty Arcuna, who owns the house. I knew her when she lived in the neighborhood. I kept an eye on the house for her, you know, as much as I could."

"Then did you ever see any suspicious activity around the house? Any strangers, anyone who looked like they didn't belong?"

She pursed her lips and shook her head. "No, not really, not that I remember."

A sound, like something heavy falling from a shelf, crashed from the back of the house. The woman just sighed.

"How many kids do you have?" Hardin asked.

"Five," she said, looking even more tired.

Hardin saw movement over the mother's shoulder. The woman looked. Behind her, leaning against the wall like she was trying to hide behind it, was a girl—a young woman, rather. Sixteen or seventeen. Wide-eyed, pretty. Give her another couple of years to fill out the curves and she'd be beautiful.

"This is my oldest," the woman said.

"You mind if I ask her a few questions?"

The young woman shook her head no, but her mother stepped aside. Hardin expected her to flee to the back of the house, but she didn't.

"Hi," Hardin said, trying to sound friendly without sounding condescending. "I wondered if you could tell me anything about Ms. Manuel."

"I don't know anything about her," she said. "She didn't like kids messing in her yard. We all stayed away."

"Can you remember the last time you saw her?"

She shrugged. "A few days ago maybe."

"You know anyone who had it in for her? Maybe said anything bad about her or threatened her? Sounds like the kids around here didn't like her much."

"No, nothing like that," she said.

Hardin wasn't going to get anything out of her, though the girl looked scared. Maybe she was just scared of whatever had killed Manuel. The mother gave Hardin a sympathetic look and shrugged, much like her daughter had.

Hardin got the names—Julia Martinal and her daughter Teresa. She gave them a card. "If you think of anything, let me know."

Two houses down was an older, angry white guy.

"It's about time you got here and did something about those Mexicans," he said when Hardin showed him her badge.

"I'm sorry?" Hardin said, playing dumb, seeing how far the guy would carry this.

"Those Mexican gang wars, they got no place here. That's what happened, isn't it?"

She narrowed her gaze. "Have you seen any Mexican gangs in the area? Any unusual activity, anything you think is suspicious? Drive bys, strange people loitering?"

"Well, I don't get up in other people's business. I can't say that I saw anything. But that Mexican broad was killed, right? What else could have happened?"

"What's your name, sir?" Hardin said.

He hesitated, lips drawing tight, as if he was actually considering arguing with her or refusing to tell. "Smith," he said finally. "John Smith."

"Mr. Smith, did you ever see anyone at Dora Manuel's house? Anyone you'd be able to pick out of a line up?"

He still looked like he'd eaten something sour. "Well, no, not like that. I'm not a spy or a snitch or anything."

She nodded comfortingly. "I'm sure. Oh, and Mr. Smith? Dora Manuel was Filipina, not Mexican."

She gave him her card, as she had with the others, and asked him to call her. Out of all the people she'd left cards with today, she bet Smith would be the one to call. And he'd have nothing useful for her.

She didn't get much out of any of the interviews.

"I'm sorry, I never even knew what her name was."

"She kept to herself, I didn't really know her."

"She wasn't that friendly."

"I don't think I was surprised to hear that she'd died."

In the end, rather than having any solid leads on what had killed her, Hardin walked away with an image of a lonely, maybe even ostracized woman with no friends, no connections, and no grief lost at her passing. People with that profile were usually pegged as the killers, not the victims.

She sat in her car for a long time, letting her mind drift, wondering which lead she'd missed and what connection she'd have to make to solve this thing. The murder wasn't random. In fact, it must have been carefully planned, considering the equipment involved. So the body had been moved, maybe. There still ought to be evidence of that at the crime scene—tire tracks, footprints, blood. Maybe the techs had come up with something while she was out here dithering.

The sun was setting, sparse streetlights coming on, their orange glow not doing much to illuminate past the trees. Not a lot of activity went on. A few lights on in a few windows. No cars moving.

She stepped out of the car and started walking.

Instead of going straight through the gate to the backyard, she went around the house and along the fence to the alley behind the houses, a narrow path mostly haunted by stray cats. She caught movement out of the corner of her eye; paused and looked, caught sight of small legs and a tail. She flushed and her heart sped up, in spite of herself. She knew it was just a cat. But her hindbrain thought of the other creatures with fur she'd seen in back alleys. The monsters.

She came into Manuel's yard through a back gate. The shed loomed before her, seeming to expand in size. She shook the image away. The only thing sinister about the shed was her knowledge of what had been found there. Other houses had back porch lights on. She could hear TVs playing. Not at Manuel's house. The rooms were dark, the whole property still, as if the rest of the street had vanished, and the site existed in a bubble. Hardin's breathing suddenly seemed loud.

She couldn't see much of anything in the dark. No footprints, not a stray thread of cloth. She didn't know what she was hoping to find.

One thing she vowed she'd never do was call in a psychic to work a case. But standing in the backyard of Manuel's residence at night, she couldn't help but wonder if she'd missed something simply because it wasn't visible to the mundane eye. Could a psychic stand here and see some kind of magical aura? Maybe follow a magical trail to the person who'd committed the crime?

The real problem was—how would she know she was hiring an actual psychic? Hardin was ready to believe just about anything, but that wouldn't help her figure out what had happened here.

The next day, she made a phone call. She had at least one more resource to try.

Hardin came to the supernatural world as a complete neophyte, and she had to look for advice wherever she could, no matter how odd the source, or how distasteful. Friendly werewolves, for example. Or convicted felons.

Cormac Bennett styled himself a bounty hunter specializing in the supernatural. He freely admitted he was a killer, though he claimed to only kill monsters—werewolves, vampires and the like. A judge had recently agreed with him, at least about the killer part, and sentenced Bennett to four years for manslaughter. It meant that Hardin now had someone on hand who might be able to answer her questions. She'd requested the visit and asked that he not be told it was her because she didn't want him to say no to the meeting. They'd had a couple of run-ins—truthfully, she was a little disappointed that she hadn't been the one who got to haul him in on charges of attempted murder at the very least.

When he sat down and saw her through the glass partition, he muttered, "Christ."

"Hello," she said, rather pleased at his reaction. "You look terrible, if you don't mind me saying." He looked like any other con, rough around the edges, tired and seething. He had shadows under his eyes. But it was a lot different than he'd looked the last time she'd seen him, poised and hunting.

"What do you want?"

"I have to be blunt, Mr. Bennett," she said. "I'm here looking for advice."

"Not sure I can help you."

Maybe this had been a mistake. "You mean you're not sure you *will*. Maybe you should let me know right now if I'm wasting my time. Save us both the trouble."

"Did Kitty tell you to talk to me?"

As a matter of fact, Kitty Norville had suggested it. Kitty the werewolf. Hardin hadn't believed it either, until she saw it. It was mostly Kitty's fault Hardin had started down this path. "She said you might know things."

"Kitty's got a real big mouth," Bennett said wryly.

"How did you two even end up friends?" Hardin said. "You wanted to kill her."

"It wasn't personal."

"Then, what? It got personal?" Hardin never understood why Kitty had just let the incident go. She hadn't wanted to press charges. And now they were what, best friends?

"Kitty has a way of growing on you."

Hardin smiled, just a little, because she knew what he was talking about. Kitty had a big mouth, and it made her charming rather than annoying. Most of the time.

She pulled a folder from her attaché case, drew out the eight by ten crime-scene photos, and held them up to the glass. "I have a body. Well, half a body. It's pretty spectacular and it's not in any of the books."

Bennett studied the photos a long time, and she waited, watching him carefully. He didn't seem shocked or disgusted. Of course he didn't. He was curious. Maybe even admiring? She tried not to judge. This was like Manuel's shed; she only saw Bennett as sinister because she knew what he was capable of.

"What the hell?" he said finally. "How are they even still standing? Are they attached to something?"

"No," she said. "I have a set of free-standing legs attached to a pelvis, detached cleanly above the fifth lumbar vertebra. The wound is covered with a layer of table salt that appears to have caused the flesh to scorch. Try explaining that one to my captain."

"No thanks," he said. "That's your job. I'm just the criminal reprobate."

"So you've never seen anything like this."

"Hell, no."

"Have you ever heard of anything like this?" She'd set the photos flat on the table. He was still studying them.

"No. You have any leads at all?"

"No. We've ID'd the body. She was Filipina, a recent immigrant. We're still trying to find the other half of the body. There has to be another half somewhere, right?"

He sat back, shaking his head. "I wouldn't bet on it."

"You're sure you don't know anything? You're not just yanking my chain out of spite?"

"I get nothing out of yanking your chain. Not here."

Scowling, she put the photos back in her case. "Well, this was worth a try. Sorry for wasting your time."

"I've got nothing but time."

He was yanking her chain, she was sure of it. "If you think of anything, if you get any bright ideas, call me." As the guard arrived to escort him back to his cell, she said, "And get some sleep. You look awful."

Hardin was at her desk, looking over the latest reports from the crime lab. Nothing. They hadn't had rain, the ground was hard, so no footprints. No blood. No fibers. No prints on the shed. Someone wearing gloves had cut off the lock in order to stuff half the body inside—then didn't bother to lock the shed again. The murderer had simply closed the door and vanished.

The phone rang, and she answered, frustrated and surly. "Detective Hardin."

"Will you accept the charges from Cormac Bennett at the Colorado Territorial Correctional Facility?"

It took her a moment to realize what that meant. She was shocked. "Yes, I will. Hello? Bennett?"

"*Manananggal,*" he said. "Don't ask me how to spell it."

She wrote down the word, sounding it out as best she could. The Internet would help her find the correct spelling. "Okay, but what is it?"

"Filipino version of the vampire."

That made no sense. But really, did that matter? It made as much sense as anything else. It was a trail to follow. "Hot damn," she said, suddenly almost happy. "The victim was from the Philippines. It fits. So the suspect was Filipino, too? Do Filipino vampires eat entire torsos or what?"

"No," he said. "That body *is* the vampire, the *manananggal.* You're looking for a vampire hunter."

Her brain stopped at that one. "Excuse me?"

"These creatures, these vampires—they detach the top halves of their bodies to hunt. They're killed when someone sprinkles salt on the bottom half. They can't return to reattach to their legs, and they die at sunrise. If they're anything like European vampires, the top half disintegrates. You're never going to find the rest of the body."

Well. She still wouldn't admit that any of this made sense, but the pieces fit. The bottom half, the salt burns. Never mind—she was still looking for a murderer here, right?

"Detective?" Cormac said.

"Yeah, I'm here," she said. "This fits all the pieces we have. Looks like I have some reading to do to figure out what really happened."

He managed to sound grim. "Detective, you might check to see if there's been a higher than usual number of miscarriages in the neighborhood."

"Why?"

"I used the term vampire kind of loosely. This thing eats the hearts of fetuses. Sucks them through the mother's navel while she sleeps."

She almost hung up on him because it was too much. What was it Kitty sometimes said? Just when you thought you were getting a handle on the supernatural, just when you thought you'd seen it all, something even more unbelievable came along.

"You're kidding." She sighed. "So, what—this may have been a revenge killing? Who's the victim here?"

"You'll have to figure that one out yourself."

"Isn't that always the way?" she muttered. "Hey—now that we know you really were holding out on me, what made you decide to remember?"

"Look, I got my own shit going on and I'm not going to try to explain it to you."

She was pretty sure she didn't really want to know. "Fine. Okay. But thanks for the tip, anyway."

"Maybe you could put in a good word for me," he said.

She supposed she owed him the favor. Maybe she would after she got the whole story of how he ended up in prison in the first place. Then again, she pretty much thought he belonged there. "I'll see what I can do."

She hung up, found a phone book, and started calling hospitals.

Hardin called every hospital in downtown Denver. Every emergency room, every OB/Gyn, free clinic and even Planned Parenthood. She had to do a lot of arguing.

"I'm not looking for names, I'm just looking for numbers. Rates. I want to know if there's been an increase in the number of miscarriages in the downtown Denver area over the last three years. No, I'm not from the EPA. Or from *Sixty Minutes*. This isn't an exposé, I'm Detective Hardin with Denver PD and I'm investigating a case. *Thank* you."

It took some of them a couple of days to get back to her. When they did, they seemed just as astonished as she was: Yes, miscarriage rates had tripled over the last three years. There had actually been a small decline in the local area's birth rate.

"Do I need to worry?" one doctor asked her. "Is there something in the water? What is this related to?"

She hesitated about what to tell him. She could tell the truth—and he would never believe her. It would take too long to explain, to try to persuade him. "I'm sorry, sir, I can't talk about it until the case is wrapped up. But there's nothing to worry about. Whatever was causing this has passed, I think."

He didn't sound particularly comforted, and neither was she. Because what else was out there? What other unbelievable crisis would strike next?

Hardin knocked on the Martinal's front door. Julia Martinal, the mother, answered again. On seeing the detective, her expression turned confused. "Yes?"

"I just have one more question for you, Mrs. Martinal. Are you pregnant?"

"No." She sounded offended, looking Hardin up and down, like how dare she.

Hardin took a deep breath and carried on. "I'm sorry for prying into your personal business, but I have some new information. About Dora Manuel."

Julia Martinal's eyes grew wide, and her hand gripped the edge of the door. Hardin thought she was going to slam it closed.

Hardin said, "Have you had any miscarriages in the last couple of years?"

At that, the woman's lips pursed. She took a step back. "I know what you're talking about, and that's crazy. It's crazy! It's just old stories. Sure, nobody liked Dora Manuel, but that doesn't make her a—a—"

So Hardin didn't have to explain it.

The daughter, Teresa Martinal, appeared where she had before, lingering at the edge of the foyer, staring out with suspicion. Her hand rested on her stomach. That gesture was the answer.

Hardin bowed her head to hide a wry smile. "Teresa? Can you come out and answer a few questions?"

Julia moved to stand protectively in front of her daughter. "You don't have to say anything, Teresa. This woman's crazy."

"Teresa, are you pregnant?" Hardin asked, around Julia's defense.

Teresa didn't answer. The pause drew on, and on. Her mother stepped aside, astonished, studying her daughter. "Teresa? Are you? Teresa!"

The young woman's expression became hard, determined. "I'm not sorry."

"You spied on her," Hardin said to Teresa, ignoring her mother. "You knew what she was, you knew what that meant, and you spied to find out where she left her legs. You waited for the opportunity, then you broke into the shed. You knew the stories. You knew what to do."

"Teresa?" Mrs. Martinal said, her disbelief growing.

The girl still wouldn't say anything.

Hardin continued. "We've only been at this a few days, but we'll find something. We'll find the bolt cutters you used and match them to the cut marks on the padlock. We'll match the salt in your cupboard with the salt on the body. We'll make a case for murder. But if you cooperate, I can help you. I can make a pretty good argument that this was self-defense. What do you say?"

Hardin was making wild claims—the girl had been careful and the physical evidence was scant. They might not find the bolt cutters, and the salt thing was pure television. And while Hardin might scrounge together the evidence and some witness testimony, she might never convince the DA's office that this had really happened.

Teresa looked stricken, like she was trying to decide if Hardin was right, and if they had the evidence. If a jury would believe that a meek, pregnant teenager like her could even murder another person. It would be a hard sell—but Hardin was hoping this would never make it to court. She wasn't stretching the truth about the self-defense plea. By some accounts, Teresa probably deserved a medal. But Hardin wouldn't go that far.

In a perfect world, Hardin would be slapping cuffs on Dora Manuel, not Teresa. But until the legal world caught up with the shadow world, this would have to do.

Teresa finally spoke in a rush. "I had to do it. You know I had to do it. My mother's been pregnant twice since Ms. Manuel moved in. They all died. I heard her talking. She knew what it was. She knew what was happening. I had to stop it." She had both hands laced in a protective barrier over her stomach now. She wasn't showing much yet. Just a swell she could hold in her hands.

Julia Martinal covered her mouth. Hardin couldn't imagine which part of this shocked her more—that her daughter was pregnant, or a murderer.

Hardin imagined trying to explain this to the captain. She managed to get the werewolves pushed through and on record, but this was so much weirder. At least, not having grown up with the stories, it was. But the case was solved. On the other hand, she could just walk away. Without Teresa's confession, they'd never be able to close the case. Hardin had a hard time thinking of Teresa as a murderer—she wasn't like Cormac Bennett. Hardin could just walk away. But not really.

In the end, Hardin called it in and arrested Teresa. But her next call was to the DA about what kind of deal they could work out. There had to be a way to work this out within the system. Get Teresa off on probation on a minor charge. There had to be a way to drag the shadow world, kicking and screaming, into the light.

Somehow, Hardin would figure it out.

Carrie Vaughn is the bestselling author of a series of novels about a werewolf named Kitty who hosts a talk radio advice show. The seventh installment, *Kitty's House of Horrors*, was released January 2010. Her young adult novel, *Voices of Dragons*, and fantasy novel, *Discord's Apple*, will also be released in 2010. Carrie lives in Boulder, Colorado and is always working on something new. Visit her at **www.carrievaughn.com**

Jessi Hardin is a homicide detective with the Denver Police Department. She heads the department's new Paranatural Unit and has (rather inadvertently) become an expert on emerging issues of law enforcement and the supernatural.

Deal Breaker

— A Quincey Morris Story —

by Justin Gustainis

"You're not an easy man to find, Mister Morris," Trevor Stone said. "I've been looking for you for some time."

"It's true that I don't advertise, in the usual sense," Quincey Morris told him. "But people who want my services usually manage to get in touch, sooner or later—as you have, your own self." Although there was a Southwestern twang to Morris's speech, it was muted—the inflection of a native Texan who has spent much of his time outside the Lone Star State.

"I would really have preferred sooner," Stone said tightly. "As it is, I'm almost...almost out of time."

Morris looked at the man sitting on his sofa more closely. Trevor Stone appeared to be in his mid-thirties. He was blond, clean-shaven, and wearing a suit that looked custom made. There was a sheen of perspiration on the man's thin face, although the air conditioning in Morris's living room kept the place comfortably cool—anyone spending a summer in Austin, Texas without air conditioning is either desperately poor or incurably insane.

Morris thought the man's sweat might be due to either illness or fear. Time to find out which. "Pardon me for asking, but are you unwell?"

Stone gave a bark of unpleasant laughter. "Oh, no, I'm fine. The picture of health, and likely to remain so for another" —he glanced at the gold Patek Philippe on his wrist— "two hours and twenty-eight minutes."

Fear, then.

Morris kept his face expressionless as he said, "That would bring us to midnight. What happens then?"

Stone was silent for a few seconds. "You ever play Monopoly, Mister Morris?"

"When I was a kid, sure."

"So, imagine a nightmare where you land on Community Chest, and draw the worst Monopoly card of all time—*Go to Hell. Go directly to Hell. Do not pass Go. Do not collect $200.*"

It was Morris's turn for silence. He finally broke it by saying, "Tell me. All of it."

The first part of Trevor Stone's story was unexceptional. A software engineer by training, he had gone to work in Silicon Valley after graduation from Cal Tech. Soon, he had made enough money out of the Internet boom to start up his own dot-com company with a couple of college buddies. They all made out like bandits—until the bottom fell out in the late nineties, taking most of the dot-commers with it.

That was how, Trevor Stone said, he had found himself sitting alone in one of his company's deserted offices that afternoon— bankrupt and broke, under threat of lawsuits from his former partners and of divorce from his wife. He was just wondering if his life insurance had a suicide clause when a strange man appeared, and changed everything.

"I never heard him come in," Stone said to Morris. "Which was kind of weird, because the place was so quiet, I swear you could have heard a mouse fart. But suddenly, there he is, standing in my office door.

"I look at him and I say, 'Buddy, if you're selling something, have you ever come to the wrong fucking place.' And he gives me this funny little smile and says something like, 'I suppose you might consider me a salesman of a sort, Mister Stone. As to whether I am in the wrong place, why don't we determine that later?'"

"What did he look like?" Morris asked.

"Little guy, couldn't have been more than five foot five. Had a goatee on him, jet black. Can't vouch for the rest of his hair, because he kept his hat on the whole time, one of those Homburg things, which I didn't think anybody wore anymore. Nice suit, three-piece, with a bow tie—not a clip-on, but one of those that you tie yourself."

"Did he give you a name?"

"He said it was Dunjee. What's that—Scottish?"

"Maybe." Morris's voice held no inflection at all. "Could be any number of things." After a moment he said, "So, what did this little man want with you?"

"Well, this is one of those guys who take forever to get to the point, but what it finally came down to is that he wants me to play 'Let's Make a Deal.'"

Morris nodded. "And what was he offering?"

"A way out. A change in my luck. An end to my problems, and a return to the kind of life I'd had before."

"I see. And your part of the bargain involved..."

"Nothing much." Another bitter laugh. "Just my soul."

"Doesn't sound like a very good deal to me," Morris said gently.

"I thought it was just a *joke*, man!" Stone stood up and started pacing the room nervously. "I was only listening to the guy because I had nothing else to do, and it gave me something to think about besides slitting my wrists."

Morris nodded again. "I assume there were...terms."

"Yeah, sure. Ten years of success. Ten years, back on top of the world, right where I liked it. Then, at the end of that time, Dunjee says, he'll be back. To collect."

"And your ten years is up tonight, I gather."

"At midnight, right. That's actually a few hours over ten years, since it's the middle of the afternoon when I talk to him, that day. But he says he wants to 'preserve the traditions.' So, midnight it is."

"Did he have you sign a contract?"

"Yeah."

"Something on old parchment, maybe, smelling of brimstone?"

"No, nothing like that. He says he's got the template on a disk in his pocket. We were all still using disks, back then. He asks to use my PC to fill in the specifics, so I let him. Then he prints out a copy, and I sign it."

"In blood?"

"Nah, he says I can use my pen. But then, once I've signed, he comes up with one of those little syrettes they use in labs, still in the sterile wrapper, and everything. Dunjee says he needs three drops of blood from one of my fingers. What the fuck, I've played along this far, so I say okay, and he sticks my left index finger, and lets three drops fall onto the contract, right over my signature."

"Then what happened?"

"He says he'll see me in ten years plus a few hours, and walks out. I tell myself the whole thing's gonna make a great story to tell my friends, assuming I have any friends left."

"You felt it was all just an elaborate charade."

"Of *course* I did. I wouldn't have been surprised if one of my former partners had sent the little bastard, just to mess with my head. I mean, deals with the devil—come on!"

Morris leaned forward in his chair. "But now you feel differently."

"Well...yeah. Yeah, I do."

"Why? What changed your mind?"

Stone flopped back onto the sofa. "Because it fucking *worked*, that's why. My luck changed. Everything turned around. *Everything*. My partners dropped their lawsuits, some former clients who still owed me money decided to pay up, a guy from Microsoft called with an offer to buy a couple of my software patents, my wife and I got back together—six months later, it was like my life had done a complete one-eighty."

"So you decided that your good fortune meant that your bargain with the Infernal must have been real, after all."

"Yeah, eventually. It took me a long, long time to finally admit the possibility. Denial is not just a river in Egypt, you know what I mean?"

"I do, for sure."

"But the bill comes due at midnight, and I'm scared, man. I have to admit now that I am really, big-time terrified. Can you help me, Mister Morris? I mean, I can pay whatever you want. Money's not a problem." Stone snorted in disgust. "Money's the *least* of my problems."

"Well, I'm not sure what—"

"Look, you're some kind of hotshot occult investigator, right? There's a story about a bunch of vampires, supposed to have taken over some little Texas town." Stone stopped, and sat studying the palm of one hand for several seconds. "Vampires. Jesus." He shook his head a couple of times, slowly. "I didn't use to believe in vampires—but then, I didn't use to believe in demons, either. The dude who told me about that Texas business, a guy I've known and trusted for years, said you took care of it in, like, four days flat."

Stone leaned forward, and Morris could see panic moving just below the surface of his demeanor, like a snake under a blanket.

"And, yesterday," Stone said, "I talked to a guy named Walter LaRue, he's the one told me how to find you, finally. He said you saved his family from some curse that was, like, three centuries old, but he wouldn't tell me any more about it. Christ, you must deal with this kind of stuff all the time! There's *gotta* be a way out of this fucking box I've got myself in, and if anybody can find it, I figure it's you. Please help me. *Please*."

Morris studied Trevor Stone in silence for almost a full minute. Unlike his unexpected visitor, Morris was dressed casually, in a gray Princeton Tigers sweatshirt, blue jeans, and sandals. The once coal-black hair was shot through with streaks of gray that made him look older than his years. The black hair came from the Morris family tree. The gray was put there by the family profession, begun over a century ago by a man who died in the shadow of Castle Dracula.

Getting to his feet, Morris said, "You're probably pretty thirsty after all that—how about something to wet your whistle, before we talk some more?"

Stone asked for bourbon and water, and Morris went to a nearby sideboard to make it, along with a neat Scotch for himself. There was precision and economy to his movements that Trevor stone might have found mildly impressive, under other circumstances.

Morris gave Stone his drink and sat down again. "You know, my *profession*, if you want to call it that, isn't exactly regulated. There's no union, no licensing committee, no code of ethics we're all expected to follow. But my family has been doing this going back four generations, and we have our own set of ethical standards."

Stone took a big sip from his glass, but said nothing. He was watching Morris with narrowed eyes.

"And it's a good thing too," Morris went on. "Because it would be the simplest thing in the world for me to go through a bunch of mumbo-jumbo, recite a few prayers over you in Latin, maybe splash a little holy water around. Then I could tell you that you were now safe from the forces of Hell, charge an outrageous amount of money, and send you on your way. You would be, too."

Stone blinked rapidly several times. "I would be—what?"

"Safe, Mister Stone. You'd be safe, no matter what I did, because you were never in any danger to begin with."

After a lengthy silence, Stone said, "You don't believe I made a deal with the Devil. Or *a* devil."

"No, I don't. In fact I'm sure you didn't."

Hope and skepticism chased each other across Stone's face. "Why?" he asked sharply. "What makes you so goddam certain?"

"Because that kind of thing—a deal with the Devil—*just doesn't happen*. It's the literary equivalent of an urban legend. I don't know if Chris Marlowe's "Doctor Faustus" was the start of it or not, but bargaining away your soul to a minion of Hell has become a...a cultural trope that has no basis in actual practice. Sort of like the Easter bunny, but a lot more sinister."

"You're saying you don't believe in Hell?"

Morris shook his head slowly. "I am saying no such thing, no sir. Hell really exists, and so does Satan, or Lucifer, or whatever you want to call him. And the other angels who fell with him, who were transformed into demons as punishment for their rebellion—they exist, as well. And sometimes one of them *can* show up in our plane of existence, although that's rare. But selling your soul, as if it was a used car, or something?" Morris shook his head again, a wry smile on this face this time. "Just doesn't happen."

"But...how can you be *sure*?"

"Because, among other things, it makes no sense theologically. The disposition of your soul upon death is dependent on the choices you make throughout your life. We all sin, and we all have moments of grace. The way the balance tips at the end of your life determines whether you end up with a harp or a pitchfork, to use another pair of cultural tropes."

"What makes you such an authority on this stuff?" Stone asked.

"Apart from what I do for a living, you mean? Well, I reckon my minor in Theology at Princeton might give me a little credibility if I need it, along with the major in Cultural Anthropology. But, far more important: we're talking about the essence of the Judeo-Christian tradition, Mister Stone. The ticket to Heaven, or to Hell, is yours to earn. You don't determine your spiritual fate by playing the home version of "Let's Make a Deal"—with anybody."

"But it *worked*, goddammit! I bargained for a return to success, and success is what I got."

"What you *got* was *confidence*. You may have had a little good luck, too, but most of it was just you."

"Are you *serious*?"

"You bet I am. A fella like you has got to know how important confidence is in business. If you believe in yourself, it shows, which causes other people to believe in you, too. And that's where success usually comes from. You were convinced your business problems were going to be fixed, and thus you acted in such a way as to fix them. You assumed your failing marriage could be repaired, and so you went and repaired it. And so on. They call that a 'self-fulfilling prophecy,' Mister Stone." Morris held up spread hands for a moment. "Happens all the time."

"My God." Stone sat back, relief evident on his face. But in a moment, he was frowning again. "Wait a minute—Dunjee, with his contract and the rest of it. I didn't imagine that, I didn't dream it, and I don't do drugs, anymore. None since college, and nothing that would give me those kinds of hallucinations."

"I have no doubt he was there. That's why I asked you what name he was using, and what he looked like. Your description was very accurate, by the way."

"You've heard of him?"

"Oh, yeah," Morris said with a sigh. "When you deal with the occult, it pays to keep track of the various frauds who pretend to have supernatural powers. A lot of my work involves debunking con artists."

"Con artists? That's what Dunjee was—nothing but a fucking *con artist*?"

"Exactly. His real name, by the way, is Manfred Schwartz, and he ran that particular scam very lucratively for a number of years. It's a version of the long con. Pretty damn ingenious, really. He would look for successful people who had fallen on very hard times. He'd show up, go through the routine he used on you, get a signed contract, then fade away."

Stone's brow had developed deep furrows. "I don't get it—how could he make money doing that? He didn't ask me for a dime."

"Not at the time, no. His approach was to visit a number of people, across a wide geographical area. He would go through his 'deal with the devil' act, then wait."

"Wait for what?"

"For his 'clients' fortunes to improve. Some of them would never recover from their adversity, of course. Those folks would never see 'Dunjee' again. But Manny chose his victims carefully—people with brains, guts and ambition, who had just been dealt a few bad hands in life's poker game. People who might very well start winning again, especially if Manny convinced them that supernatural powers were now on their side. Then, after they started to pull themselves out of their hole, Manny would show up again."

"Before the ten years were up?"

"Oh, yes, long before. He'd say he was just checking to confirm that they were receiving what he had promised—and to remind them what the ultimate price would be. Then he'd sit there, looking evil, and wait for them to try to buy their way out of their contract."

"Oh, my God," Stone said. "I see what he was doing, the little bastard."

"Sure. Manny would act reluctant, which would usually prompt the victim to offer even more money, which he would finally accept—in cash, of course. If asked what the Devil wanted with money, anyway, he'd say something about money being the root of all evil, and the more money the forces of darkness had to work with on this plane, the more evil they could create, et cetera. He'd wait while the mark went to the bank, if necessary. Then he'd make a ritual of tearing up the contract, and go off to spend his loot. It's a perfect con, because the mark never even knows that he's been ripped off."

"Wait a minute—Dunjee never came back to see me. Never!"

"I'm not surprised," Morris said. "Because Manfred Schwartz was picked up by the FBI on multiple counts of interstate fraud—something like nine years ago."

"Son of a bitch!"

"Manny never came back to extort money out of you after your life got better, because Manny's life took a turn for the worse. He's currently serving fifteen to twenty-five in a federal pen—Atlanta, I think."

"But I never heard a thing from the FBI—they never asked me to testify."

"Probably because Manny hadn't received any money from you yet, so technically he hadn't committed a crime. Besides, I expect the government had plenty of other witnesses to present at his trial."

Stone appeared to really relax for the first time since he had shown up at Morris's door.

"Feeling better?" Morris asked with a quiet smile.

"*Better* doesn't begin to describe it," Stone said. "I feel like... like I can take a deep breath for the first time in years."

"Well, then, I'd say that calls for another libation."

Morris took their empty glasses back to the sideboard. While mixing Stone's second bourbon and water, he unobtrusively opened a small wooden box and removed a couple of capsules. Using his body to shield what he was doing, he popped open the capsules and poured their contents into the drink he was making. He stirred the contents until the powder dissolved, then poured another Scotch for himself.

Morris gave Stone his drink and sat down again. The two of them made small talk for a while, Stone asking Morris questions about his "ghostbusting." Then Stone said, "Man, I suddenly feel really wiped out."

"Not surprising," Morris said. "With the release of all that tension, you're bound to feel pretty whipped. Anyone would."

A few minutes later, Stone's speech started to slur, as if he had consumed far more than two drinks. His eyelids began to droop, and then they closed all the way. Stone's head fell forward onto his chest, and the nearly empty glass dropped from his fingers and rolled across the carpet, before coming to rest against a leg of Morris's coffee table.

"Stone?" Morris said. No reaction. Then more loudly: "*Stone! Wake up!*" Receiving no response, he slowly stood and went over to the unconscious man. He put two fingers on the inside of Stone's wrist and held them there for several seconds, while looking at his watch. Satisfied, he gently released Stone's arm.

Morris then left the room, and came back carrying a small, rectangle-shaped bottle with a glass stopper. Back at the sideboard, he poured several ounces of what looked like water from the bottle into a clean glass, then returned to his chair. He put the glass on a nearby end table, but did not drink from it. Then he glanced at his watch again, picked up the latest issue of *Skeptical Inquirer* from the end table, and settled down to wait.

Morris did not check the time again, but he knew the witching hour had arrived when an elegant grey Homburg suddenly plopped onto the middle of his coffee table. Looking up, Morris saw a small man in an elegant gray suit and maroon bow tie sitting on the sofa next to the unconscious form of Trevor Stone. The new visitor absently stroked his goatee as he frowned in Morris's direction.

"I was about to say that I'm surprised to see you, Quincey." The little man's voice was surprisingly deep. "But, on reflection, I really shouldn't be. My last client tried to hide out in a cathedral, for all the good it did him. So I suppose it was only a matter of time before one of them came crying to you for protection."

"I'm a little surprised myself, Dunjee," Morris said calmly. "Surprised, I mean, that you even bothered with this one. He was contemplating suicide when you showed up to make your pitch, you know. You guys would have had him anyway—and a lot sooner."

The little man shook his head, frowning. "Our projections were that he wouldn't have given in to his suicidal ideations, more's the pity. Even worse, there was a 70-30 probability that, after hitting rock bottom a couple of years later, he was going to enter a monastery and devote the rest of his life to prayer and good works. Ugh."

Dunjee stood up. "I hope we're not going to have any unpleasantness over this, Quincey." He reached inside his jacket and produced a sheet of paper, which he waved in Morris's direction. "I have a contract, duly signed of his own free will. My principals have lived up to their part of the agreement, in every respect." He glanced over at Stone, and his expression reminded Morris of the way a glutton looks at a choice cut of prime rib, medium rare. "Now it's his turn."

"You know that contract of yours is unenforceable in any court, whether in this world or the next," Morris said. "The only thing you've got working for you is despair. The client thinks he's damned, and his abandonment of hope in God's mercy ultimately makes him so."

Dunjee shrugged. "Say you're right. It doesn't matter a damn, you should pardon the expression. If it's despair that makes him mine, so be it. Bottom line: the wretch *is* mine—for all eternity."

"Not this time," Morris said quietly.

"Surely you're not claiming he didn't accept the validity of the deal. Did he come running to you because he was eager to hear stories about that famous ancestor of yours? I don't think so, Quincey. He *knew* he was damned, and he was hoping you could find him an escape clause."

"You're absolutely right," Morris told him.

Dunjee stared at him, as if suspecting a trick. "So, why are we talking?"

"Because I found one."

"Impossible!"

"Not at all. Despair is the key, remember? Well, he doesn't despair any more. I convinced him that his soul isn't his to sell.

Further, I spun him a yarn about how you were a con artist planning to come back when his luck changed and extort money from him, except you got arrested before you could return." Morris shook his head in mock sympathy. "He doesn't believe in the deal anymore, and that means there's no deal at all."

Dunjee's eyes blazed. "He doesn't *believe?*" Before Morris's eyes, the little man began to grow and change form. *"Then I will MAKE him believe!"* The voice was now loud enough to rattle the windows, and Dunjee's aspect had quickly become something quite terrible to behold.

Morris swallowed, but did not look away. He had seen demons in their true form before. "That won't work, either. I slipped him a Mickey—120 milligrams of chloral hydrate, combined with about four ounces of bourbon. He'll be out for hours, and all the legions of Hell couldn't wake him."

Morris stood up then, facing the demon squarely. "The hour of midnight has come and gone, Hellspawn," he said, formally. "You have failed to collect your prize, and consequently any agreement you may have had with this man is now null and void, in all respects and for all time."

Morris picked up the glass he had prepared earlier. Pointing the index finger of his other hand at the demon he said, in a loud and resolute voice, "I enjoin you now to depart this dwelling, and never to enter it again without invitation. Return hence to your place of damnation, where the worm dieth not, and the fire is never quenched, and repent there the sin of pride that caused your eternal banishment from the sight of the Lord God!"

Morris dashed the contents of the glass—holy water, blessed by the Archbishop of El Paso—right into the demon's snarling face, and cried *"Begone!"*

With a scream of frustration and agony, the creature known on Earth as Dunjee disappeared in a puff of gray smoke.

Morris took in a deep breath and let it out slowly. He carefully put the glass down, then pulled out his handkerchief to mop his face. His hands were trembling, but only a little.

He looked over at Trevor Stone, who had started to snore. He would never know what Morris had accomplished on his behalf, but that was all right. In the ongoing war that Morris fought, what mattered were the victories, not who received credit for them.

Sniffing the air, he realized that the departing demon had left behind the odor characteristic of its kind.

Quincey Morris frowned, and wondered if a good spray of air freshener would get the pungent scent of brimstone out of his living room.

Justin Gustainis is a college professor living in upstate New York. He is author of *The Hades Project, Black Magic Woman, Evil Ways* and the forthcoming *Hard Spell* and *Sympathy for the Devil*. His website may be found at **www.justingustainis.com**

Quincey Morris, who is descended from the man who gave his life in the fight to destroy Count Dracula, is an occult investigator living in Austin, Texas.

SEE ME

— A Smoke and Shadows Story —

by Tanya Huff

"Mason, you want to move a bit to the right? We're picking up that very un-Victorian parking sign."

Huddling down inside Raymond Dark's turn-of-the-19th-century greatcoat, Mason Reed shuffled sideways and paused to sniff mournfully before asking, "Here?"

Adam took another look into the monitor. "There's fine. Tony, where's Everett?"

Tony took two wide shots with the digital camera for continuity and said, "He's in the trailer finishing Lee's bruise."

"Right. Okay...uh..." Adam was obviously looking for Pam, their PA, but Pam had already been sent to the 24-hour drugstore over on Granville to pick up medicine for Mason's cold. He'd already sneezed his fangs out once, and no one wanted to go through that again. Tony grinned as Adam's gaze skirted determinedly past him.

Although he'd been the 1st Assistant Director since the pilot, this was Adam's first time directing an episode of *Darkest Night*—the most popular vampire/detective show in syndication—and he clearly intended to do everything by the book, including respecting Tony's 2AD status. Or possibly respecting the fact that Tony was one of the world's three practicing wizards. Even if he didn't get a lot of chance to practice given the insane hours his job required.

CB Productions had never had the kind of staffing that allowed for respect.

"I'm done here, Adam. I'll get him."

"If you don't mind..."

Chris on Camera One made an obscene gesture. "Dude, he's with Lee."

Tony flipped him off as he turned and headed for the trailer that housed makeup, hair, wardrobe, and, once, when the writers were being particularly challenging, three incontinent fruit bats.

Halfway there, he met Everett and Lee heading back.

Everett rolled his eyes and cut Tony off before he got started. "Let me guess, Mason's nose needs powdering."

"It's a little ruddy for one of the bloodsucking undead."

"My sister's wedding is in *four* days," Everett growled, hurrying toward the lights. "I've already rented a tux. If he gives me his cold, I'm putting itching powder in his coffin. And you can quote me on that."

Tony fell into step beside Lee, who, unlike Mason, was dressed in contemporary clothing.

"I get that it's artistic, the real world overlapping Mason's angst-ridden flashback, but, after four seasons, I can safely say that our fans could care less about art and the only overlapping they want to see is James Taylor Grant," he tapped his chest, "climbing into the coffin with Raymond Dark."

"Not going to happen."

"Jealous?"

Tony leaned close, bumping shoulders with the actor. "It's basic geometry. Mason's bigger than me and you and I barely fit." At the time, they'd been pretty sure they weren't coming back for another season and had wanted to go out with a bang. Tony still had trouble believing the show had hung on for four years. He had almost as much trouble believing he and Lee had been together for over two years—not exactly out, although their relationship was an open secret in the Vancouver television community.

Their own crew had survived a dark wizard invading from another reality, a night trapped inside a haunted house trying to kill them, and the imminent end of the world by way of an immortal Demongate hired to do some stunt work. Relatively speaking, the 2AD sleeping with the show's second lead wasn't worth noting.

Tony handed Lee off to Adam and headed down the block to check out the alley they'd be using as a location later that night. Stepping off the sidewalk and turning into the space between an electronics store and a legal aid office, he switched over to the Gaffer's frequency with one hand as he waved the other in front of his face.

"I think we're going to need more lights than Sorge thought, Jason. There's bugger all spill from the..."

He paused. Frowned. The victim of the week was an impressive screamer. Pretty much simultaneously, he remembered she wouldn't be arriving for another two hours and realized that the scream had come from in front of him, not behind him.

Had come from deeper within the alley.

"Tony?" Adam, in his earbud.

"I'm on it." He was already running, muttering the night-sight spell under his breath. As it took effect, he saw someone standing, someone else lying down, and a broken light over a graffiti-covered door at the alley's dead-end. Still running, he threw a wizard lamp up into it. People would assume electricity.

The someone standing was a woman, mid-twenties maybe, pretty although overly made-up and under-dressed. The someone on the ground was an elderly man and, even at a distance, Tony doubted he'd be getting up again.

"Tony?" Lee, leading the pack running into the alley behind him.

"Call 911!" Tony snapped without turning. He'd have done it himself, but these days it was best to first make sure the screaming was about something the police could handle. Like called to like, as he'd learned the hard way. Having Henry Fitzroy, bastard of Henry VIII, romance writer, *and* vampire based in Vancouver was enough to bring in the fine and freaky. Since Tony had started developing his powers, the freaky vastly outnumbered the fine.

Dropping to one knee beside the body, he checked for a pulse, found nothing, checked for visible wounds, found nothing. The victim wasn't breathing, didn't begin breathing when Tony blew in two lungfuls of air so Tony shifted position and started chest compressions.

One. Two. Three. Four. Five.

A smudge of scarlet lipstick bled into the creases around the old man's mouth.

Six. Seven. Eight. Nine. Ten.

A glance over his shoulder showed Lee comforting the woman, her face pressed into his chest, his arms around her visibly trembling body.

Eleven. Twelve. Thirteen. Fourteen. Fifteen.

The old man was very old, skin pleated into an infinite number of wrinkles, broken capillaries on both cheeks. He had all his hair but it was yellow/white and his teeth made Tony think of skulls.

Sixteen. Seventeen. Eighteen. Nineteen. Twenty.

His clothes belonged on a much younger man and, given what he'd been doing when he died—fly of his jeans gapping open, hooker young enough to be his granddaughter—he was clearly trying too hard.

Twenty-one. Twenty-two. Twenty-three. Twenty-four. Twenty-five.

Where the hell was the cavalry? There'd been a police cruiser at the location. How long did it take them to get out of the car and two blocks down the street?

A flash of navy in the corner of one eye and a competent voice said, "It's okay. I've got him."

Tony rolled up onto his feet as the constable took over, stepping back just in time to see Lee reluctantly allowing the other police officer to lead the woman away.

She was pretty, he could see that objectively, even if, unlike Lee, he'd never been interested in women on a visceral level. Long reddish brown hair around a heart-shaped face, big brown eyes heavily shadowed both by makeup and life, and a wide mouth made slightly lopsided by smudged scarlet gloss. Tears had trailed lines of mascara down both cheeks. Below the neck, the blue mini dress barely covered enough to be legal and he wondered how she could even walk in the strappy black high heels. She wasn't trying as hard as the old man had been but Tony could see a sad similarity between them.

"She's terrified she's going to be charged with murder." Lee murmured as Tony joined him.

"Death by hand job?"

"Not funny. You don't know that she..." When Tony raised an eyebrow, Lee flushed. "Yeah, okay. But it's still not funny. She really is terrified."

"Sorry." Tony moved until they were touching, shoulder to wrist.

The police seemed a lot less sympathetic than Lee had been.

"I'm going to see if she needs help," he said suddenly, striding away before Tony could reply.

"This is not a reason to stop working," Adam called from the sidewalk at the end of the alley.

"Does anyone care that I'm fucking dying over here?" Mason moaned beside him.

Standing at the craft services table, drinking a green tea, and trying very hard to remember that the camera really did put on at least ten pounds, Lee attempted to ignore the jar of licorice rope. The memory of the woman in the blue dress had kept him on edge for two days and he kept reaching for comfort food.

Movement on the sidewalk out beyond the video village caught his eye and, desperate for distraction, Lee gave it his full attention. He'd have liked to have been able to tell Tony later that he was surprised to see the woman in the blue dress again, but he honestly wasn't. Grabbing a muffin and sliding a juice box into his jacket pocket, he picked his way through the cables toward her.

"These are for you." When she looked down at the muffin in her hand, a little confused, Lee added, "The other night, you felt...looked like you weren't getting enough to eat."

She had on the same blue dress with a tight black cardigan over it. The extra layer did nothing to mask her body but, he supposed, given her job, that made sense.

"So, the other night, did the police ever charge you?"

"No."

Something in her tone suggested he not ask for details. "Were they able to identify the old man?"

"No." Her hair swept across her shoulders as she shook her head. "I don't think so. They wouldn't tell me anyway, would they?"

"I guess not." He heard a hundred unpleasant encounters with the police in that sentence and he found himself hating the way she seemed to accept it. "I never got your name."

"Valerie."

"I'm Lee."

"I know." She smiled as she gestured behind him at the barely organized chaos of a night shoot.

The smile changed her appearance from attractive to beautiful. Desirable. Lee opened and closed his mouth a few times before managing a slightly choked, "Right. Of course." He glanced down, unable to meet her gaze any longer, noticed her legs were both bare and rising in goose bumps from the cold, looked up to find her watching him, and frowned. "Are you warm enough?"

Expectation changed to confusion and she was merely attractive again. "I'm fine."

"You sure? Because I could—"

"Lee!" Pam trotted up, breathing heavily, one hand clamped to her com-tech to keep it from bouncing free. "They're ready for you."

Tony watched Lee take his leave of a familiar hooker and follow Pam onto the section of street standing in for Victorian Vancouver. Tony met him just before he reached his mark and leaned in, one hand resting lightly against the other man's chest. "You okay?"

"I'm fine. I was just talking to—"

"I saw."

"Her name's Valerie."

"I know. Police let it drop when they questioned me about finding the body. They didn't charge her."

"Yeah, she said."

"Apparently you don't scream if you've just killed someone and there was still five hundred and twenty-seven dollars in the guy's wallet." Tony frowned. "They said there was no ID, though."

Lee frowned as well, a slight dip of dark brows. Not quite enough to wrinkle his forehead. "They said a lot."

Tony shrugged. Past experience had taught him that a lot of cops weren't too concerned about maintaining a hooker's privacy, but he had no intention of getting into that with Lee. "She say why she came by? Are we on her stretch of turf?"

"No." Lee shook his head, careful not to knock James Taylor Grant's hair out of place. "Well, maybe. But I don't think that's why she came by."

"Get a room, you two!" Adam's shout moved them apart. "And Tony, unless you've been cast as Grant's new girlfriend..."

"And the Internet goes wild," someone muttered.

"...get your ass out of my shot."

Lee handed Tony his green tea, and visibly settled into his character as Tony moved back beside the camera. When he looked for Valerie, she was right where Lee'd left her, cradling the muffin in both hands. Suddenly becoming conscious of Tony's regard, she turned her head slightly and their eyes met.

Tony almost recognized her expression.

"Upon reflection," he said softly to himself, hands wrapped around the warmth of the paper cup, "I don't think that's why she came around either."

"You don't have to come in now, you know." Eyes half closed, Tony stared blearily across the elevator at Lee. Early mornings were not his best time. "Cast call isn't for another hour."

Lee waved it off. "Five thirty, six thirty—they both suck. But my car's back in the shop, it's too early to haul one of the drivers out when you're going in anyway, and once I'm there, I can always grab some shut-eye on the couch."

"I don't know." He sagged against the elevator wall, the stainless steel cold even through three layers of clothing. "We've been seen a lot together lately, and that roommates thing only goes so far."

"Tony, it's five o'clock in the morning, even the paparazzi are still asleep. What's up with you?"

"I've just been thinking about it, that's all. About the choice you're making for..." He waggled his coffee between them. " ...us. And I want you to know that I appreciate it."

"What the fuck brought that on?"

Lee's eyes started to narrow, as if he could read the world *"Valerie"* in the space between them so Tony hurriedly muttered, "I don't know. Lack of sleep."

After a moment, Lee leaned in, gently bumped the sides of their heads together—a manly embrace for the security cameras—and stepped away as the elevator reached the parking garage. "You're an idiot."

Unlike Lee's expensive hybrid, Tony's elderly car seldom broke down, and Tony gave thanks that his ancient brakes worked as well as they did when he pulled out of the underground garage and nearly ran down a brown-haired woman in a short blue dress.

"Is that...?"

"Yeah, I think it is." Lee twisted in his seat as she disappeared behind a panel van in the small parking lot. "Pull over."

"What?"

"I should talk to her."

"About what?"

"I don't..." Sighing, he faced front again. "Doesn't matter. She's gone. Maybe it's the way we met, maybe it's just that she's so vulnerable in spite of...everything. I think she needs a friend." When Tony glanced over, Lee was frowning slightly. "There's just something about her, you know?"

"Yeah." Tony could feel her watching from wherever she'd tucked herself and worked very hard at unclenching his jaw. "I know."

Finished at four thirty—almost like a person with a real job —and back home by six, thanks to traffic, Lee sagged against the minivan's seatbelt and muttered, "I should never have gotten rid of the bike."

Richard, CB Productions' senior driver, shrugged as he pulled into the condo's driveway. "Well, you got domestic."

"Jesus, Tony had nothing to do with it." Lee wondered which of them Richard thought had lost their balls. "CB *suggested* the insurance wouldn't cover me if I kept riding."

Richard shrugged again. "Yeah, that's a good reason too. You going to need a ride in tomorrow?"

"No, my car'll be ready in the morning; I'll drive. I've got a late call, it's all Mason and the..."

Girl. Woman. She was standing on the other side of the street. Watching him through the breaks in the rush hour traffic. Smiling. Looking good. Looking beautiful. Looking even better than he remembered, actually. The black sweater had fallen open and soft curves filled out the drape of the dress.

"Lee?"

Lee was already out of the car. "Thanks for the ride, Richard."

By the time the traffic cleared and he had a chance to get across the road, she'd disappeared. He crossed anyway, although he had no idea which way she'd gone or what he'd do if he caught up to her. He knew better. He was on a syndicated vampire show, for crying out loud, he'd had crazy stalking fans before. Not as many as Mason, but then, Lee wasn't the one actually wearing the fangs.

He wondered if she was homeless. The unchanging wardrobe suggested as much. There really wasn't much he could do, except give her money, but he found he wanted to do something. Be the hero.

He didn't get much chance to do that these days.

It had been another fifteen-hour day, and all Tony wanted was a chance to spend some time with Lee before falling into bed and starting the whole grind all over again in the morning. The flashing lights on the patrol cars and other emergency vehicles, not to mention the bored looking police officer approaching his car, suggested otherwise.

"Sorry, only residents are allowed into the building right now."

"I live here."

Her gaze flicked down to his car. When it flicked back up, she didn't even pretend to hide her disbelief. "Driver's license, please."

Tony handed it over and stared past her as she checked his name against a list. Two EMTs were rolling an elderly man wearing sweatpants and a UNBC t-shirt out of the building on a stretcher.

Tony knew dead.

He knew freshly dead.

He knew long dead and decaying.

He knew undead.

This guy, he was dead.

"Who is he?" he asked, as a man in a rumpled trench coat zipped up the body bag.

The officer glanced over her shoulder. "No idea, no identification. Custodian found him in the mechanical room." She handed Tony back his license. "ME says natural causes. You're good to go, Mr. Foster."

Lee was distracted that night but hey, dead guy in the mechanical room so Tony figured he had cause.

Hoped that was the cause.

Next morning, when Tony pulled into the studio parking lot, he found himself parking next to Constable Jack Elson's red pickup. Jack had started coming around when a bit player had died under suspicious circumstances, had hung in there when the circumstances had changed from suspicious to really fucking strange, and continued to come around because he was dating the production company's recently promoted office manager. Leaning on the tailgate, he was obviously waiting for Tony.

"Go easy in there," he said, as Tony joined him. "Amy's..."

"In a mood?"

"That'll do." Jack rubbed his hand over his head, ruffling his hair up into pale blond spikes. "I had to cancel on her again. I'm working a missing person case and unless he magically appears

in the next twenty minutes there's no way I'll be free for lunch."
Blue eyes narrowed. "He's not likely to magically appear in the
next twenty minutes is he?"

Tony rolled his eyes. The RCMP constable had been a part of
what Amy liked to call "CB Productions and the Attack of the Big
Red Demon Thing" where all cards had been laid on the table—
and then incinerated—and was remarkably open-minded for a
cop, while still managing to maintain his profession's suspicious
nature. "Not as far as I know. Why?"

"He was seen four days ago in Gastown. You were in
Gastown four days ago. Know a twenty-seven year old named
Casey Yuen?"

"Name doesn't sound familiar." He rubbed the back of his
neck. "You know they...well, we found a body in an alley down
the street from our shoot?"

"The John Doe? I heard *you* found him. And I checked him
out, but he's about seventy years too old."

"They found another elderly John Doe in the mechanical
room at Lee's condo last night."

"I heard. You weren't there when it happened."

"You checked?"

Jack shrugged. "Things happen around you. But I also heard
it was natural causes both times. And that the first guy's heart
had a good reason to give out."

Valerie. Who he'd seen outside their building the morning of
the day the old man had died. It hadn't even occurred to him to
tie her to the second death until Jack's innuendo.

"The death occurred in the early evening," Jack pointed out
after Tony filled him in, "and I think I'd have heard if it was a
second death by hand job. That'd make it a pattern and we watch
for those."

"Neither man had ID."

"That's not as uncommon as you might think." Jack studied
him shrewdly. "I'll check to see if the second body gave any
indication of recent sexual activity but I suspect there's another
reason your working girl is hanging around. Lee was playing
white knight at the scene and she showed up at the shoot later."

"How—" Tony cut himself off. "Amy."

Jack shrugged. "All I'm saying is that if the girl was outside
your building, odds are good she was there for Lee not because
she's been helping absent minded old men die happy."

"I'm not jealous."

"Did I say you were?" But he was thinking it. Tony didn't need to be a wizard to see that on his face. "Look, Tony, old men die. It happens. Sometimes they get confused and wander off without identification. Before he went into the nursing home, we got my granddad an ID bracelet, just in case. But, right now, I'm more concerned about that missing twenty-seven year old."

"I could—"

"No." Jack held up a hand. "I don't want you out there playing at Sam Spade with a wand. I just wanted to know if you knew him." *If you were involved* said the subtext. "If I run into any weird shit, trust me, I'll call you."

Tony didn't have an office. He had a corner of a table in one end of the soundstage near the carpentry shop where craft services occasionally set out the substantials rather than have cast and crew tromp through the truck. Barricaded in behind a thermos of coffee and a bagel, he alternated between working on a list of what he needed to do before they started the day's shooting and thinking about the woman in the blue dress.

Sure, Lee seemed taken by her, but Tony wasn't jealous.

He was suspicious. Not the same thing.

The old guy in the alley had five hundred and twenty-seven dollars in his wallet and was dressed to score. Tony remembered his initial impression of trying too hard and anyone trying *that* hard—not a lot of eighty year olds would shoehorn themselves into a pair of tight, low slung jeans—hadn't been wandering around randomly.

When he called lunch, Tony reminded everyone to be back in an hour, then told Adam he might be late. That there was something he had to investigate downtown. If Adam believed the investigation was necessary to protect the world from a magical attack, well, Tony wasn't responsible for Adam's misconceptions.

Jack Elson could go fuck himself. Tony wasn't playing at anything. Two men were dead, Valerie had a connection to them both, and she was hanging around Lee.

And he didn't have a fucking wand.

The drive into Vancouver from Burnaby wasn't fun, traffic seemed to be insane at any time of the day lately, but Tony wanted the car with him, just in case. In case of what, he had no idea. Stuck behind an accident on McGill Street, he pulled out his phone and realized that of the three people he could call for advice, two of them would be dead to the world—literally—until sunset. His third option, Detective Sergeant Mike Celluci, would likely tell him the same thing Jack had. Stay out of it.

Lee was in it.

So was he.

As the car in front of him started to move, he pocketed his phone and hit the gas.

Gastown was an historic district as well as an area the city was fighting to reclaim and, in the middle of the day in late fall, the only people out and about were a few office workers hurrying back from lunch, a couple of bored working girls hoping to pick up some noon trade, and a man wearing a burgundy fake fur coat passed out in a doorway. The alley didn't look any better by daylight.

Tony walked slowly past the graffiti and the dumpster and the other debris he hadn't noticed that night. He walked until he stood on the spot where the old man's body had lain, checked to make sure no one was watching, and held out his left hand. The scar he'd picked up as a souvenir of the night in Caulfield House was red against the paler skin of his palm. The call wasn't specific; he had no idea of where the old man's identification was or even *what* it was exactly, he just knew it had to exist.

That would have to be enough.

Come to me.

It took Tony a few minutes to realize what he was seeing—that the fine, grey powder covering his palm was ash. He traced the silver line back to a crack where the lid of the dumpster didn't quite fit. Watched it sifting out and into his hand. There was quite a little stack of it by the time it finished. Mixed in with the ash were tiny flecks of crumbling plastic and what might have been flecks of rust.

The old man had ID with him. Someone had burned it, then dusted it over the garbage in the dumpster. Even if they'd looked, the police would never have found it.

Tony flicked his hand and watched the ash scatter on the breeze.

Most modern identification was made of plastic.

It would take more than a cheap lighter to destroy it so thoroughly.

Lee wasn't exactly surprised to see Valerie standing at the end of the driveway when he headed out to work. He pulled over and unlocked the passenger side door. She stared at him for a long moment through the glass—although, given the tinting, he doubted she could see much—and then, finally, got into the car.

Enclosed, she smelled faintly cinnamon. He loved the smell of cinnamon. Her lips were full and moist, the lower one slightly dimpled in the middle. Her eyes made promises as she said, "I know places we can go where we won't be interrupted."

"That's not why I stopped."

"That's why everyone stops." A deep breath strained the fabric of the dress. "I can give you what you need."

"I have what I need." As a line, it verged on major cheese, but it was true. "What do *you* need?"

"What do I...?" She blinked and the promises were unmade. "No one's ever asked me that before."

"I'm sorry."

She looked startled by the sympathy. He had a feeling no one had ever apologized to her before, either. Slender fingers tugged at the hem of her dress. "I...I could use a ride downtown."

"Okay." Lee pulled into traffic. "That's a start."

Amber snapped her gum and pushed stringy hair back off her face. "So you're not a cop?"

"No."

"Or some kind of private dick?"

Tony spread his hands. "I don't even play one on TV."

"Then why are you askin'?" She sagged back against the building and yawned. "You don't look like some kind of religious nutter. What'd this girl do for you that was so fucking great you need to find her?"

"It's not what she did for me—"

"Ah." Amber cut him off. "I get it. Jealous boyfriend." She laughed at Tony's expression. "Honey, you haven't looked at my tits once, and even the nutters check the merchandise. And..." Her voice picked up a bitter edge. "...you turn, just a little, when a car goes by. Enough that a driver could check us both. You've got a history. Afraid he's going to find out about it?"

"He knows."

"Uh huh."

Tony had no idea how this had suddenly become about him. "Look, I just need to find Valerie. Reddish brown hair, short blue dress."

"Black heels? Black sweater, kind of cropped? She just got out of one of them expensive penis-mobiles on the other side of the street," Amber added when he nodded. "At least someone's making the rent today."

Tony turned just in time to see Lee's car disappear around the corner and Valerie walk into a sandwich shop. He shoved the fifty he'd been holding into Amber's hand and ran across Cordova, flipping off the driver of a Mini Cooper who'd hit the horn.

The sandwich shop was empty except for the pock-marked, middle-aged man behind the counter.

"The woman who just came in here, where did she go?"

The man smiled, looking dazed. "I didn't see a woman."

"She just came in here."

His smile broadened. "I didn't see a woman."

The guy was so stoned he wouldn't have seen a parade go through. The only other door was behind the counter. When Tony moved toward it, he found himself blocked.

"Where the fuck do you think you're going?" Counter guy didn't look stoned now, he looked pissed.

"Look, I *need* to find that woman."

And the smile returned. "I didn't see a woman."

It wasn't magic, at least not magic Tony recognized, but it wasn't right.

"I gave her a ride, Tony, what's wrong with that?"

"Nothing's wrong with it." Tony paced the length of Lee's dressing room and back again, wishing he had another ten or twenty meters to cover. "It's just...she wants something from you."

Lee rolled his eyes. "No shit. But I'm not going to give it her. I feel sorry for her. She's in a bad situation." He caught Tony's wrist as he passed and dragged him to a stop. "You should know about that."

Except this *still* wasn't about him. "I think she had something to do with those two deaths."

"Then why did she scream that night in the alley? Why did she scream and attract attention to herself if she had something to do with the guy's death?"

"She screamed because I was already on my way into the alley. She knew she was going to be discovered and screaming would shift suspicion away."

"You have any evidence to support this theory?"

"I found the old man's ID..."

"Tell Jack."

"It's been destroyed. I'm guessing that between the time he died and the time she screamed—and he was still warm so that wasn't long—something reduced his ID to a fine ash." Tony twisted out of Lee's grip. "Your average hooker couldn't do that."

"*You* could." From the look on his face, Lee knew exactly how that had sounded. "Look, you have no proof Valerie's involved in anything but bad timing. You're not a detective..."

"And you only play one on TV."

"Is this about me? Because I'm paying attention to her? For fuck's sake Tony."

"I saw how she looked at you."

"I'm an actor. Lots of people look at me."

Tony meant to say, "*I think you're in danger.*" but when he opened his mouth, what came out was, "I saw how you looked at her."

Before Lee could respond, Pam rapped on the dressing room door and called, "They're ready for you on set, Lee."

Lee took a deep breath and shrugged into the overlay of James Taylor Grant. "We're done talking about this," he growled, opened the door, pushed past Pam, and slammed the door so hard two framed photos fell off the wall.

"I think you're in danger," Tony said, staring at the broken glass.

"Lee..."

"I've got that promo thing tonight." Lee shrugged out of Grant's leather jacket. "With the American affiliates. There's going to be a lot of liquor, so I'll probably get a room at the hotel."

Not the sort of hotel a basic streetwalker could score an entry to. "Okay." Tony held out the next day's sides. "You've got a 10 AM call tomorrow."

Lee looked down at the paper, up at Tony, closed his eyes for a moment and sighed. "She's very beautiful and I'm not dead but I would never..."

"I know." And ninety percent of the time, he did.

If he wanted to talk to a hooker, Tony had to go back to where the hookers were. Back in Gastown, he wrapped himself in a notice-me-not and wandered along the sidewalks, searching for Valerie among the men and women who had nothing left to sell but themselves.

A little voice in the back of his head had started trying to tell him that she was with Lee when he spotted her outside the

Gastown Hotel on Water Street. Same blue dress. She was stand-ing by a car. A classic Chevy Malibu. Mid-sixties probably, jet black. Tony couldn't see much of the driver except for the full tribal sleeve tattoo on the arm half through the open window.

He was a block away on the wrong side of the street so he started to run. Stopped when she half turned and looked right at him.

Her eyes widened and he had no doubt she could see him clearly.

As clearly as he could see her. Surrounded by traffic and people, she was entirely alone. Her need to be *seen* hit him so hard it nearly brought him to his knees.

Then she shook her head, got into the car, and by the time he reached the curb in front of the hotel, Tony couldn't tell which set of taillights he needed to follow.

Nine-thirty the next morning, Tony was out in the studio parking lot waiting for Lee, pretending he wasn't. He stepped back as Jack's truck pulled in and then stepped forward again when the constable stopped a mere meter away. "Listen, Tony, can you do me a favor? Tell Amy..."

"No."

"I'm just going to be late, that's all. I've got another missing person and my time is fucked."

Tony closed his hand over the edge of the open window. "This missing person, does he own a classic Chevy Malibu?"

He got his answer from the look on Jack's face when he pushed up his sunglasses. "Tony?"

"Check around. See if an old John Doe with a tribal sleeve turned up. Left arm."

Jack glanced down at the paperwork on the seat beside him. "My missing person has a tribal sleeve. Left arm." When he looked up, his eyes had narrowed to the point where they were nearly cliché. "What do you know?"

"I spooked her and she got careless." He drew in a deep breath and let it out slowly. "And this isn't a police case."

Jack stared at him for a long moment and finally nodded. "You want me to call you when this old John Doe turns up?"

"You can."

"But I don't need to."

Tony shrugged.

"So while I'm dealing with this case that isn't a police case, what are you going to be doing?"

"Research."

"Where do you research *this* kind of shit?"

"I work on a vampire/detective show, Jack." Backing away from the truck, Tony spread his hands. "I'm going to talk to the writers."

Lee half expected Tony to be waiting for him in the parking lot. They were used to spending nights apart—hell, they'd spent five weeks apart during hiatus while he was in South Africa shooting a movie—but this... He couldn't fucking believe they were fighting over a woman. Wasn't that what straight guys did?

When Tony finally appeared forty minutes later, Lee stepped toward him only to be yanked back into place by the stunt coordinator.

"Trying to keep you from breaking bones," Daniel growled. "Pay attention."

They moved directly from set-up to rehearsing the fight scene to shooting the fight scene.

By the time Lee was free and the crew had scattered for lunch, Tony was behind closed doors in CB's office.

"How long's he going to be?"

"Jesus, Lee, how should I know?" Amy reached under a fall of matt black hair to adjust her headset. "Stupid PA quit and it's not like I don't have the whole office to..." She rolled her eyes as the phone rang. "CB Productions, can I help you?"

His scene later in the day was all weird, esoteric dialogue, the vampire/detective version of techno babble. He should go to his dressing room and run lines, but all Lee could think of was brown eyes and chestnut hair and a blue dress. "I'm done until three. Tell Tony I've gone into downtown."

Amy nodded, rolled her eyes at whatever was being said on the other end of the phone, and waved him toward the door.

Valerie was waiting on the corner of West Cordova and Homer Streets. Well, not waiting for *him* but since he was the one who drove up beside her, Lee figured she might as well have been. "Hey!"

Her smile made him feel immortal.

"You hungry?"

"Hungry?"

Her confusion made him feel like pounding the men who'd all asked her a different question. "You *do* eat, don't you? Come eat with me," he continued, not waiting for an answer. "You and me. Just food. I promise."

"Just food?" She pushed her hair back off her face.

"Lunch." It felt like they were speaking two different languages. "I'll pay for your time, if that's what you're worried about."

"He went *where*?"

"Downtown."

"Son of a bitch!"

"Hey!" Amy lunged up from behind her desk, grabbed Tony's wrist and hung on. "You want to explain yourself!"

Faster to explain than fight. "Lee's hooker is something like a succubus."

"She's a demon? Tony, do not tell me we're starting that demon shit up again because we barely survived the last time they came visiting!"

"No, I'd know if she was a demon." After Leah and the Demongate, if there was one thing Tony could recognize, it was a demon. "I said she was something *like* a succubus. All her victims are men, probably men sexually attracted to her but..." He waved a hand. He didn't have a lot of actual fact although the show's writers had come up with a lot of theories. "Anyway, she's definitely sucking the life out of them and she wants Lee."

"Who doesn't," Amy muttered, using her grip to fling him toward the door. "Don't just stand here talking, move!"

The sandwich shop was not the place Lee would have chosen, but Valerie seemed comfortable there, so he tried not to think about health code violations.

"Why don't you want me?"

The upper curve of her breasts was creamy white.

"I do want you."

She gave him a twisted smile and stood. "Then why don't we..."

Lee reached out and pulled her back down into her chair, trying not to think about the feel of her skin. "Look, I want to *help* you. You can get out of this life. I know people...a person ...who has."

It wasn't until she glanced down at the bracelet his fingers made around her wrist that he realized he was still holding on. When he let go, she frowned.

"Why are you doing this?"

He shrugged and went with the truth. "I can't stop thinking about you."

She licked her lips and he couldn't look away from the glistening moisture her tongue left on the pink flesh. "We should deal with that."

He gave her back a twisted smile. "I'm trying to."

Her laugh stroked him. "Not what I meant."

"I know. Why are *you* doing this?"

Suddenly, she was only Valerie again. "What?"

"You asked me, I'm asking you."

She stared at him for a long moment, and, just as suddenly, she wasn't Valerie, she wasn't anything he knew. To begin with, she was one hell of a lot older than mid-twenties and when she spoke, her voice sounded as though it came from very far away as well as from inside his head. "I take them into me but it never lasts and I'm alone again."

Over the last few years, Lee had seen a lot of things that terrified him. This wasn't one of them. *"...maybe it's just that she's so vulnerable, in spite of...everything."* What he'd said to Tony still stood. A word like *everything* covered a lot of ground.

"You don't have to be alone." And he was back in the sandwich shop again, sitting across a grimy, laminate table from an attractive woman in a blue dress. "I think you could use a friend."

"A friend?" This expression, the staring like she couldn't believe what she was seeing, he recognized although he was usually the one wearing it. "You don't know..."

"I have a pretty good idea." He shrugged. "I'm the second lead in a vampire/detective show. I read some weird shit. Not to mention, my life has gotten interesting lately."

"And you still think we could be friends?" She stared at him like she couldn't believe what she was seeing. All things considered, Lee found that kind of funny. "I'm a..."

"Hooker." He grinned when the corner of her mouth twitched. "Yeah. I know people who've got out of...*that*."

"That?"

"Something very like that. My partner's ex is kind of..." It was as if thinking of Tony magically made him appear. There he was, suddenly standing on the other side of West Cordova and even through the sandwich shop's filthy windows, he looked...

Terrified.

"There's something wrong." Lee shoved his chair back and tossed his card onto the table. "That's got my cell number on it. You can call any time. We'll work this out. But I've got to..."

"Go."

"Yeah." He gripped her shoulder as he passed, and ran out the door. "Tony!"

Tony'd found the car but he couldn't find Lee and his hand was shaking too much to use his phone and...

"Tony!"

He turned in time to see Lee start across the road toward him.

To see the SUV come out of nowhere.

To hear the impact.

To see Lee flung into the air. To see him land crumpled by the curb in a position the living could never hold.

Tony knew dead.

He froze. His heart shattered like Lee had been shattered. Then he took one step. And another.

She reached the body first. Stood there for a moment, searching Tony's face. Then she dropped to her knees, gathered Lee up onto her lap and pressed her mouth to his.

"Oh my God! I didn't see him."

Panicked hands grabbed Tony's arms, fingers digging painfully deep in a grip he couldn't break.

"He was just *there*."

All Tony could see was a red face and wide eyes and a mouth that wouldn't stop moving.

"I swear I didn't see him. I wasn't going that fast. He didn't *look*. He was just *there*!"

Then other hands grabbed and other voices started to yell out words that stopped making sense and Tony finally managed to break free.

He found Lee sitting on the edge of the road, his jeans were torn and there was blood on the denim, blood on his shirt, and a smear of scarlet lipstick on the corner of his mouth.

His heart starting to beat again, Tony bent and picked the blue dress up off the pavement.

Together, they watched a cloud of fine silver ash blow away on the breeze.

Tanya Huff lives and writes in rural Ontario and is probably best known for her Vicki Nelson *Blood* books—although there's another twenty novels out there including *Smoke and Shadows*, *Smoke and Mirrors* and *Smoke and Ashes*, the Tony Foster books.

The Enchantment Emporium is her most recent. She maintains an active LiveJournal page at **andpuff.livejournal.com**

Tony Foster is the second assistant director on "Darkest Night", the most popular syndicated vampire detective show on television. He's one of only three wizards currently practicing in the world and he intends to keep practicing until he gets it right. Given the amount of supernatural flotsam showing up in Vancouver lately, he's being given a lot of opportunity.

SOUL STAINS

— A Vampire Babylon Story —

by Chris Marie Green

A chill was trying to worm past her skin and deep into her bones, but Dawn Madison didn't even shiver. She'd first learned how to handle the willies as a Hollywood stuntwoman, and her later "career" as a vampire hunter had taught her the rest, even if it'd been a while since she'd been in the hunting game.

"*Something's* sure as shit here," Kiko said, sensing her disquietude. The psychic PI was more than a foot shorter than her, a little person, former actor, and former hunter. Today he was garbed in his version of a business suit: cargo pants and a white dress shirt covered by a dark pea coat. Since their last and final hunt together, he'd grown out his blond hair a bit, grown back the soul patch on his chin.

The old Coconut Coast showroom was quiet now that the staff had wrapped up their post-show duties and left. With its faded burgundy velvet-curtain glamour, booth seats curled around scratched mahogany tables—your basic old school luxury and tackiness rolled into one—the Bahia Resort and Casino was one of those Vegas stalwarts on the north end of the Strip that cried out for a corporate takeover. But the owner, "Tigerman" Lee, had held on to it, even though the place had to be on its last legs.

They called him Tigerman, apparently, because of the gray sideburns he wore like feral slashes under his cheekbones. He may have been over sixty years old, but as he stood next to Kiko, he still seemed like someone Dawn wouldn't want to mess with in a dark alley. Actually, he didn't seem all that keen on her, either, what, with the marks on *her* face. Gifts from her final hunt.

His voice was a cigarette-hewn rasp. "The past two years, there've been a few sightings here in the showroom, but Gigi Calhoun's more active backstage."

A ghost haunting the Bahia.

Or maybe it wasn't that at all, and that's why Kiko, the PI, had come here—and why Kiko had brought in his old friend Dawn.

They'd already done their own background check on Gigi Calhoun. She was a secret vampire who'd sold her soul in preparation to recycling her declining Hollywood career after she'd "died" spectacularly in the auto accident that had supposedly decapitated her. With the help of the vampires and their servants, her body had sure looked headless enough to the Coroner and Medical Examiner; the Underground had fooled the press, fooled everyone into thinking she was dead and gone. Gigi's legend grew as she wiled away her time Underground. But, unfortunately for her, Dawn and the team had wiped out the Hollywood hive before the actress and singer could complete her release cycle; that would've included plastic surgery, a name change, then reemergence Above as a similar star—but one who only used vampire Allure to remind everyone of the original Gigi Calhoun.

Tigerman's gaze had taken on a longing softness, just like every other fan who'd nursed a fervent need to never see his idols die. "When Gigi first headlined here in the early Seventies, Vegas was like a woman just finding out how powerful she could be, wearing her neon like jewels she got from all the men buzzing around her. Gigi opened this place, sang and danced on this very stage. Then she..."

"Died," Dawn said, going along with the lie.

Tigerman sighed.

"That's why you think she came back here," she added, "even in the afterlife? Because she had a special attachment to the Bahia?"

"I like to think so. And, pretty soon, ghosts might be all that's left. Maybe I'll even be one myself when they finally strong arm me into giving up this place."

Kiko was wily enough to walk past Tigerman, "accidently" brushing his hand against the owner's. He was trying to get a reading with his psychometric abilities while the elderly man's mind was on Gigi.

When the psychic frowned, Dawn knew he'd come up blank.

"Why do you think Gigi waited so long to show up here after all these years?" she asked. "Why didn't she come to the Bahia to hang out just after her death?"

"I thought that's why you two were here—so you could ask *her* about that stuff. That's what most of you paranormal types do, with your societies, right? But I don't mind. Gigi's been a draw, bringing us a little more business since word got out about her."

Kiko wandered toward the stage, avoiding this subject. He'd told Tigerman that he was a garden-variety paranormal enthusiast, creating the impression that there'd be some free publicity from an article Kiko said he'd write for a trade journal.

Bullshit. He and Dawn were only here to find out if Gigi was the last surviving remnant of the vampire Underground they'd destroyed in Hollywood. If she was, they'd deal with her.

Dawn felt her skin prickle on her right side. She waited for the heaviness in the middle of her own body to weigh her down, too, just like it had before she'd gone into self-imposed exile after the last Underground—the one in London—had been vanquished.

Rehab. That's what her lover and companion, Costin, called it.

As a former vampire who'd been turned human again with the termination of her maker, Dawn knew just what it was like to feel the darkness as it tried to drag you under.

The chill came to her again, but this time, there was valid reason for it.

A curtain by the stage.

A hand that appeared briefly before disappearing behind the velvet, leaving it stirring.

Adrenaline rose in Dawn, leaving her heartbeat sharp and fast.

But no one else had seen. In fact, Tigerman left Dawn standing there as he caught up to Kiko, then began leading them backstage. Kiko slowed down to talk to Dawn, cocking his eyebrow as she sent one last look to that stilled curtain. Maybe she'd just been imagining things, if Kik hadn't sensed anything amiss.

"Tigerman was closed off," the psychic whispered to her. "He blocked out my touch reading."

"Not everyone is open to them."

"Bad guys never really are."

As they followed Tigerman out a side door, Dawn's skin kept crawling, and it wasn't just because of what she thought she'd seen back in that showroom.

They'd agreed that Kiko's hotel room was the best place to talk in private. Dawn perched on the king-sized mattress, opposite where the psychic was leaning against the dresser. She caught a glimpse of herself in the mirror, and didn't much care for what she saw. Dawn didn't look like a normal person, even with makeup covering the black marks on one side of her face—her very own physical manifestation of the anger in her soul. The splotches of red on the other side were a souvenir from the dying high master of the Undergrounds, who'd splashed her with his blood. Thank God they just looked like inexplicable tattoos.

"So how're...*things*...right now?" Kiko asked.

"Things?"

"You know."

Dawn shot him a sarcastic glance. "All we've done so far is tour the showroom and backstage. *Things* are cool."

"But we'll be going back to get readings with my equipment. I just wanted to see if you need...well, rest. Stuff."

"Kik, this isn't so bad when you consider that my days used to consist of slicing off vamp heads."

"Are you sure that—" Kiko started.

"Hey—I won't turn into a raging monster that'll bite your head off because Costin's not around to temper me." She took a long breath and made herself relax. "Besides, before he got me to the airport this morning, he took care of me."

Just like every morning, they woke up before sunrise and Costin had used his psychic energies to push back the dragon's blood that always threatened to join with the vampire darkness inside her. With the death of her own maker, she'd gone human again, but the heaviness within had remained, growing in force and hunger until Costin had found a way to curb it. He kept the dragon away from the soul stain, because they feared a collision would resurrect the big master...in *her.*

"I'm sure you're as mellow as ever, Deepak," Kiko said, "but I'll get you back to San Diego by tomorrow morning so you can be with Costin anyway. I just wanted your take on Gigi here."

"If she turns out *not* to be a ghost, Costin's gonna join us, you know."

"Yeah." Kiko didn't sound happy. Not because he didn't like Costin, but because if Gigi *wasn't* a ghost, that'd throw a curveball into their new lives.

"Before Tigerman gave us the tour," he continued, "I didn't realize that Gigi has been appearing to everyone in her prime, just like she never aged a day past her supposed death decades ago. But I guess her looking that way would make sense if she's a ghost now. I mean, there've been plenty of reports of spectral Elvises and Marilyn Monroes who show themselves at the peaks of their gorgeousness, before they went downhill."

"So that proves Gigi's a ghost, and not a humanized survivor of the Underground?"

"If she isn't an apparition, she'd resemble an old woman now, since all the Elite vampires went back to their real human ages when their maker died. Even if Gigi found another vampire to turn her recently, she wouldn't look brand spankin' young again." Kiko seemed troubled. "I guess maybe I'm just lookin' for reasons for her to be a ghost, because what if it ends up that Gigi *did* survive? And what if she's not the only ex-Underground vamp running around?"

"We never did hear of her or some of the other Elite vampires after they turned human again and fled the L. A. Underground." They'd thought those humanized vamps had committed suicide, just like all the others who'd found themselves un-beautiful and aged. "Maybe her soul stain never got to her, like it did with the others, and she made her way to Vegas."

The soul stain—the curse of a humanized vampire in the dragon's line. Dawn only knew this because she'd survived it, in spite of the marks her rage had brought out on her skin—badges that no other survivor had. Maybe that made her real special. Yay.

Her ex-vamp father and mother had gotten through their soul stains by dealing with the despair in their own ways, but...

Kiko said, "So what're we going to do?"

His meaning was clear: if they found suicidal ex-vamps—remnants of the hunts—didn't the team have a moral obligation to help them? Shouldn't they deal with the damage they'd caused?

Dawn faced away from the mirror, where she could see the vague reflection of her "tattoos," even when she wasn't really looking.

Despite her obvious discomfort, Kiko persisted. "Like you said, Gigi could've been different from the other ex-vamps.

Maybe she fought the soul stain because she had more to live for. Just like you did."

"Or maybe she's only a ghost." It was as if the more often she said it, the better chances were that it'd be true. "We could just be seeing the first case of a soul stain causing a manifestation of grief."

Kiko looked doubtful.

"Is it out of the question?" she asked. "Can't extreme loss or tragedy bind a spirit to a place they loved or to an area where they need to right a wrong? I wonder if a soul stain did make Gigi commit suicide, then left behind something we can all see now."

"And that's why she's here—because the Bahia represents her at her best, and that makes this a heaven for her."

Dawn could picture how many other ex-vamp ghosts might have already appeared elsewhere, too, plunged into the deepest sadness from their stains as they haunted the earth.

Maybe ghosts weren't a better option than humanized vamps, after all.

"Costin never mentioned it," Kiko said. "He destroyed so many Undergrounds over the centuries, and he never saw something like *this* before."

"He never stayed around to tend to the mental health of a master's surviving progeny, Kik. He had to move on from one Underground to another as fast as he could." God dammit. "This could be the first time those consequences have come back to bite one of his hunting teams in the ass."

"Fuck a duck," Kiko said.

Dawn closed her eyes. "Fuck a million ducks."

A security guard allowed Dawn and Kiko into the showroom again, thanks to instructions left by Tigerman, who wasn't very interested in watching the "ghosthunters"; he'd just told them to be done by the time the staff came in for a rehearsal of the showroom's feature, *Heat!*, which was dark today. He'd also arranged for some employees who'd witnessed Gigi to be interviewed for the "article," and they'd be here in about an hour.

Meanwhile, Dawn and Kiko wandered around backstage with an electromagnetic field detector and an ambient temperature gauge, but they found nothing ghostly. Then Kiko set about trying to capture some Electronic Voice Phenomena with his recording equipment.

As he worked, Dawn could hear her heartbeat, which felt like it was coming from the center of the earth, shaking the floor, pounding at her neck, temples. She waited for the skin on her right side, where the dragon blood marked her, to throb also, but it didn't.

Don't answer our summons, Gigi, she thought. *Be dead.* Stay *dead.*

Kiko guided Dawn away from the recorder because he wanted to allow Gigi some time alone with it, just in case she was a ghost who'd be reluctant to talk to them. Then they went out to the main showroom to sit in a booth, not talking much, until it was time for the interviews.

The subjects waited in the backstage area: "Roberto," the emcee of the show, with his butterfly-collar shirt and smile-crinkled gaze; a fifty-something magician whose tamed country accent belied the name "Trevor Barkley"; his button-nosed, Bambi-eyed blond assistant Naomi; and an unsmiling, reedy theater usher who seemed coolly intrigued not only to be asked about a ghost, but to be interviewed about it by a soul patch-wearing little person, too.

"I saw Gigi first," Roberto said, as he sat on one of the vanity tables in the large common dressing area. Behind him, bulbs lined a mirror, and Dawn could see hair plugs dotting the back of the emcee's scalp. "Gigi was on those steps leading to the stage, just as bold as life."

He pointed at the stairs to their right, and everyone looked, as if expecting to find her there.

Much to Dawn's gratitude, they didn't.

Kiko asked, "How do you know it was her?"

"No mistaking Gigi Calhoun," Roberto said. "I'm her *numero uno* fan."

The magician's assistant, Naomi, cleared her throat, and Roberto chuckled.

"Okay. Maybe I share that honor."

Naomi smiled at him and picked up a brunette wig behind her, starting to comb it out. In spite of her attempt at humor, frown lines decorated her forehead.

Kiko asked, "Could you see Gigi's face? Tigerman said she appears with her hair half-hiding her features. Her dress and gloves cover the rest of her."

Roberto had that dreamy fan expression—he was in Gigi-land, and Dawn wondered if his love for the star had been strong enough to conjure up a ghost.

"I've been a fan since I was old enough to watch old movies on TV," he said. "I know my Gigi."

Dawn asked, "How long did she stay?"

"Not long. She walked to the top of the stairs, then turned right once she got to the stage. It was during a show, and I was—"

The magician broke in" —flirting with the showgirls while you waited for your next cue?"

Everyone else but Naomi laughed, and Trevor slid her a grin, as if he liked teasing her about Roberto having a wandering eye. She didn't seem as amused, and Dawn guessed that there was probably something hearts-and-flowery between the *numero uno* fans.

"As I was saying," Roberto said, "I was able to run up those stairs pretty fast, but Gigi was gone." He snapped his fingers. "Just like that."

"I saw her in the back of the showroom about a month ago," Naomi said, "while Travis and I were rehearsing a new trick on stage. When I said something, Travis thought he saw her, too."

"Maybe I did, maybe I didn't." The magician settled back in his chair, all fading boyish good looks. "The lights were in my eyes. You should ask Victor about it, though." He nodded to the usher. "He's seen Gigi more than anyone."

In response, Victor just shrugged. Dawn narrowed her eyes at him.

"How many times?" she asked.

"Three." He had a voice as dry as a half-drunk martini. "She comes and goes."

So nonchalant. "You see a lot of ghosts?"

Victor's attention seemed focused on the pseudo-tattoos that Dawn's makeup barely covered. She didn't flinch. Let him stare.

"If Gigi has decided to hang out with us," the usher said, "I say let her be."

"I agree," Trevor the magician said. "I was even hoping to put her in my act."

Victor rolled his eyes. "Classy."

Travis grinned at the rest of them. "Gigi was never shy about publicity, from what I hear. She'd be a boost for all of us. A draw. God knows we need the PR."

Ah, the sweet stench of show biz, Dawn thought. She'd grown up in Hollywood, so she knew it well. It smelled just like piles of bloodstained money.

As Kiko went on to question them about details—how solid did Gigi's form seem? What were the exact times and dates? —Dawn realized that there wasn't much of a pattern to her appearances.

When showgirls and other staff began to arrive, Dawn and Kiko's time was up. Tigerman had invited them to watch the rehearsal—a few tweaks to a rain forest number featuring the statuesque young ladies in towering diamond-shower head-dresses, and not much else. Dawn and Kiko had asked to watch from backstage, since Gigi had been seen here the most.

They stood out of the way while the topless showgirls quickly moved past them on their way to the stage. Since Dawn wasn't much for boobs, she lost interest early, wandering down to the common dressing room and finding a quiet corner in front of a darkened dressing station. She should call Costin and update him, but she was dreading it. He'd hoped to live the rest of his life with her in peace, not picking up the pieces from former Undergrounds.

She looked up, into the mirror. Her eyes, which had gained clarity during this past year of rehab, were shaded again. It was almost like she could see straight to her dormant soul stain.

Just as she was about to look away, she caught a flutter of movement in back of her—

Red.

A dress?

She whipped around, her pulse pounding and, at first, her mind refused to believe what it was registering.

A person...a...thing. One eye barely visible under a curtain of red hair. Shoulders hunched, gloved arms curved by its sides.

All of Dawn's hunting instincts came screaming back, and she flipped open her jacket, going for the silver-bullet loaded revolver she'd strapped on, just for this case.

No time to get Kiko, so she grabbed a tube of lipstick from a nearby table and scribbled on the mirror: *Gigi!*

Then she drew an arrow toward the spot where she'd seen the vision. On her way, she caught the eye of Roberto, who was laughing with a showgirl.

Dawn yelled over the music. "Tell my friend where I am!"

She saw him spy the note about Gigi on the mirror. Then she thought she saw...anger?

She didn't have time to think about his expression as she darted toward the dark nook where she'd last seen the vision—the superstar who'd already disappeared into the dimness.

Her revolver drawn—*dammit, would bullets do anything to ghosts?* —Dawn entered what seemed to be a maze of wooden pillars, but they faded as it got darker...and darker.

Please be a ghost...

Still, even if that's what Gigi was, Dawn knew this wouldn't be the end of it. They'd have to see if they needed to help put Gigi at peace.

To put all of them at peace...

A sound in front of her...a door opening, the hinges yelping ...weak lighting...

Dawn sucked in a breath because, right there, solid as could be in the soft illumination, was a woman, half her face revealed under all that falling hair. But this close up, there were wrinkles on her skin. And her expression...

Twisted. Her mouth, pulled down, like gravity had tugged on it and wouldn't let go. She seemed to be forming a word.

Or maybe she was just smiling—

Something crashed into Dawn and, as she hit the floor, her forehead banged against wood, leaving her gasping under the weight of a body, her world going black over the hazy image of a nightmare in red.

As Dawn came to, she barely heard the voice through the fog in her mind.

"Are you here to kill me?"

Husky. But the tone seemed whittled down from its former glory: thinner, an imitation of seduction. The words were slurred, too, like they were coming at Dawn through a filter.

Fighting the needled pain in her temples, Dawn forced her eyes open. It took an instant for the room to come together, so the smell got to her before anything visual did.

Blood: coppery, strong.

She jerked, and that's when she realized that she was sitting slumped, her back to a wall. As her vision slowly cleared, her stomach roiled.

There were three of them confronting her—people wearing surgical masks, just like cops at a crime scene would, the material coated by Vapo-Rub or something to block the smell. They hovered, stared. Dawn already knew who two of them were because she and Kiko had interviewed them.

Roberto, with his slicked emcee hair and butterfly-collar shirt. Naomi and her Bambi eyes. Also, a dark-eyed man Dawn had never seen before.

Her pulse was racing, but she told herself to calm down because she could already feel the dragon's blood marks on her right side shifting, like they were connected to her shuddery wariness.

d inside of herself—the power and anger she'd quieted within
rself in an effort to keep the blood away from her soul stain.
e *couldn't* allow the dragon to join with the darkness to resur-
ct itself within her.

She sucked in breaths, thought of ocean waves. Thought of
ostin, who'd always kept her in control.

Breathing.

Breathing.

"One thing we know for sure," Naomi said, "is that Gigi's
oing to stay happy. And we'll do anything—*anything*—to make
re she's always that way."

The gutted body next to Naomi told Dawn the rest. Gigi, the
-vampire, still liked her blood, and Dawn might just be her
ext meal if the fans could find a way to cover up their own
unting. And her fans would always indulge her, just as long as
e kept touching them with her stardust.

While Naomi kept petting Gigi, the star watched Dawn, as if
e was pleading with her.

Then Gigi spoke. "The only time I'm not watched is when I
an escape to the theater, but they always catch me..."

"Gigi," Roberto said soothingly, "we're just keeping you safe."

Dawn kept sucking in the diseased air, not only to calm her-
elf, but because she'd heard the agony in Gigi's tone. Felt the
espair, just like it was her own.

As it scraped through her, from her awakened dragon-blood
kin down to her soul, something consumed the room like a
lash and bang of lightning, obliterating Dawn's vision.

Then it all went into fast-forward.

Nothing but a field of white from the flash bomb—footsteps
.running...

It was Kiko—shoving a gun into her hands while Dawn
eard Naomi, Roberto, Steve, and Gigi calling out to each other
n their own temporary blindness. She could hear him cocking a
istol while Dawn's vision gradually turned to color, then solid
mages, again.

The first thing her gaze latched onto was her partner. *"Don't
move,"* Kiko said, aiming at the fan club, cool and collected.
They'd dealt with a hell of a lot worse on hunts.

The devotees had their hands up, but Gigi...

Gigi was turning around, toward a table where Dawn's con-
fiscated weapons lay.

"Stop moving!" he yelled. Then to Dawn, "Are you okay? A
showgirl saw you and I—"

Breathe, she thought, going to that place she'd found in rehab.
Right away a sense of control eased through her. It smoothed out
her heartbeat first, then everything else.

She'd be fine. Kiko would be down here soon.

But then she remembered she'd hadn't told anyone but Roberto
where she'd been going.

The female voice came again from behind the wall of humans.

"Are you here to *kill* me?"

Still dizzy—there was a pounding bump on her head from her
fall—Dawn tried to answer, but the stench in the room made her
gag instead.

Naomi's voice was muffled behind her mask. "We know who
you are now. She just told us."

She. Gigi.

Roberto added, "You're one of the hunters who took it all away
from her."

He backed away from Dawn, revealing the movie star right
behind him: the vision in the red dress, red gloves, red hair. She
was dressed like a younger version of herself, but Dawn could see
how her skin was withered, her one visible eye droopy. An appall-
ing mockery of the young movie star.

But she looked human enough...

Lipstick blurred Gigi's mouth, one side of it limp, like she'd suffered a stroke.

"I saw you Underground," she slurred. "Eva's daughter. You
killed my master."

No sense in denying that. "Me and my friend are here to help,
Gigi. That's all." Dawn's words...they were just as slurred as the
star's. "All the rest of the vampire Elites in the Underground...
we weren't sure what happened to some of you after you turned
human and ran away."

"The others killed themselves, right in front of me." Gigi's voice
was ragged. "They couldn't live after you made us ugly. *Mortal*."

The soul stain—it'd made the Elites' loss of youth worse, hadn't it?

"You're the only one left?" Dawn asked.

Gigi's sideways mouth dipped as she whispered, "I think so."

Collateral damage, Dawn thought, as there was with all wars.

Bile inched up her throat. All of them were just the smoking
aftermath of a war.

"The weight," Dawn finally said. It was hard to talk because
of the smell. "How did you survive the weight in your soul when
others didn't?"

Gigi started, then rested her gloved hand over her chest. It only confirmed to Dawn that the soul stain really was there.

"It stays with an ex-vamp," Dawn added, "as if you never deserved to be human again anyway. It destroys."

Her voice choked off, and it wasn't just because of the charnel house odor.

Roberto adjusted his slipping mask as he walked closer to Gigi. "You can tell her, darling. Tell her what kept you going after you turned human again."

Dawn had already assumed that the masked people around her were servants. The star was still the queen who held court, just like in the Underground. But with the way the old, grotesque woman glanced at Roberto, Dawn could see that there was an imbalance of power here.

Things weren't the same as they'd been in Hollywood...

At Gigi's hesitation, Roberto sighed, as if resigning himself to speak for her. "Naomi and I were so happy to get jobs at the Bahia, because Gigi used to work here. We collected old dresses of hers, even put up a web site..."

The *numero uno* fans exchanged fond glances.

"And, what do you know," Roberto went on. "While Gigi was Underground, waiting until she could resurface, she'd kept tabs on all her press—which she still got, even if she'd been dead for a few decades. Servants would print out reports for her and bring them below ground, where she'd read about the continuing devotion of her fans. She was so close to her release date. Did you know that? She'd waited such a long time..." He swallowed. "It's only natural, when she turned back human, that she tracked us down, using our site information. She knew we would still love her, no matter what misfortunes she'd endured."

So the undying devotion of fans had kept Gigi alive this long. Maybe the other stars hadn't connected to that—*remembered* that in their urgent anguish—as this star had.

Dawn focused on the third man, still silent under his mask. Still wary, as if he expected her to attack him. She didn't feel her revolver on her, and she was sure they'd taken the other weapons she'd strapped on, too. The knife. The throwing blades she hadn't used in such a long time.

Roberto turned toward Gigi, who'd lowered her head, as if in shame.

"When she came to us," he said, "she was a gray, shriveled thing, wearing a ripped evening gown. I found her backstage

one day, watching us. At first, we thought she wa[s] who'd wandered in, but..."

"But," Naomi finally said, "Roberto recognize[d] she told us what she'd been through, it just broke never said it outright, but we knew she'd want us [to] if she was just as beautiful as she'd always been. [So] of her, dressed her in her favorite outfits, fed her,

Like their own Gigi doll, Dawn thought. A fan

"She never wanted to come home with us, th[en] continued. "She likes it at the Bahia, so we made old storage room. Steve—" she nodded at the th[ird] another fan who helped with the web site. He's now. I'm afraid he overreacted when he found you

Steve didn't give any sign that he'd heard or w[ord] of the conversation. He just kept staring with thos[e] Dawn.

"We didn't intend to make her a legend again," "Not this way—with her as a 'ghost.' But then we this is what Gigi needs—a legend that keeps gr[owing] make up stories about seeing her. But sometimes...'

"Sometimes," Naomi added, "Gigi gets out on [her]

The old woman kept peering at the ground.

"Just like another Underground," Dawn said, rattle. They were keeping Gigi alive because tha[t] needed. Fans who could never let go.

Across the room, Gigi finally raised her face, me[t] gaze. Darkness filled her eyes, and Dawn saw the of a captive.

Are you here to kill me?

The woman's question took on a whole new m deep within Dawn, she felt the burden—the sorr[ow] fusion after everything Gigi loved had been take[n] gnarled into an existence she'd never expected.

Her admirers loved her, and it had kept her goi[ng] But these fans loved her *too* much.

Naomi abandoned the circle to stand next to Gig bigger hole that revealed the source of the room's ste

A half-gnawed corpse hanging from a series of [hooks] into the wall, its face chewed, its stringy hair matte[d] its entrails squiggling out of its bared stomach.

Dawn gagged again. Then the dragon's blood je[rked] skin, *under* it, as if it was yelling that she didn't ne[ed] to rescue her from this. She didn't need anything bu

"Gigi's not a ghost," Dawn said. "She's human."

Kiko looked sick about that. But Gigi had heard Dawn, too, and her gaze drifted to the corpse on the wall, then back to Dawn and Kiko.

Human? she seemed to ask.

Gigi was already reaching across the table for Dawn's revolver. Dawn felt like her own soul was lead, an echo of what was in Gigi, and she couldn't call out for the star to stop because she knew what would make the ex-Elite truly happy now.

Knew all too well.

Before anyone but Dawn understood what was happening, let alone why, Gigi shoved the barrel into her mouth.

Later, Dawn could have sworn that a smile appeared on Gigi's ravaged face in the half-second before she pulled the trigger.

Chris Marie Green is the author of the "Vampire Babylon" series, which includes *Night Rising* and *A Drop of Red*. In 2011, Ace will publish her new postapocalyptic urban fantasy western noir "Bloodlands" series. She has a website at **www.vampire-babylon.com**

Former Hollywood stuntwoman **Dawn Madison** is currently in retirement from vampire hunting and resides near San Diego. Kiko Daniels, who lives nearby, runs a paranormal detective agency with his partner, Natalia Petri.

Under the Hill and Far Away

— A Black London Story —

by Caitlin Kittredge

A shadow fell across Pete Caldecott like a bird flickering across the sun. She looked up from her drink, and immediately wished she hadn't.

The Fae was a head and a half taller than she was. Pete was short for a human, so that likely made him short for a Fae. He tilted his head when Pete made eye contact. "Madam Caldecott?"

Pete straightened up, fixed him with her worst copper stare. "I think you have the wrong Madam Caldecott, mate."

The Fae spread his hands. "No, miss. I'm quite certain it's you she wants." He had pupiless eyes, silver. Beautiful, if you were into that Tolkien bullshit. Or Shark Week.

Pete deliberately put her eyes back on her pint. The Lament was theoretically a neutral zone in the Black, the ebb and flow of magical London that existed out of most people's sight. No fighting, no magic and no Fae.

Pete told it, "I'm waiting for someone."

"Sir Jack Winter." The Fae inclined its head again. It looked a bit like David Bowie and a bit like it wanted to turn her into a skin handbag. Pete felt the back of her neck crawl and a faint scent of orchids and earth crawled up her nose. The Fae had its magic up—it would have to, to cross the iron bands in the Lament's door and the assorted protection hexes that surrounded the pub like a cocoon of ethereal razor wire. To penetrate it, the Fae was stronger than any Pete had ever seen. Not that her experience with Fae was vast.

"It's none of your bloody business," Pete said, "but, yes."

"He won't be coming," the Fae intoned. "Madam Caldecott..."

"Look, if you *insist* on speaking to me, lay off of that before I call the bouncer and get you thrown right the fuck out," Pete ordered.

"Petunia," the Fae tried, her given name looking like it caused it—him? —pain. "I bear a request from the Senechal of the Seelie Court. I need you to come at once."

The Fae reached for her, and Pete lost what little patience she had for the creatures. "You lay that pretty hand on me and you're getting a pretty stump back," she said, swatting. Contact with its skin sent a spiraling jolt of power up her arm and into her heart. Pete didn't make it her practice to cause a scene in the middle of pubs—at least not when she was sober—and when the Lament's few patrons looked over, she felt herself flush. "Look, I'm sorry," she said. "But here, you don't just swan in and grab people..." she waited for the Fae's name.

"You can call me Rowan," it said. Pete crinkled her nose.

"That's a bit swishy for a strapping thing like yourself." The expression on Rowan's face showed he had no idea what she meant. Pete sighed. "Rowan, what do you want? You're making me conspicuous."

"You *must* come," Rowan said. "If I don't deliver you..." The magic about him changed subtly, a darkening, a chill across Pete's bare skin. "If I don't," Rowan whispered, "they cut off my head."

Pete blinked. "How medieval," she said dryly. "You expect me to believe that?"

"Don't you know?" he said. "Seelie Fae can't lie. We are bound by blood. Our very nature forbids it."

That caused Pete to consider. Jack, the one with actual experience of the pasty bastards, had only spoken of Fae in the most dismissive of terms. She had no idea whether to trust Rowan or laugh at the audacity of his put-on.

"They told me you were smart," Rowan said. "That you were a detective."

Pete took a sip of her dark beer. "Used to be. Not any more." It was hard to reconcile murders and robberies and the orderly procession of the Metropolitan Police with magic and curses and a place like the Lament Pub. Too hard. Six months next week, she'd been off the job.

"That's why they want you," Rowan continued. "The puzzle. The bloody business. Human eyes are needed."

Pete raised her eyebrow at that. Rowan was growing more fidgety by the second, like a first-former itching to tattle on a classmate. "Come out with it!" she said.

"A murder," Rowan said. "It's the first in...well, a very, very long time, even for us. Honor killings are one thing. Duels. Assassination. But this..." He scrubbed his hand against his forehead. "It has no sense behind it."

Pete sighed. "You look for murder to make sense, you might as well be looking for meaning in 'Whiter Shade of Pale'. Don't Fae have...I dunno, investigative types?" The idea of Fae police, in everyday Met uniforms, made her smirk a bit. Most of the Black was lawless as the American West, and it was by pure meanness and cunning that you kept your blood and entrails inside your body. Jack had taught her that. Where the fuck *was* Jack?

"We used to have Inquisitors," Rowan said. "But the Queen disbanded them, long ago. It's said...they said Petunia Caldecott was the cleverest human in the Black. And this needs a human's eyes."

Pete looked at the door again, at Rowan's haggard face, and finally back at her mostly-still-full pint glass. "Fine," she sighed, tossing down a few pounds for it. "Let's have a look at your corpse, then."

They left the Lament, which opened onto an alley that was never in the same place twice. Rowan visibly relaxed once they were outside, and Pete felt him shift something, the enchantment that had allowed him inside in the first place, though his magic still prickled her. "Have you ever visited Faerie?" he asked Pete. His voice was stronger, with the clearbell-like quality she associated with Fae.

"Never have, never wanted to," she said. Feeling in her pockets for her pack and a lighter, she lit up, inhaled, and added a small blue cloud to the low wet fog that fell around them like frayed lace.

"This way," Rowan said, starting down the stairs of a long-abandoned tube station. In the light world, it would be full of people, buskers, newsagents. In the Black, it was boarded up and painted with graffiti in a dozen arcane languages, the steps slippery and the air dank. Pete hesitated on the top step.

"If this is a setup to get me eaten by something nasty, I'm going to be very bloody upset with you, Rowan."

Rowan held out his long pale hand, the color of a drowned man's. "I mean you no harm. I swear."

Pete didn't take his hand, but she did take the first step down to the tube platform. A shadow passed over the clouded moon, and for a moment there was perfect blackness. Something whistling and unearthly breathed in her face.

Pete's cigarette went out.

When she could see again, she was in Faerie.

Pete didn't know what she'd expected, exactly—perhaps some Froud-esque fantasy of pixies at play under giant, *Alice in Wonderland* mushrooms. Or perhaps a palace of tall, pale, ridiculously good-looking Fae straight out of *Hellboy*. She'd expected soft things, silver eyes, the scent of elderflower.

Faerie was hard, instead. It was brick and iron, blackened to the same color by soot and grit. A sign was worked into the tiles of the tube station, in a language that looked like twisting vines to Pete's eye.

Rowan slowed when she did. "Is something the matter, Lady?"

"It's, um..." Pete gestured at the wood track, broken and empty. "You have the tube here?"

"Used to," Rowan said. "When people and the Fae were much closer. We shared a great deal."

He hopped from the platform and started to walk. "The court is this way."

Pete shivered. Things lived in the dark, of the Black and of the light world. That she knew. Demons, murderers, angry ghosts. If it was a toss-up between the Fae and the dark, Pete knew which she'd choose. She hopped the platform, her feet crunching into shifting gravel between the ties, and followed Rowan into the tunnel.

The Seelie Court loomed from nowhere, when Rowan and Pete emerged onto a rail trestle. Below her, in the dark, Pete heard the rush and burble of a creek, and laughter that sounded like water on rock. Selkies, or naiads. Maybe a kelpie.

"I thought it was always summer here," she said to Rowan. Another tidbit from Jack.

"It is," he said. "The Prince's death has changed that."

Prince. "Bloody fucking hell," Pete muttered to herself. Not only was she supposed to Sherlock Holmes a culprit out of the thin Fae air, the victim was royalty. Pete had worked an overdose case once, an MP's son, and the MP himself, his supercilious face and veiled threats, still haunted her. He'd wanted it swept neatly under the rug, had actually sent a bloke in a dark suit to Pete's flat to offer her fifteen thousand pounds to say his son'd had a heart attack and blot out all mention of the pharmacy floating in his bloodstream.

Pete had told him to fuck off, in exactly those words. But she had a notion that her usual routine wouldn't play well with the ruling members of the Seelie.

She wasn't even a DI any longer. Why the fuck had she agreed to come?

Before she could find a decent answer, they had been swept through a private entrance, past a coterie of guards armed with billy clubs and short, brutal swords that Pete had no doubt would do the job they were intended for, and into chambers guarded with a twined seal of two oak leaves. "Bow your head," Rowan muttered. "You're about to receive an honor few humans ever dream of."

"Aren't I a fucking prizewinner," Pete said under her breath. Then she remembered those blades, and thought better of finishing the thought.

The Queen of the Seelie wasn't a person Pete had ever fancied meeting, and she could tell the reverse was also true. The Queen drew herself up and in when Pete and Rowan came in, patting at her cheeks with a handkerchief spun from something white and translucent. She wore a simple black gown, the kind of thing you saw in old photos of Victorian mourning. Flanking her were three more Fae, two men and a girl.

Pete took their measure even as she smiled and inclined her head. She'd treat this like any other homicide. "You're the mother?"

The Queen's throat worked, tightening, but not with sorrow. "I am the Queen."

Pete nodded, as if that explained everything. "I'm sorry for your loss, madam." It all came back, like getting on a bloody bike. The somber tone, the sympathetic yet determined demeanor, letting the family take the lead to get the information you really needed. "I realize this is hard for you," Pete said, "but anything you can tell me about your son's last hours will likely be helpful."

The bigger of the two men stepped in. "Anything you need to know, ask me."

Pete gave him the eye. "Don't tell me you're the family barrister."

The Fae's lip curled back. His two front teeth came to points. "I am the captain of the Ash Guard."

"Ah," Pete said. A security heavy. This was familiar ground as well. "And your name, Captain...?"

"Tolliver," the Fae said gruffly. "The Queen is indisposed. You speak to me."

"Tolliver," Pete said, grasping him by the arm, "can I speak to you over here, please?" She led him to a shadowy corner, where a leaded window looked out on the storm-tossed hills of Faerie. "I understand," Pete told him.

Tolliver blinked, clearly having expected to be lectured. "You do?"

"'Course," Pete said. "You're responsible for the family, and the boy getting done in was your cock-up. But being a pillock to me is *not* going to find the bloke, so how about you step aside while the chance is still there to catch him? Or her?"

His throat worked. Pete saw a scar there, under his jaw. His clothes were fine as the rest of the group, but his hands were roughed at the knuckles, bent and square from bare-fisted fighting. Tolliver was a man who believed in blunt force. Pete hoped that also meant he believed in honesty.

"I found him," he said, and his voice went rough. "I came to get him for our daily fencing lesson and he was on the floor, like a doll with all of the stuffing gone out..." Tolliver's jaw worked and he looked away from her, out at the boiling thunderheads illuminated by a sickly green light in the eastern sky. "Unseelie land," he murmured. "They'll be putting up a ruddy festival. This is their dream come true."

"Could an Unseelie have done this?" Pete asked. Her hands felt restless and she wished for her leather-bound reporter's notebook. Ollie, her old partner in the met, had used his PDA to take notes, but Pete preferred the feel of paper and ink.

"No." Tolliver was back in control. "Our borders prevent it. The Courts are neutral ground. So it's been since the accords long past, when we made the Seelie and Unseelie lands half each of Faerie."

"So who's your money on?" Pete asked. Tolliver's eyes expanded, then contracted. Wrinkles sprouted like weeds at his cheekbones. After a moment he said, "That's your job, isn't it?"

Pete allowed herself a flicker of a smile. "You thought of someone," she said. "When I asked. You have an answer back there behind that big, ugly scar."

"I protect the Queen," Tolliver said brusquely. "I protect the family. And I've told you all I'm fit to tell." He turned his back, and stared out the window.

Pete sighed, and returned to the icy stare of the Queen. She was beautiful, of course. It was hardly remarkable in Faerie. Her beauty was that of statues, and ice—remote, chill and unearthly. Hair of the whitest white, like Rowan's, skin to match, traced only by blue veins. A young face with eyes ancient as the stones under Pete's feet. There was a little pink around them from crying, and they made Pete think of animal eyes. Hungry eyes.

"Tolliver's given me leave to ask you a few questions," Pete said.

The magic in the room, slithering and sliver, came to a boil when the Queen spoke. "I am in mourning. I have nothing to say."

Pete normally didn't open herself to the Black. Being a Weir meant she was a repository rather than a conductor, and too much magic could turn her to cinder, surely as fire. She felt it, though. Every flux and flow. Every push and pull. And the Queen was at the center of something that was alien and frozen as the surface of another planet. Pete bit her lip, and let the magic lap at the back of her mind.

"You know who we look at in my world, when someone dies?" she asked quietly. "Family. Parents. Wives. Brothers. Family knows you best. Family can hate you more than anyone else in the world."

The Queen shot a glance at the other man, who was slender as Tolliver was enormous. He cleared his throat. "Perhaps Miss Caldecott would care to examine the body and the scene of the deed?"

Pete knew when she was being brushed off, but she didn't expect the young woman next to the Queen to pipe up. "I'll come."

"Snowblood, no," the man insisted. "You'll only upset yourself."

"Shut up, Crowfoot," she hissed. "You may have my aunt fooled but you don't fool me!"

"Snowblood!" The Queen's voice snapped like the lightning outside. "That's enough."

"All right," Pete spread her hands. "You, young miss—you're with me. The rest of you, stay put. I'll have more questions once I've seen the body."

The prince was kept in a chamber below the Court, older than the building above, cool arches dripping water into drains that lead to places only rats would know. Pete scented the familiar rotten-orchid scent of decay, along with something foreign, a bit like char. Blood, she guessed. Fae blood.

"Snowblood's quite a name," she said to the girl. "You the queen's niece?"

"Yes," Snowblood said tightly. "And the prince's intended."

The body was covered with a sheet, whiter than white— like any white in Faerie—but dotted all over with blossoms of red, like a first bloom after a snowfall. Pete stopped her hand before she moved it back.

"The prince...he's your cousin."

Snowblood lifted one boneless shoulder. "That's the way it works, isn't it?"

Pete let that one go. It wasn't like royals and inbreeding were strangers. "And Crowfoot?"

"He's the leader of the majority. The Seelie Council." Snowblood paused. "He's perfectly hideous."

"Politicians usually are," Pete said, and twitched the sheet back. She wasn't looking at the prince, but at Snowblood's face. The girl betrayed absolutely no reaction. Her eyes were dull and glassy as a stagnant pond.

"Crowfoot wanted to marry me. Before my cousin," Snowblood said. Pete looked at the body. It was a clean job, exit wounds in the chest ragged and black and, when she rolled the body, two stab wounds in the back, angled upward into the heart and lungs.

Pete realized something. "I don't know his name,"

"Oh," Snowblood said carelessly. "Don't you? It's Caliban. Like the play."

"Half-savage mortal man?" Pete said. "Bloody odd choice, for your firstborn son."

"Yes," Snowblood agreed tonelessly. "For your firstborn."

"Mind if I ask you some questions while I get this business done?" Pete asked. The little stone room didn't have any tools, but she got out her pen light and flashed it over Caliban's hands and fingers. They were limpid, like flower bulbs. The damp wasn't doing him any favors of preservation.

"I suppose not," Snowblood sighed. She sat on a ledge, kicking her feet and dislodging mortar.

"Caliban was a fencer?" Pete asked. She examined the wounds more closely. They hadn't even had time to bleed much.

"A good one," Snowblood said, perking for the first time. "He could beat any man but Tolliver. Tolliver wanted him made a captain of the Ash Guard, rather than taking up his royal duties. Caliban was merciless in battle and in the court. Tolliver said he didn't have the delicacy for politics, but he had the blood for battle. They're similar, I suppose."

"Both big smashy bastards?" Pete peeled back the prince's eyelid and checked his eyes. Wishing for a glove, she stuck a finger in his mouth and checked his tongue as well.

"I suppose," Snowblood said. "Tolliver knew him better than anyone. Better than me."

"Ah," Pete said. She stepped back and looked at the dead prince. She had a fair notion now, but it was only a notion. She didn't have any facts.

"And the Queen, at last," she asked Snowblood. "Some dodgy magic on her—what's that about?"

Snowblood chewed one shockingly crimson lip. "The Unseelie took her, many years ago, kept her for a time before Tolliver and the Ash Guard brought her back. They placed a wasting curse. It's held at bay with other magic, but she was with them a long time. It clings."

It did, indeed. The winding, smoky trail of the curse was apparent to Pete even now, here, layers and layers below the Queen's chamber. "Bit of a short stick for her," Pete said. "Might explain that temper."

"Rowan did the right thing bringing you here," Snowblood said suddenly. Pete cocked an eyebrow at her as she pulled the bloody sheet over Caliban's face once more.

"Really?"

"This is rotten," Snowblood said. "It's not the kind of thing we do. Not the Fae."

"'Course," Pete muttered, thinking that every fairy tale in her world would disagree with the slender girl. "I'm done. Can you do me a favor and get everyone together in one room? The smaller and hotter the better?"

Snowblood looked curious, but she bit down on her question and merely nodded. "Of course."

"I'll be in after a time," Pete said. "Can you have Rowan show me the place where he died?"

That'd give the Queen and her entourage time to get good and pissy about being locked up.

"Just you and me," Pete told Caliban, after Snowblood's footsteps faded away. The prince made no reply.

Caliban's rooms would be opulent even by Las Vegas standards. Heavy velvet in waterfalls of blue and green and midnight purple cascaded from the walls. The bed was gold, and enormous. A mirror made in the shape of an oak leaf stared back at Pete from the ceiling.

"He did like his creature comforts, eh?" she said to Rowan.

He shrugged, staying far away from the bloodstain in the center of the rich blue carpet. Pete didn't even smell the coppery—or charred, she supposed, as this was a Fae–scent that usually accompanied a fresh stabbing scene. The prince's chamber was heavily perfumed, and a garden of scents cloyed at Pete's nose.

She noted that the door locked from the inside with a heavy bolt, and the windows were barred over with grates that had rusted into place.

Pete brushed off her knees reflexively and stood, coming back to Rowan. "I've seen enough. Go join the others, and I'll make an entrance in a bit."

Rowan obeyed, and Pete was alone again, with the last moments of Caliban's life.

She could hear the Fae long before she came upon the door to what the guard told her was Crowfoot's private library. They were complaining. Vociferously. That was good. She wanted them off balance and receptive to the truth.

The member of the Ash Guard outside the door tightened his grip on his short blade when she approached. "Lady," he said, just the proper amount of deference in the tone.

"You can just call me Pete," Pete told him. "What's your name?"

"Juniper," he said. Pete winced. The flower names, to her mind, were just cruel.

"You know how to use that pig-sticker, Juniper?" she inquired. He gave a curt nod, much less polite. He could use it well enough that the question had offended him.

"Good," Pete said. "Stay sharp." She shoved the door open. Tolliver exploded out of the seat he occupied next to the Queen, jabbing his finger into her face.

"How dare you herd us together like cattle? Like we're criminals?"

Crowfoot was on his heels. "Do you have any idea my position in the Seelie Court? I am Senechal...*I* brought you here."

The Queen didn't get up, she just raised her voice. "I am the Queen of all Faerie..."

Only Rowan and Snowblood stayed silent, and they looked anxious as pigs on market day.

"Oi!" Pete made a slashing motion through the air at the trio of shouters. "Simmer down, yeah? The lot of you. You're in here for a reason."

Tolliver's scarred throat worked. "And that'd be...?"

Pete shooed them back to the four corners of the room. She went to Tolliver, then Crowfoot. Rowan, Snowblood, and lastly the Queen. She asked them each a question. Then she went to the fire and warmed up her hands. It was stuffy in the library, but outside the storm was only getting worse.

"*Lady* Caldecott," Crowfoot huffed. "I really must insist that you share your findings."

"Yeah, yeah," Pete rubbed her hands together and then faced them. As a point of self-preservation, she made note of the heavy fireplace poker near her right hand. "I know who killed your Prince Caliban."

"First," Pete held up a finger. Her stomach was twisting and her heart was thudding, even though she kept her face blank. Hercule Poirot never had to face down a roomful of fucking Fae. "Snowblood tells me that Caliban was one hell of a fighter, and he was a big bastard besides. Nobody was taking him by force."

"So?" Crowfoot said rudely. Pete crimped her mouth into her smuggest smile just for him.

"So he was topped by someone he trusted, someone he opened the door to."

"And?" Crowfoot demanded. Pete reached up and patted his bony shoulder.

"And that lets you out. You're a bit of a slimy fuckwit, according to everyone here, and you were sniffing around his woman. Sorry, mate."

Crowfoot blinked, confusion and relief flitting on his features. "I didn't...I mean...of course I didn't! My loyalty is to the Court!"

"You didn't," Pete said. "But somebody here did."

Tolliver's eyes darted to the door. Pete folded her arms. "That's Juniper outside. One of yours. You trained him, I imagine. Like you trained the prince." She approached Tolliver. "I asked you if the Prince could beat you in a low-down brawl, and you said yes. You're not the kind who stabs in the back, and I don't think you did it." Pete lowered her voice. Tolliver was a big man, and probably had some magic riding him to boot. If he didn't like her next words, she'd be in two pieces before she could help it. "But I think you know why it happened."

"Excuse me," the Queen. "But where do you—"

"Not that you're any better," Pete interrupted her. It was the MP and his son all over again, and she was bloody sick of it. "What kind of a mother names her only son after a monstrous savage? I asked you and all you said? "That was his name." That's cold, miss. Ice water all through your veins, no mistake."

"Please." Snowblood's word cut off the Queen's outcry. "Just tell me. Who killed Caliban?"

Pete swiveled, her finger landing on Rowan. "He did."

Silence, for a tick of clock-hands. Then Snowblood exploded toward Rowan, who yelped and ducked, but not quickly enough. Snowblood's small, sharp fist landed a blow on his perfect nose and blood blossomed, trickling over Rowan's lips.

Pete slapped the door with the flat of her hand. "Juniper, get your arse in here!"

Juniper and another of the Ash Guard held Snowblood and Rowan apart. Snowblood panted, her face crimson, while Rowan folded in on himself, trapped in the far corner of the library. Crowfoot and the Queen were talking all at once, their words tripping over each other like tangled vines.

Tolliver came to Pete's shoulder. "How did you know?"

Pete gave Rowan a regretful smile. "Flowers." She sighed, her head suddenly throbbing. "I smelled flowers when Rowan came into a supposedly Fae-proof pub to find me, and again when we were in Caliban's room. I thought it was some kind of shield hex, but it's not, is it?" She fixed Rowan with the copper stare. To his credit, he didn't flinch or change his visage, he just stared back, his eyes like drops of mercury on glass, blood the only motion on his form.

"It's a glamour," Pete continued. "And that means he's not who he says he is."

Snowblood turned her head to Rowan, her small frame quivering. "Who *are* you?"

"Burn in the Underworld," Rowan said quietly. Snowblood turned back to Pete.

"*Who is he?*" she demanded, voice sharp and high with distress.

"My guess?" Pete said. "He's an Unseelie." She stepped closer to Rowan, close as he must have been to Caliban when he stabbed him with one of the short, vicious blades the Ash Guard carried. "And that means he can lie. Been spinning me a fat one since the start of things."

She ticked off the points she'd assembled while she went over the prince's body. "Your Queen was a prisoner of the Unseelie some time ago. I'm guessing, about as long ago as you are old. Is that right, Rowan?"

Crowfoot was the first to catch on. "You begot an heir?" he whispered. "A half-breed heir?"

"Caliban is an odd name for a beloved firstborn son. But he wasn't her firstborn," Pete said. "It's you, Rowan. Isn't it?"

She saw all of the defiance run out of him. The strange ethereal gleam of his skin dulled, and his eyes turned from silver to plain grey as he let the glamour flow out of his grasp. His hair was the same, though—white as the Queen's.

"He was plotting against you, Mother," he said softly. "Tolliver told me one night, in his cups. He would have let the death-curse overwhelm you so he could take your place and obliterate anyone who stood in his path."

"Could be," Pete said. "Could be a load of bollocks. We'll never know, will we?" She jerked her chin at Tolliver. "In any event, Tolliver guessed, did he? He knew what you were going to do, after he found out what you were?"

"I loved my mother," Rowan went on, softly. "I knew what I had to do, even if she wanted nothing to do with me." He raised his eyes to the Queen as Juniper started to drag him away. "Hate is strong. But love is stronger. Mother. Please."

The Queen raised her head, nostrils flaring. Pete saw no tears on her face, just unfathomable rage. "*Never* speak that word to me. I am *not* that. Not to *you*."

"Mother—" Rowan shouted, but more Ash Guard surrounded him and led him away.

"And him," said Crowfoot, pointing at Tolliver. "He's a conspirator. He knew full well and did nothing to stop it."

Tolliver stopped by Pete, walking under his own power, dignity holding his spine straight. "I knew what he was," he murmured. "I saw it when we trained. Cruel. Honorless. He'd torture a lesser opponent for the sport of it. He talked about the mockery he'd make of his cousin's virtue and the atrocities he'd visit on the Unseelie when his mother passed on from her curse. He would have left the Seelie Court in embers if he took the throne." Tolliver swallowed, hard. "You won't get any guilt from me, Lady."

Pete nodded. "I'm sorry you got caught," she told him. "Rowan was blinded, but you aren't."

"Don't be sorrowful," Tolliver said. "You bested me at wits, fairly. No shame in that."

Pete watched Rowan and Tolliver disappear down the opulent hall, no doubt bound for a place much darker and much less sympathetic to his motives.

Crowfoot gripped her arm. "You've done very well, Lady Caldecott. And you've earned a favor of the Fae. Anything you wish. Ask it."

Pete glared at the hand, and then at Crowfoot, until he removed it. "Yeah, I've got a favor," she said. "Take me the bloody hell back to the pub."

When Pete walked back into the Lament, she saw a familiar platinum-dyed head hunched on the far stool at the bar. She practically tripped over her own feet to join him.

Pete didn't know how she felt about condemning a man only trying to help his mother. She didn't know how she felt about the sudden attention of the Fae.

But she did know that she'd enjoyed being a detective again. It had felt good.

She missed it.

In the morning, she'd probably end up calling her old DCI, Nigel Newell, and inquiring about positions that were open in the Major Crime Squad. But for now, at least, she was content to bask in the knowledge that she'd still got her old skillset.

Jack regarded her over a whiskey glass. "Where've you been, then? Missed you, luv."

Pete signaled the publican for a glass of the same. "Trust me, Jack," she said. "You wouldn't believe me if I told you."

Caitlin Kittredge is a full-time writer who lives in Seattle with collections of comic books, cats and vintage pinup clothing. She's the author of the bestselling "Nocturne City" and "Black London" urban fantasy series, and the novel *The Witch's Alphabet*, a steampunk adventure for young adults. Her website is **www.caitlinkittredge.com**

Petunia Caldecott is a former Detective Inspector with the Metropolitan Police, London. She graduated from London City College and currently resides in Whitechapel. **Jack Winter** is a mage and a pain in her arse, but he sometimes makes himself useful. He hails from Manchester, England.

An Ace in the Hole
— A Sazi Story —

by C. T. Adams & Cathy Clamp

"I said...*empty your wallet.*" I glared across the table at Carmine Leone and let a slow growl roll up and out of my chest. Blame the werewolf in me. When I get annoyed, my mask of humanity slips a little, even with my former employer

"And *I said*, go to hell." He matched my growl with one of his own. No werewolf in him, but mob boss isn't that far of a leap. "Nobody touches my wallet. Not my wife, not my staff and not even you. There's nothing in there that's of any interest to anyone."

I let out a sigh, and looked over at Lucas Santiago, who was sitting in the corner of the room. He was my new boss, for Wolven, the law enforcement branch of the shapeshifting community known as the Sazi, and up until a month ago, had been arguably the second most powerful being on the planet. But he'd been attacked, like I'd been two years ago, and now he was a vanilla human, trying to get a handle on *not* being the toughest dog in a fight. I'd thought coming on this case with me would make him realize he didn't need to be a wolf to stay boss of the organization. He'd saved my butt a couple times and I figured I owed him.

Lucas had been trying to stay out of this, but I could smell that he was getting fidgety. There were three emotion scents in the room right now—determination, which smells similar to a heated cast iron pan; and anger, which reminds me of hot peppers roasting. The final scent was frustration; which is a weird mix of scents, including boiling water, black pepper and other stuff.

I shook my head. "See, there's a flaw in that logic, even if you're too stressed to see it."

Carmine narrowed his eyes, but then he grudgingly nodded. "Go on."

"First, neither of you are going to like me blabbing all this, but you both need all the information at hand to see my point, so just get over it." Now both sets of eyes were mere slits under narrowed lids. "You called me up here to Canada to find out the status of the job you gave me, which is finding and killing the guys who beat the crap out of you, using the knife they sliced you with. Just so we're clear, I don't have that knife anymore, but the job's still on"

Carmine made a small, strangled noise, and then started scanning the ceiling and walls—probably looking for some sort of bug.

I shook my head again. "This isn't some sort of trap, Carmine. I'm not state's evidence material. I'm just laying out the facts. The job's already been approved by the Sazi Council, so while Lucas might not *like* that it's been allowed, he knows why I'm here. No, the question is...why are *you* here?"

He shrugged. "Vacation. Just a quick get-away with Linda and Barbara before the baby's due. Calgary's nice this time of year." The black pepper scent told me he was lying.

"Just knock it off, okay? Lying isn't going to help any of us." I held up a hand to forestall further bluster. "You own a flippin' *island* in the Caribbean where there's no extradition treaty. The feds know it, so you're a flight risk. What odds would you give me that there's an order out there restricting your movements?"

Lucas crossed his arms over his chest and let out a light growl. It wasn't precisely a wolf growl, but close enough. While Carmine was a full human, he was also the significant other of Barbara Herrera, an alpha werewolf...and the woman about to give birth to his son. He had thus become a fringe "family member," who Wolven and the Council would keep an eye on.

Carmine didn't respond at all. But I noticed he didn't deny my guess.

"So," I continued, "It's unlikely you'd be allowed on a commercial flight out of the country, meaning you *snuck* here, probably in the middle of the night—and I know you're not stupid enough to do that without a damned good reason."

"There is one." A simple acknowledgment with a short nod. At least I didn't have to dig on that point deeper.

"Now, when I walked in the hotel room, we shook hands." He stared down at his hand suddenly like I'd infected him with something, or passed him some poison. I snorted. "No, it's nothing like that. But I *did* do a hindsight on you without your knowledge."

Now Lucas glared. That was supposed to have been a secret.

"Goddamn it, Giodone!" The same words came out of two mouths as they both rose to their feet and advanced toward me threateningly.

"Knock it off!" I had to yell over the blue language that was now searing the paint off the walls. "Would you *please* give me a second to explain why it's important you *both* know?" After a moment, their scents settled down, but they still arched over me like vultures waiting for a death twitch.

My head tipped up until I could watch Carmine's face. "I figured that my arriving would put your mind on the day you were attacked and stabbed in the condo in Colorado, so I snuck into your head to watch what happened. It *is* a hell of a lot easier to find people when you know what they look like, y'know."

"It's not like I had a camera handy while they were slicing me up." His mouth was bitching, but his scent was impressed I'd thought to do the hindsight.

The Sazi magic that turned me into a werewolf also did other stuff to me. Most shifters get heightened senses—better eyesight or super-sensitive hearing. But a very few become 'seers,' those with a sixth sense. Lucky me. In my case, I don't get the future popping into my head. No, I get the *past*. Usually it's a specific past, an event that's important or emotional to the one who lived it. I've learned to be able to step outside the memory to see tiny details that happened, but which aren't readily evident until the person is pressed or under hypnosis.

"Precisely. But your mind is a perfect camera." I tapped my forehead. "It just takes the right software to download it."

"So what's my wallet got to do with anything?"

"One of the guys nicked it out of your pocket while you were getting slapped around."

Now he frowned, with his whole body. His muscles stiffened and there was a scent that told me he was hiding something. "I checked it after I came to. It was *in* my pocket and nothing was missing."

"Precisely. They put it *back*. Interesting, huh? Those South American guys didn't come to the condo to rob you. They were *looking* for something. And from the expression on the guy's face in your memory, he found it. So, I say again...empty your wallet. Let's find out what they wanted."

"There's nothing to find! There's personal...stuff about business that's none of yours."

I glared at Carmine, meeting those cold eyes with steel blue ones that were beginning to glow with magical fire. "So you're telling me that even though I'm *positive* the reason you were beaten up was only to *distract* you from the real reason for their visit, you don't care? You want me to just kill them, without finding out what they wanted or why? Jeez, your personal and business life have *already* been compromised! Are you positive that the damage hasn't already been done, while your people had no idea you were laid up in the hospital?" I paused while his pulse pounded under his skin so loud I'd swear it was coming out of speakers in the walls. "Tell me, Carmine. Be honest. Are you really pig-headed and stubborn enough to risk everything you have just to keep your little secrets—that I don't give a damn about anyway?"

Sometime in the middle of my little rant he went still and thoughtful. The gears I knew he had in that grey matter finally jump-started. He raised up one hip to sit partway on the table. His face, and scent, went through a dozen emotions, before finally settling on the dry heat smell of embarrassment.

"Okay, so what's the plan? Let's say I give you my wallet." He shot a glare at Lucas, who glared back—two junkyard dogs sizing each other up. "*Just* you. Do you know what you're looking for?"

I nodded. "The last thing he pulled out was a slip of paper, about the size of a post-it note with fringed edges. An old photograph, maybe? It was on the left side and he had to dig to get it out." Actually, I knew it was a photo. I'd even seen the image, but it didn't make sense. It was just a photo of a long brick wall with no other identifying marks.

Carmine had gone still again, but this time he wasn't embarrassed. He was nervous. He pulled out his wallet like a snake after a mouse. Any inhibition he'd had was lost as he nearly tore apart the soft suede. Pictures, credit cards, money, receipts and all manner of cryptic notes were tossed on the table as he frantically looked for whatever wasn't there. A solid five minutes went by while he opened every paper, made sure the missing item wasn't attached to anything, and re-probed every pocket, pouch and slit in the leather.

When he finally gave up, he stood staring at the pile of papers that constituted his life, looking older than I'd ever seen him. It only lasted a moment and then he smiled. The flash of teeth was completely empty of meaning and everyone in the room knew it. "Eh. No big deal. Wouldn't mean anything to anyone but me."

"What's missing?" Lucas demanded. "I'd suggest you talk to us before you start talking to those who can *make* you talk."

Carmine shrugged, the patently false smile abandoned. He turned his back so we couldn't see his face. "Just an old photo of some architecture. Something my dad took years ago. Like I said, only important to me."

I didn't know much about Carmine's father—only that he was raised in Chicago around the Capone era. He didn't settle down and get married until he was nearly sixty, and most of Carmine's friends thought Marco was his grandfather, instead of his dad.

Lucas made a gesture, pointing to my hands and then to Carmine. I knew what he wanted and I didn't disagree. This conversation would go a lot faster if I just did another hindsight. I don't really like doing two in one day on a person, but this was taking for-freaking-*ever*! I pulled off one of the black leather gloves I have to wear to keep from getting accidental images from people—but then froze and raised my nose in the air. Lucas did the same, but got a frustrated look on his face. He can't smell things like he used to anymore, and it drives him nuts. But he's still got eyes, and he used them...scanning around the room to try to see anything out of place. I shook my head and pointed toward the door and then thumped Carmine on the shoulder hard enough to make him jump and turn around.

The scent that was coming under the door was a peculiar one that I'd smelled before. I wasn't raised on a farm, but I've stood in a field of cantaloupes, right at the point when the whole lot was about to turn and go moldy inside. The smell is nearly over-powering—musty, sweet and slightly rotten. I carefully drew my Taurus back-up revolver from my ankle holster and wasn't at all surprised that Carmine and Lucas produced guns as well. I smeared the polish on the clean, shining mahogany table by using my finger to write: *snakes*.

There was a polite knock on the door, followed by a woman's voice. "Room service."

I raised my brows at Carmine and he shook his head firmly. He didn't order, and *we* didn't order, so it was a trap. He got the hint of me rolling my finger at him and called out "Just a second," as if he was in the bathroom.

Snakes don't have the best hearing, so they probably wouldn't hear if we kept our voices to the barest whisper. "Is there a back way out of here," I said, "or do we take them on? I'm pretty sure there's more than one out there."

Carmine paused longer than I liked, and I leaned so close to his face that he could probably smell cinnamon toothpaste. "Unless you want your kid to grow up *without* a dad, you'd better start spilling. I can take one of them, maybe two, barehanded, but understand that even one shot will bring the cops."

A second knock turned his head toward the door and to the shadows that moved across the sunlit carpeting, showing there were at least four feet on the other side. With a tiny, disgusted noise from the back of his throat, he turned and hurried into the separate bedroom. It was a gorgeous room, befitting a hotel of the Fairmont Palliser's reputation. But I was pretty sure that most rooms didn't have a bookcase that swung out from the wall when a portion of the baseboard was pressed.

He waved us through just as I heard a cardkey being inserted into the door in the outer room and the tiny high pitched whine as the lock released. He got the wall closed just in time and the thick, flat steel bar that slid into the oak header would make sure that nobody followed us—at least not *quickly.*

We had to squeeze against the wall to let him pass, then followed him down an old iron staircase that seemed like it might have been attached to the outside of the building once upon a time. I knew Lucas was burning up with curiosity, just like I was. But now wasn't the time to ask. Not until we were in a more defensible position.

The staircase descended several floors and when the temperature of the walls changed, I was pretty sure we were at the basement level, or below. In a moment, I was proved right. The sounds of metallic thumping and hissing came from behind the wall at the end of the staircase and Carmine put his eye up to what appeared to be a peep hole into the outer area. After a long moment, as I listened to the snakes tearing things apart in the upper room, he slid back a steel bar that was a twin of the one above. The door pushed outward smoothly and we stepped out, into a back corner of the boiler room.

There was something about the boiler room of the Palliser Hotel that set off alarm bells in my mind, but I couldn't for the life of me figure out why. So, rather than do something as potentially fatal as asking one of the people in the room with me, I went to the 'intercom' in my head.

While it's taken some getting used to, one unique thing about werewolf mates is that they're telepathically tied to each other. In sticky situations like this, being in instant contact with my wife was often more useful than an extra clip of ammo.

Sue?

Hey, lover. What's up? Her voice was warm and slightly sleepy. She's been working a lot of late nights, also for Wolven, and supposedly had the day off. So I've been trying to stay out of her head. We're getting better at shutting out the other person from our day to day thoughts. It had been making both of us a little squirrely.

Palliser Hotel, in Calgary. See if you can find anything online about the basement. I'm remembering something in the back of my head, but since we're being chased by snakes right now, I don't want to spend the brainpower to figure it out.

Snakes? Uh-oh. Not good. The word made her nervous enough that the walls were breaking down in our heads. I was starting to see our bedroom overlaid on the machinery. The furnace grate was wearing a burgundy coverlet and the brick walls had drapes.

Whoa, we're fine. Okay? I'm here with Lucas and Carmine and we're all armed. I don't think they even know where we are. We booked it out of the room as soon as I smelled them. But Carmine's hiding something and I need to know what. I'm going to shut the vault door now, so knock before you come back in.

She took a deep mental breath and calmed. *Okay, sorry. I'm just still having nightmares about snakes from the attack last fall. It'll pass. I'll find what I can and get back to you.*

I felt a bump against my shoulder and turned my head before I turned my gun. Sure, it was only Lucas, but still—*Getting sloppy, Giodone.*

He must have noticed that I was having trouble focusing, because he stopped and waited for a moment. "You back with us? Getting a vision?"

One of the nice things about Lucas is he's been around seers his whole life, *and* he was mated up until he turned back human.

"Having Sue do some research on her end while we're getting out of here."

He looked at me for a long moment, likely wondering just *what* I was having her research, but he didn't say anything in front of Carmine. Instead, he motioned around the room with his Ruger. "Getting anything?"

I had done a quick scan when we stepped through the hidden door, but did another just to be safe. "All clear...although there have been snakes down here pretty recently. No more than a week."

Carmine frowned, as well he should. The guys who beat the crap out of him were snake shifters. He was damned lucky he wasn't turning on the moon like me. He'd originally attributed the attack to a South American mafia trying to get back an ancient artifact one of his people stole. Now, it looked like it might be something entirely different. "I just got here a week ago. Think it's coincidence?"

Lucas and I turned at once and both stared at him. I mean... *duh.* "You tell me," I said.

He didn't respond, but just stared at me, which was weird. Here he's worried about snakes, who have been in the room recently, and he's only got *my* word the room is clear, but he's *not* looking around the room, checking out every shadow. That's very unlike him. He's even more paranoid than me.

Tony? I've got your answer.

Not the warning I asked for, but there isn't anything critical going on anyway. *What'cha got?*

There's a secret tunnel in the boiler room of the Palliser.

Ah! That's where I remember it. It was in one of those 'Secrets of' series of books—strange things about major cities. Okay. Just came down the tunnel. Staircase to the fourth floor, right?

There was a pause. *Um...no. That's not mentioned. This one is an old laundry tunnel that goes under the railroad tracks and veers east for a few blocks. Seems that years ago, the hotel cleaned all the linens a couple blocks away. It's sealed off in the boiler room, but the tunnel's still there.*

Little pieces were starting to fall together in my head, but it would require a little private detecting later, when nobody was around.

There are a lot of times when the local police are handy to our kind. One of those times is when people ransack rooms looking for things. It was short work to install Carmine at a different hotel and have Babs—my private name for Barbara Herrera, call the hotel and complain that someone with a master key broke into the room and robbed her while she was napping. We got her back up to the room the same way as we got out, long after the snakes were gone. The security cameras would definitely show the door being opened with a key. Apparently, they'd been coming and going through the secret staircase to avoid cameras showing Carmine and Linda out of the country, so as far as the cameras were concerned, they'd never left the room.

Less than two hours after I'd left, I was back in the laundry room.

I didn't smell anything I hadn't smelled before and saw no glowing evidence of other Sazi in the room before I slipped inside. But when I felt the cold press of a gun barrel to my temple, I knew I hadn't been careful enough. I dutifully raised my hands while I was relieved of my weapons. But since she was human, and it was the first night of the moon I still had an advantage.

The thick Russian accent from the woman was a surprise. "Where is the box?"

"Box?" This was news to me.

The question earned me a swipe across the back of the skull with the gun, hard enough to make me realize this was no human. I wound up sprawled face down, spitting blood from kissing the concrete. "Do not toy with me, wolf. Why else would you return to the tunnel?"

She knew I was Sazi? That lowered my brows and made me push off hard from the floor to try to take her feet out from under her. Her reaction was fast enough to avoid my leg sweep. That told me she was either a cat or a spider in her animal form. But it did give me enough time to get my feet under me and face her. She *should* have an aura, but didn't. No scent, no magic aura, but a shifter? That was just wrong on so many levels.

We squared off in the small space, but neither of us attacked. Yes, she could shoot me, but she didn't seem inclined. Apparently, she thought I had information. Unfortunately, all I had were guesses. I was betting she had actual *answers*.

I took off the gloves, both metaphorically and physically. All I had to do was get close enough to touch skin and she was *mine*. But then the hammer cocked back and her eyes narrowed.

"You will put the gloves back on. *Now!*" I paused and then dropped them to the floor. She backed away. "We have heard of your Sazi mind tricks, seer. I am willing to shoot you if I must and find another way to get the information." She raised the Taurus she'd taken from me and likewise cocked the hammer. One gun was aimed at my head now, the other at my chest. Simultaneous shots would put me down permanently. She motioned with the barrel pointed at my heart. "Pick up the gloves and put them back on."

I did as I was told. But as they say, *you can't stop me from* thinking *bad things.*

I threw open the door in my mind. Sue's consciousness slipped inside of mine seamlessly. I didn't need to speak. She'd be able to see the guns pointed at me and know instantly where I was. *Call Lucas on his cell. Tell him the nice lady with the guns wants some sort of box and thinks I know where it is.*

I don't have to. He's here with me. Carmine too.

Good. Tell Lucas to lean on him until he spills whatever the hell he's hiding from us. And tell him to hurry.

It was even money that my former boss knew *exactly* what the Russian was talking about, and I was pretty sure that even as a lowly human, Lucas was tough enough to drag it out of him.

Being in two places at once isn't all it's cracked up to be. It's a lot like trying to hear one person inside a crowded party. It can be done, but it takes concentration. Sue and I were in the same boat. She was listening to Lucas and Carmine argue, and I was trying to hear through her ears. She was also going to try to learn as much as we could from my opponent. "What makes you think I know where it is?"

She laughed. It had a harsh edge that told me she wasn't buying the stall technique. "You are friends with Leone and came here at his request. We know he has been in the tunnel recently. Either he took something out to give you, or put something in. But the photograph does not show *which* brick the box is behind."

Ah! That's what the photo of bricks was—the inside of the tunnel under the hotel. It's a map of sorts. Take the photo into the tunnel and hold it up until the pipes line up. Then just pick the right brick and there's a hidey-hole. And it was something his *father* hid. Interesting.

"You can't just sniff it out?" I asked the question with a slightly sarcastic tone, just to see how she'd respond. It might tell me what sort of shifter she was. Cats have pretty good noses. Spiders have none at all.

"Do not play dumb, wolf. You know he defeated that by putting his hands on each and every brick in the picture." She motioned with the guns toward a batch of boxes in the corner.

"Go. You will show me where it is, or I will give you to my com-rades...for *dinner.*" She paused when I glared instead of begging for my life. "It will be a *slow* meal."

I shrugged, which made her blink. "Whatever. I've been tor-tured more than once. Snakes, spiders and even a dragon have taken chunks of my hide. I'm getting pretty jaded to threats." She just motioned a second time. At the moment, I was getting more information than I was giving. But I was starting to hear bits of information through Sue's ears now, so I turned and walked to where she was pointing. I was hoping a doorway would become evident as I got closer, and it did.

The tunnel was dark, but wolves see in the dark really well. Still, the *comrade* behind me apparently wasn't willing to risk me disappearing into the blackness, so she turned on a pen light. A quick glance behind revealed it was held in her mouth. Damn. I was hoping she'd put down one of the guns.

I listened through Sue as I walked and got more nervous as I progressed. It wasn't just the darkness, but the scents and sounds that came from far ahead of me. There were snakes, all right. Lots of them, and the sounds of whimpers and screams that echoed off the walls. The fact that the lady behind me gave off the citrus scent of happiness with each scream wasn't the best encouragement for sticking around.

"What do you need from the box? Maybe we can make a deal."

I was surprised when she answered calmly. "We want the virus back, of course. But we shall see what else is inside. No doubt there are other things of value, as well."

The *virus?* What the hell!? *Pass that along, would you? What the hell is Carmine up to? I want answers, Sue. Get them however you have to before I reach this box.*

I felt her body race for the next room where Lucas had taken Carmine to *chat.* It annoyed me he wouldn't let her attend, but he'd always been really protective of Sue. I heard when she told him and heard his swearing when he threw open the bedroom door again and slammed it behind him. I needed a minute to talk to Carmine myself, so I paused and spoke with my back turned.

"Let me see the photo. I need to orient myself. I've never actu-ally been here without a guide. By the way, do you have a name?"

Hell, I hadn't been here at *all,* so I was actually doing pretty good so far. I felt a barrel press into my spine and kept my hands in the air. She didn't speak, but there was a fumbling with my back pocket and when the metal left my shirt, I reached back. There was the photo I'd seen.

"My name isn't important. Now, orient yourself and let us finish this."

I had a feeling that *finish this* didn't just mean getting the box. Clearly, I'd seen too much to live.

While I held up the photo and stared, I slipped into Sue's mind. I'd only done this a couple of times before, but it was time I got some answers from Carmine.

The bedroom door was locked, but it wasn't a high end hotel. It would only be a hollow core door with a flimsy lock. I pushed into her further, almost too much. I nearly dropped the photo. Stepping this way and that, all with the light trained beyond me into the darkness, I stepped forward in one body and kicked outward in another. The door to the bedroom slammed open and Sue caught Lucas with both hands clutching Carmine's shirt, mid-threat.

It was Sue's voice speaking, but my words. "Goddamn it, Leone! I've got a gun pointed at my head and another at my heart, and if you don't spill what the hell this is about, I swear to God that I'm going to rip your chest open and shove your beating heart up your ass!" He'd be able to see Sue's eyes glowing blue. They always did when I slipped into her body.

I advanced threateningly toward the bed and Lucas backed up a little in surprise. He probably knew I was subject to Sue's physical limitation as a human, but those limitations had extended somewhat recently, ever since she'd done a magic ritual that saved her life. Nobody was really sure what we were capable of together. I didn't want to find out right this second, but nobody else had to know that. Trouble was, I was starting to feel hot, and that wasn't a good thing. On the first night of the moon, I may or may not shift, and have no control over the process.

Carmine scrambled backwards on the bed, apparently believing whatever he saw. I didn't want to look in the mirror to see what that was. "Okay, okay! Fine, Tony. I'll talk."

"Be quick about it. I've only got a few more minutes to stall here."

I slipped back into my own body and stepped forward a few paces, then zig-zagged and pointed for the woman to aim the light at the ceiling where the pipes were. "This would be a lot easier with more light."

"Just keep walking. We have time."

The scent of snakes was getting stronger, and I was liking this less and less. I slipped back into Sue. "How do I find the box? I won't turn it over if I can avoid it, but I need to know what I'm looking for."

Carmine sighed. "Right wall, six rows up, and look for a thumbprint in the mortar."

"Tell me about the *virus*. What the hell, Carmine? When did you get involved in bioweapons?"

I couldn't really smell through Sue's nose, but he actually looked contrite. "It wasn't intentional. We raided a warehouse to get hold of an ammo shipment we heard was being stockpiled. It was in a briefcase that was handcuffed to the wrist of a guy with a Russian diplomatic passport. We couldn't figure out what he was doing there, but decided it needed to be in safekeeping while I decided what to do with it."

The logic escaped me. "Uh, turn it in to the CDC maybe? Why would you *keep it*? Jesus, Leone. Are you *insane*? What kind of virus is it?"

He shrugged and stood up before starting to pace back and forth. "I don't know. I really don't, Tony. That whole situation put me in a hell of a bind. There was stuff in that warehouse that I don't want, but also don't want anyone else to get hold of." He paused and stared right at me through the eyes of my wife. "Not even our government. Y'know? Stuff that ought to not exist at all. So, I put it in the box my dad started. He called it his *ace in the hole* box. It started out with a bunch of gold coins. He'd been transporting them from Capone's vault to a new location, when the Feds started moving in. While he was en route, Capone was arrested and the place Dad was going to was raided. So, he headed north and wound up here in Calgary. Over the years, he put in other things that made life easier—blackmail photos, audio tapes of corrupt politicians and cops, and anything he fenced for people that was too hot to handle for a while. By the time Dad died, I was already doing well enough that I didn't need to raid the gold." He shrugged. "I've added to it a few times. It keeps life...*comfortable*."

Yeah, I'll just bet it does. I know a dozen people who would love to get their hands on that box. I was smelling Carmine's cologne in the tunnel now and understood what my Russian captor meant about him spreading his scent. It was everywhere. He must have brought down a bottle of cologne and sprayed it across every brick. I'll bet Babs taught him that. It was quickly burning out my nose.

That's when I spotted the thumbprint. I tried to give no sign of it, but scuffed my foot sideways, like I had tripped, and caught myself against the tunnel wall. Hopefully I'd be able to find it again. Once I was another dozen feet further down the tunnel, I stopped again and held up the picture. Apparently, Lady Russia was getting antsy, because a moment later I heard her let out an annoyed sound and then her voice rang out into the darkness. "Boris! Andrei, come here! I have the wolf seer, and he's stalling. I think we will have to cut some...pieces...off him to get the location."

Great. Just great. Well, I had what I needed from Carmine. I turned Sue's head toward Lucas. "However you need to do it, you need to get back to the Palliser and give me a hand. I'm about to be overrun with Russian and South American snake shifters. I'll do what I can, but bring enough ammo for an army."

That was all the time I had to talk, because the moon had finally reached full height in the sky and we must have been just barely under the street, because it cut through me like a laser. I'm pretty sure I screamed. I definitely dropped to the floor of the tunnel like a puppet with its strings cut. "Get up!" She shouted at me, but it wasn't like I had a choice.

I tried to choke out words, because I knew her fingers were getting itchy on the triggers. "If you did your research, you must know I'm a three-day. You want the box, you need to shield the moon."

She swore in Russian and tucked one of the guns in her waistband. Only the very best alpha shifters can shield a lesser animal from a distance. Most need direct touch to control a shift. She reached out to grab my sleeve and at the last second, I pulled off my glove and grabbed her hand.

The moon faded with her power and I latched onto her mind in a hindsight. Her eyes glazed over as she slipped into her own past. I dragged her backwards with me and extinguished the light. I could hear the footsteps ahead of me increase in speed and a bright flash of light told me someone else had shifted. The low buzzing sound that resulted said there was at least one rattler among the snakes.

Terrific.

Once I was back at the spot where I'd stumbled, it wasn't hard to find the place where Marco's thumb had dug into soft mortar. As I suspected, the brick was loose in the wall. It would be tricky to pull it out with one hand, but I couldn't afford to let go of the Russian babe to use both. I did, however, take back my gun, and hers to boot, before yanking the brick loose to let it drop to the ground. The sound echoed and the voices, boots and scales moved faster still. The snakes sounded *big*.

The box was just behind the brick and had a handle on front that made me think of a safe deposit box. Maybe it was. All I knew is that I only had time to drop Natasha, grab the handle, and take off running. I couldn't risk that box staying here, even if there was only a slim chance of them finding it before we could get back to retrieve it.

The moment I let go and started to run, I felt the moon slice through my skin once more. Just to be safe, I put the handle of the box in my teeth. It was a good thing I did, too, because it wasn't more than a dozen feet before I couldn't stand the pressure anymore. The howl that tried to leave my mouth was forced to escape through locked jaws and then I was running on four legs instead of two, pulling behind the tattered remains of my clothing as I ran.

Bullets started to ricochet off the brick and I felt a flash of pain in my ribs. There were shouts behind and the scent of rotten cantaloupe enveloping me as I made one final leap through the door of the boiler room, tearing at least two leg muscles in the process.

But I was luckier than my pursuer. The giant snake ran fang first into the boiler I barely missed and cold-cocked himself. Lucas and two wolves I'd never seen before rushed past me into the tunnel shouting for everybody to give themselves up, as I crawled under the massive machine with my prize.

A week later I was still nursing an ACL tear and broken collarbone from a bullet, which had felt like my ribs at the time. As a three-day, I don't heal very fast. But I'd be back on my feet a lot faster than a full human.

Even Lucas hadn't been able to get the box away from me that night. He said he'd have had to break my jaw to unlock it. We went through it together the next morning. There was lots of interesting reading. Most of the blackmail evidence was destroyed, but Lucas saw no reason not to give the gold back to Carmine. Anyone it might have belonged to was long dead now and he'd need money to pay his legal bills for being out of the country. Turns out the Feds were watching him closer than we'd imagined. The RCMP picked him up at the hotel while we were all out, to deliver him to the Feds. I'll be laying low for some time to come because it turns out I was caught on film as well. Since

I was supposed to be dead, and now I'm not, I'll probably need a make-over so I don't wind up in the cell next door. However, Lucas is going to see what he can arrange for us to get a clean bill—a full pardon from the President for both me and Carmine, owing to us turning over the weapons cache and virus we dis-covered and the terrorist spies...at least the full human ones. The others? Well, the snake attackers who I was able to finger through the hindsight on Carmine will never see trial. Not only is Carmine watched by the Sazi now, he'll be *protected* by them. At least, so long as he's not breaking the law.

That's Wolven law enforcement, and it's why I stick around.

C. T. Adams and **Cathy Clamp** are real people with slightly twisted minds who write strange fiction for fun. They are hap-pily the award-winning, *USA Today* bestselling authors of the "Tales of the Sazi" and "Thrall" series for Tor Books. They are also now writing urban fantasy as "Cat Adams" and released a new series, "The Blood Singer" in June, 2010. Both C.T. and Cathy spend their days working in a law office in central Texas, which is what many claim warped their brains. They share a website at **www.ciecatrunpubs.com**

Tony Giodone's skill as a hit man has resulted in a stack of cold case files in the homicide divisions of a number of major cities. Even before he was attacked and turned into a werewolf, if you met Tony in a dark alley, he'd be walking back into the light alone. Although still an assassin, he's now working for Wolven, the police force of the Sazi council—in other words, the good guys.

HELL BOUND

— A Hell on Earth Story —

by Jackie Kessler

"Stupid fucking name." The incubus Daunuan shook his head. "Why do so many human magicians pick stupid fucking names?"

"Aw, sweetie," I said. "Don't be like that. They're just being creative. They think it makes them sound exotic."

"It makes them sound like assholes."

"Not everyone can have a name like yours, Don Juan," I said with a wink, emphasizing the human pronunciation. The demonic version was more sensual, called for more use of the tongue and lips. We creatures of Lust were nothing if not sensual. And all about the tongue and lips. "Besides," I said, " 'Noel Le Noir' isn't the worst name I've ever heard."

"No, but it *is* hopelessly cheesy."

"I like my men hopelessly cheesy."

"You like your men, period." Daun smiled. "And your women."

"I'm an equal-opportunity succubus," I agreed happily. Whatever the gender, whatever the form, I loved humans. To death. Speaking of which...

From our secluded table in the corner, I gazed at my new client, who was sipping a drink all by his lonesome at the bar.

To look at him, you'd never guess that Noel Le Noir—born Leon Siegal—was a Satanist (which put him on my side) and a master magician (which did not). At first glance, he looked bookish and plump, with a weak chin and acne scars. And talk about overkill on the black: silk shirt, slacks, shoes, socks, dyed hair. A gaudy silver necklace with a pentacle dangling point-side down hung around his fleshy neck. He looked like he'd tried going Goth when he'd hit 35 and didn't quite make it.

Based on his reputation Below, I'd expected to feel his magical power teasing his flesh like foreplay. One didn't become a master of the dark arts without radiating a little menace, or at least seeming like the sort who'd go out of his way to kick puppies and drown kittens. This guy? He radiated as much power as a limp dick. Maybe someone was fooling around Downstairs and mislabeled Noel's file as that of an actual mage, instead of a wannabe who chanted his "Hail Satan's" and pretended his rod of power was something other than what lay between his legs.

He didn't need magic, however, to score a one-way ticket to Hell, even without the Satanism. Noel Le Noir was personally responsible for nineteen human sacrifices and too many animal killings to count, to say nothing of all the pain and suffering he'd caused others over the past dozen years or so. He was a serial killer with the face of a nebbish.

Yum.

"I still don't understand why you scored this assignment," Daun said, casting a dark look at Noel.

"What's to understand? Queen Lillith gave it to me personally." And never mind how she'd gloated as she'd handed me the paperwork. "Besides, I haven't eaten a magician in *centuries*. And the last one was a charlatan."

"This guy's supposed to be the real deal, babes."

"Even if he is"—which I seriously doubted—"I can take him. The queen wouldn't have given me the assignment if I couldn't."

"I'm sorry, I think you've mistaken your queen for someone who's on Team Jezebel." Daun leaned in close. "She's making it known far and wide that you intend to corral an evil magician's soul down to the Pit, and that it wasn't sanctioned by Lust."

Gosh, Lillith had lied. What a shock.

Daun's eyes sparkled with mirth. "Demons of Greed are already taking bets on whether you get completely destroyed or just bound to the mage as his slave."

"What're my odds on actually nabbing his soul for Hell?"

"Against? I can't count that high." He grinned, his fangs flashing momentarily through his human disguise. "Your queen has set you up, Jez. If you do your job, it's a win for Lust, and she gets the credit. If you fail, it's because you overstepped, and she's not responsible."

I pouted. Lillith, the first mortal demon and my eternal tormentor (read: my boss) had it in for me, for reasons that I still didn't know. She was why I was stuck as a fifth level succubus, even though I'd been around for almost four thousand years. She absolutely despised me. Maybe one day I'd know the reason why. Or not. "I know what I'm doing, Daun."

"So do I. You're getting in over your head."

"You just prefer it when I'm giving head."

"Not the point." He looked at me intently, studying my features. Which was a waste of time, since, like him, I was in a human guise at the moment. "There's a reason even the Lower Downs don't like getting assigned to magicians. If this guy isn't a phony, he very well could overpower you and then boom: instant bondage. And not in the fun-filled, handcuffs way. You'd be his servant until Judgment Day."

"He's not going to live that long."

"Or you could just be vaporized."

"Why, sweetie," I said, cooing. "It's almost like you actually care about me."

He chuckled, low and lush. "You're the best lay in all of Hell. I'd hate to see your ass incinerated by mortal magic."

Awww. For a demon, that was practically a love sonnet. "Strip away the human magic, and all you have is another flesh puppet. He's got his temptations, just like any other mortal." I patted Daun's thigh. "No worries. When I'm done with Noel Le Noir, he'll be ten minutes dead before he realizes he lost his soul."

"Big talk for a little succubus."

"It's my chance to finally prove to my queen that I deserve to be promoted. Besides, I'm sure Noel's a fraud. I'm not sensing anything from him." Real magicians reeked of magic, like garlic in an Italian restaurant. "What about you?"

Daun glanced in Noel's direction, sniffed loudly, then rubbed his nose. "Only thing I smell on him is his aftershave."

"See that? Nothing to worry about."

"He could have a shieldstone. That would mask his power."

"You've been screwing the role-playing folks again, sweetie. There's no such thing as a Shield Against Evil."

"Some would say there's no such thing as demons."

"The difference is they'd be wrong. Bye-bye, Daun. I've got work to do."

"Fine, go get lusty with the master magician. If he destroys you, don't say I didn't warn you." He kissed me, very thoroughly, then disappeared in a puff of evil intent.

I fluffed my hair (currently jet black), adjusted my boobs (double-D), and retouched my lipstick (blowjob red). Then I stood up, grinning like a cat after a serving of canary.

All right, Noel Le Noir. Time to say hello to the best—and last—lay of your life.

I shimmied over to him with practiced ease, the clacking of my four-inch heels announcing my presence well before I reached his side. The bartender, who was sliding another drink in front of Noel, paused to give me an appreciative glance, his gaze stopping at my boobs. I gave them an added jiggle by way of saying hello. And then I slid onto the barstool next to my new client.

"What would you like?" the bartender asked me.

"Sex on the beach." Yes, I like the drink, too.

He grinned and got right on it. I watched him work, enjoying the way he wore his black tee-shirt, feeling Noel's gaze on me. Noel Le Noir was into power games; being a multiple murderer proved that. He'd make the first move. And if he didn't, a lick of my infernal power would turn up the heat. I preferred not to resort to my Hellish magic to hook a client—that gets old after the first thousand years—but I had no qualms about whammy-ing a hesitant one with lust, if that's what it took to get the job done. I'm a demon, after all. We cheat.

As the bartender slid the drink in front of me, Noel dropped a twenty on the bar and cleared his throat. "I've got this one, Dave. Keep the change."

Dave the bartender flashed a perfunctory smile and took Noel's cash, then also took the hint and sidled away.

Me, I beamed at Noel. "That's sweet," I said. "Thanks for the drink."

"You're welcome." Noel actually talked to me and not to my chest. Hmm. To fix that, I took a deep breath. Yep, there we go—now he was staring at my twin assets. Much better. He introduced himself to my breasts: "I'm Noel."

"Jesse," I said, offering him both my nickname and my hand. He pressed my palm to his lips—old fashioned and wonderfully, inappropriately intimate. The kiss was warm, and lingering, and hinted at many things. As did his tongue.

Ooh. Whether or not Noel had any real magical power, he sure knew how to use his mouth. Bonus!

He released my hand, and I sipped my drink and smiled inanely as I let him talk for a bit, telling me about himself (yawn) and that I was beautiful (well, duh) and that he wasn't seeing anyone now because his last girlfriend didn't work out (that often happens when you use the girlfriend as a human sacrifice, but whatever).

"I'm not seeing anyone either," I chirped. "My last boyfriend wanted a relationship, but all I wanted was hot and sweaty sex."

Noel spluttered his drink.

"Love your necklace," I said, making with the Bambi eyes. What serial killer didn't love a big-busted gal with huge Bambi eyes?

"This?" He dangled the pentacle between his fingers, and I made sure to lean forward in appreciation. My boobs nearly popped out of my dress as I admired the silver necklace. Being near the jewelry actually made me feel itchy, but I figured that was my impatience; I really wanted Noel to get on with seducing me. Talking to my nipples again, he said, "It's a pentagram. I do magic," he added in a low voice, ending with a smile that was probably supposed to make him seem mysterious.

Cue my wide-eyed curiosity: "So you saw girls in half?"

"Not *stage* magic. Real magic." His smile pulled into a leer. "Sex magic."

I giggled. Couldn't help it. He was so earnest. It was adorable. "Is sex magic hotter than regular sex?"

"Oh yeah." He paused. "Want me to show you?"

"Like you would not believe," I said with a smile. "Your place?"

"Wouldn't have it any other way."

He helped me down from the barstool, grinning like a lovestruck idiot. As I clasped his hand tightly, I sent out a pulse of power, exploring him, testing for magical ability. Nothing. The guy was a blank page.

Some tough assignment. Hah. At this rate, I'd have his soul within the hour.

As we waited for a cab, he babbled about his prowess as a magician. I made all the appropriate oohs and ahhs. Oh yes, he'd call my name as he came inside me, and I'd hold him tight as he died. And then, once his soul was bound to me, I'd take him down to Hell.

No need for Lillith to know that Noel was a fraud. Hell had marked him as a high-level dark magician; that was all that mattered. I'd complete my assignment easily, and Lust would get major kudos for a powerful catch. In doing so, I'd finally prove my mettle to my queen and get the promotion I deserved. Everyone would be happy.

Well, except for Noel. But hey, you can't win them all.

The apartment wasn't bad. I'd expected Ikea-chic and some secondhand accoutrements, but instead I found tasteful furniture (modern) and framed paintings (abstract). I recognized one of the artists as someone who'd recently been claimed by Hell—the man had sold his soul for the opportunity to be immortalized by his artwork—and I took a moment to admire the bold strokes of black in the otherwise colorful painting.

"That's an original," Noel said, after naming the artist.

It looked like road kill with tire streaks. I liked it.

Noel took me by the arm and led me to his bedroom, a thing of black walls and overflowing bookshelves. Oh yes: this was where the power happened. Not magic, no—still coming up blank on that end—but the *sex*...I smelled the lingering energy, felt the ripples in the stagnant air, tasted the aftermath of death. It was enough to make me tipsy. Sweet Sin, this room had seen many active nights. And days. And afternoons. To say nothing of the weekends. Clearly, Noel was a man who got his jollies right here— sex before, during and after the ritual sacrifices. His sheets must be easily washable.

I couldn't wait for us to get started. I bet his soul would taste like licorice and rum—steeped in evil, dripping with lust. Yum!

As Noel started lighting some candles (black, naturally) around the room to "set the mood," I stepped over to the bed: a four-poster with a metal frame, its sheets satin and red as a beating heart. The comforter was a lush thing of sensual black—not the dead no-color of rot but the enticing inky darkness of nightmares.

I almost shivered with anticipation. Setting the mood, indeed.

He walked up behind me, his hands resting on my shoulders, then stroking down my arms. "Ready?"

"Sweetie," I purred, turning around to face him, "I thought you'd never ask."

Noel kissed me hard, mashing his lips against mine and forcing his tongue into my mouth. He was aggressive. Possessive. Just like I knew he'd be. I went along with it, encouraged him with little moans that could have meant pleasure or surprise or fear—whatever he needed, I'd give it to him. He was my client, and I'd make sure he was satisfied. So instead of me seducing him, I simply reacted as he kissed me down my jaw and my throat, bruising me with passion. His tongue teased me, darting, painting me with small licks; his teeth grazed me, the threat of pain in the midst of building pleasure.

He hit a sweet spot, and I bit my lip to keep myself from tearing his pants off and throwing him onto the bed. Let him be in control, I told myself. Let him have his power. Let the moment stretch. It would be over all too soon. Sex with humans always was. His hands moved down my back until they cupped my ass.

"No panties," I breathed. His fingers quickly discovered I was telling the truth. Then I said, "No bra."

As if that had given him permission, with one hand he tugged down the front of my dress, then stared in obvious glee at my very large, very bare breasts. (Infernal magic: way better than an underwire bra.) My nipples were already erect, thanks to Noel's rough kisses and blunt fingers, but now the sheer hunger in his gaze as he stared at my tits made me slick with need. He was murder and sex and brute humanity in one black-clad package.

Oh, Gehenna, he was *fabulous*.

And then his mouth latched onto my nipple, and my reaction was very loud and very positive. For the next who knew how long, he suckled me and stripped me down until I was shining from his licks and wearing only my stilettos and a huge smile.

One of his hands was doing marvelous things between my legs when he asked me, "Can I tie you up?"

"So polite," I murmured.

"The magic is stronger when it's consensual." He emphasized the importance of consent with a waggle of his fingers.

"Of course you can tie me up." I adored bondage—Lash Me, Thrash Me is a particular favorite among the succubi. Besides, no mortal ties could truly keep me pinned; a teensy burst of power would sear through even the strongest of bonds. Or I could always just bamf myself down to Hell if I really needed to make a quick exit. But I was still sure the only thing I had to worry about from the wannabe magician was premature ejaculation.

Noel steered me to the bed and eased me down, his fingers dancing all the while. "Spread yourself wide for me," he panted.

I obliged.

Leaning over me, he opened the drawer of his nightstand and took out four pairs of handcuffs. Soon I was bound to the bedposts, still in my heels.

Noel sat back and smiled at me. "Perfect. You're perfect." He got off the bed and rummaged through the drawer again.

"What are you looking for, sweetie? A blindfold?"

"Nope. Just this." He pulled out a pouch and dangled it in front of me before he loosened the drawstrings. "Salt." He sprinkled the white crystals on the ground in a white trail, going around the bed. As Noel walked out of my line of vision, I realized the bed hadn't been flush against the wall. "Don't mind me," he said from behind me. "Just have to finish the circle."

Bemused, I chuckled softly. The handful of magicians I'd dealt with over my thousands of years had drawn circles too. Usually in blood. Noel was certainly acting the part. Shame he had no ability whatsoever.

"There we go," Noel said. He was just out of eyesight, but I heard him drop the pouch, then open and close another drawer. He said, "This next part's going to sting a little."

That's when he plunged a dagger into my stomach.

Shock hit me more than the pain. Steel can't kill me, even though getting stabbed with a foot-long curved blade hurts worse than an angel's blessing. But the notion that this mortal man had actually stabbed me stunned me into silence. How *dare* he? Sure, he was a serial killer who performed human sacrifices as a matter of course, so that should have been a tip-off he had a pair of balls on him...but *still*. The nerve!

The thought took me all of a second—long enough for Noel to pull the blade out of me and step back. And that's when I felt the magic snap like electricity. A hungry buzz filled the air, the sound of flies over a corpse.

Right, all done with playing along.

I reached within me for my infernal power, ready to overwhelm Noel Le Noir with lust and then ride him until his bones broke and I sucked out his soul.

Except nothing happened.

Ignoring the agony in my belly and the sweat on my brow, I tried again. And again, nothing happened.

What the fuck ...?

"Sorry about stabbing you before we got to the good part," Noel said, sounding quite cheerful. "But if it's any consolation, I promise to fuck you silly after you're dead."

Terrific.

"I said I'd show you magic, right? Well, the circle you're in just sealed, thanks to me spilling your blood. It's a magic circle, honey. The circle negates evil magic. So nothing evil in it can get out."

My mouth dropped open. Screw me on Salvation Day, Noel wasn't a fraud after all. Thanks to his fucking spell, I had no power while I was trapped in the circle. Why couldn't I sense his magical ability?

And how did he know I was a demon?

"You're perfect," said Noel. "Those legs...those tits. Ah, man, those tits. You're just the right sacrifice for the demon I mean to summon."

Back the truck up. *Summon* a demon?

"Sweetie," I said—okay, croaked, but give me a break, I'd been stabbed in the stomach and was bleeding and in a lot of pain—"what're you talking about?"

"I traffic with demons," he said proudly. "I get power in exchange for souls. Magic. Stock tips. Fashion advice. All I have to do is kill someone and leave the offering in the circle, and then my demon sponsor gives me goodies after I summon him. So I had to sacrifice you, Jesse. I hear Hell's lovely this time of year. I bet you'll love it there."

Actually, I did. But that was beside the point.

"Listen, Noel, you're obviously not in your right mind." Fuuuuuuuuck, it hurt to talk. And because I was in a magic-free circle, I couldn't even heal myself. Stupid magic spell. "Demons are the big, bad evil. Whatever you summon is going to steal your soul." Unless I could steal it first.

"I've been doing this for years, Jesse. I'm not worried. Especially because I'm not the one in the circle." He grinned, a predator's smile I normally would have admired. "Seems like your soul's the one in jeopardy."

It would be, if I had a soul. "You're making a mistake," I gritted. "And the demon you summon will destroy you."

"Uh-huh. I'd say that's what they all say, except by now they're usually dead or too busy dying to bother with talking." He sighed. "This much spirit in you, you must be phenomenal in the sack."

"Oh, I am. Why don't you come here and find out yourself?"

"Sorry, honey. Can't break the circle. Now you hush up and go ahead and die while I summon the demon, okay?"

I clenched my teeth against the pain throbbing from my stomach. "Demons don't care for being called like dogs. Tends to make them grumpy. Even if you get one to serve you now, it'll come after you when you're not looking."

"Talk, talk, talk." Noel grabbed something off the nightstand—his pentagram necklace. "This is a Shield against Evil, honey. No demon can harm me while I wear it."

No freaking *way*. Really? That stupid thing was real? "You probably want to put that on, so that the demon you summon won't, you know, slaughter you." No way was I letting another one of the nefarious kill him. That would be *my* job when I got out of here.

"Unfortunately, the shieldstone blocks my magic. So, no wearing it for me right now."

Satan spare me. Daun had been right.

"It's sweet of you to be concerned, though." Noel smiled down at me. "Don't worry. Between the circle, which will hold the demon, and my shieldstone for when I'm done, I'm completely safe. Now if you'll excuse me, I have a creature of the Pit to summon."

I didn't know which was worse: me being captured by a mortal with intentions of magical grandeur, or Daunuan being right.

Even before the chanting stopped, the shadows had pulled together until there was a black mass hovering over me. It stretched and filled out, taking on the shape of an obscenely well-muscled man. Skin the hue of burnished copper. Hairless. Wonderfully naked, but his most important muscle was covered by a leather apron.

Only one demon made it a point to wear a workman's apron of tanned human skin: Baruel, so-called Master of All Arts. He was a creature of Pride, one of Lust's natural enemies. Baruel was also an asshole, but that had nothing to do with him being one of the Arrogant. He was one of Hell's elite, and as befitted any infernal Lower Down, he had an ego that dwarfed Mount Everest.

Baruel would have no qualms about destroying me; it was a Pride thing.

Snarling, I struggled against the handcuffs, to no avail. Think, Jesse. There's got to be a way out of this that didn't end with my severed head on a silver platter.

Baruel loomed over me, his red eyes glowing with malefic presence. He took in my naked, bleeding mortal form, then squinted and looked past the temporary shell. He sneered, baring his fangs. "Magician!" he boomed. "You dare to disgrace me with this paltry offering?"

"Hey now," Noel said, affronted. "She's sexy and dying. What's wrong with that?"

"She's even lower than mortals! Her kind are nothing more than clap-carrying, pox-ridden dogs!"

I could almost hear Noel's brain try to process the demon's words. He said slowly, "You mean she's...a prostitute?"

"No, you ass," I sighed. "He means I'm a succubus."

The confused look on Noel's face would have been funny if not for (A) me being trapped in his magic circle, (B) me still bleeding and in pain, and (C) a demon of Arrogance standing over me with murder in his eyes.

"I'll destroy you for this insult, Noel Le Noir," Baruel promised, his voice rumbling like doom. "I'll make a new apron out of your hide."

Noel raised his weak chin and declared: "You can do nothing to me, demon. You're bound by the circle. You can't break it."

Easy for him to say. He was safely outside of the circle. Anyone can taunt a tiger when it's on the other side of the bars.

Baruel smiled slowly, stretching his mouth impossibly wide. Then he leaned over until he was at the edge of our prison, and he blew out a breath. The candlelight flickered...and part of the salt outline of the circle vanished. The hum of magic sputtered and died.

Yes! Score one for evil! I grinned as I felt my power surge through me. Now at least I had a fighting chance.

Poor Noel looked like he'd just crapped in his boxers. "You *can't*," he stammered. "The circle...!"

Baruel cracked his huge knuckles. "I'm the Master of All Arts. I taught you more about magic in a dozen years than other humans can learn in a dozen lifetimes. Do you really think I don't know how to break a human magician's circle?"

Noel paled. "But you never did before..."

"The sacrifices were tasty. Until now." Baruel grinned hugely. "I'm not in the mood for succubus. I think I'll dine on magician."

"Told you so," I said to Noel. But he was too busy calling up some magic spell or another to pay any attention to me.

Baruel, for his part, launched himself off the bed and out of the desecrated circle, his fingernails already lengthened into claws. Noel barely got a shield of light up in time to deflect the blow. Screaming like a nun at an orgy, he let loose a magical blast that would have singed off Baruel's hair, if he had any. The demon bellowed and slammed his fists down. Noel threw himself to the left, avoiding getting pounded into pudding. Baruel's hands momentarily stuck in the ruins of the bedroom floor. Still screaming, Noel made a "Here, boy" motion, and a black-bladed sword appeared in his outstretched hand. He lunged at Baruel, slicing at the demon's neck.

Don't mind me, boys. Keep yourselves entertained as I poof away my bonds like so...

Free, I sat up and rubbed my wounded belly. With a wisp of my power, the bleeding stopped, the cut scabbed over and faded, and I was back up to full strength.

The demon and the human were tearing into each other, no holds barred. I frowned, debating whether I should help Baruel. Even though he was an Arrogant bastard, and one of Hell's elite to boot, he was still one of my own kind. Noel, furthermore, tried to sacrifice me. I expect that sort of thing from demons, not humans.

And it would irk Baruel for the next two millennia if I helped him. Creatures of Pride didn't do well with charity.

I aimed at the back of Noel's head, ready to throw my magic at him, but Baruel saw me. He lobbed a bolt of power at me, and I yelped as I scampered out of the way.

"I'm coming for you next, little whore!" he roared. "I'll destroy you for your part in this!"

Well, fuck that noise. I plopped down on the bed and let them fight it out.

A minute passed as Noel and Baruel danced—the one a high-level magician of the dark arts, the other his demonic teacher. The two struck and parried and struck and scored and struck and dodged. Blood and ichor flew. Curses rang out. I buffed my nails.

Before another minute passed, they both scored fatal blows. It took them both two more minutes to figure out they were dying. (Men, whether human or demon, could be a bit slow on the uptake.) Noel crashed to the ground, limbs quivering. Baruel sank to his knees. Dark stains pooled beneath them both.

I stretched and stood up.

By the time I picked up the black blade that had slipped from Noel's fingers, the carpet was saturated with blood and other body fluids. I stepped carefully so that I wouldn't slip. Balancing in four-inch heels could be such a bitch. Baruel, I noted, was half-way to decapitated.

No one likes a half-assed job. I separated the demon's head from his neck.

Then I turned to Noel. The master magician lay dying, too far gone to mutter any anti-death spells. His body was nothing more than strips of bloody flesh.

Yum.

I sliced away the scraps of clothing that covered him from torso to thigh. With a pulse of my power, the most important part of him stood at attention. And then I straddled him there on the ground. I even took his hands and put them to my naked breasts. I thought he'd like that; clearly, he'd been a boob man.

Smiling, I gave Noel Le Noir the last ride of his life. With his final breath, he called my name...and his soul was mine.

Turns out, practitioners of the dark arts taste like chicken.

You'd think a place called Pandemonium would be chaotic. But no, the administrative level of Hell was frighteningly orderly. There was paperwork for everything...and with every additional form, you had to get back on line and wait your turn to file the new paper. And the line tended to be three years long.

I was consoling myself by humming Michael Jackson tunes when Daun popped in, grinning from ear to ear.

"Figures," he said, shaking his head. "The only time a fifth-level succubus has ever taken out a Master of the Dark Arts, and it gets cancelled out as a Wrongful Termination of one of the elite. Babes, I don't know whether to be impressed or bust a gut laughing."

I sniffed. "My reputation precedes me."

"Jezzie, it's all over the Pit. Demons and damned alike are taking bets on whether you get everything squared away before Salvation Day."

Terrific.

It was grossly unfair. Even though Noel had delivered the fatal blow to Baruel, my cut had been the final one—so in Hell's book, the kill was mine. And that meant I was stuck with miles of paperwork. And if that weren't bad enough, Lillith was furious with me. Apparently, offing one of the elite demons of Hell is something that she, as my queen, was answerable for. Oopsie. She'd already promised me a decade's worth of torment.

And it was all because I'd done my job and hadn't died in the process, even with her setting me up.

Not like I could complain about it. I worked for Hell. Shockingly, management tended not to be overly sympathetic.

"And," Daun said, "I was right about the Shield Against Evil, wasn't I?"

Fuck me with a halo.

"Don't fret, babes. I won't remind you that I was right. Well, not much. I'll probably stop after a century or so."

I sighed. "Great."

"Did you at least keep the thing?"

"Couldn't," I said. "It went kablooey when Noel died."

"Charmed items tend to do that when the charmer expires."

"My afterlife sucks," I said with a sigh. "I wish I could just give it all up, run away and start over."

Chuckling, Daun stroked my cheek. "Even if you could run away, you wouldn't. There are plenty of things worth staying in Hell for."

I arched an eyebrow. "Like what?"

"Like the promise of sex so steamy, the Lake of Fire would be a cool dip in comparison."

Ooh.

"Why don't you get off line," Daun murmured, "and come with me. I promise I'll make you forget about your troubles for a few days."

"Are you tempting me, sweetie?"

"Of course."

Bless me, Daun always knows just what to say. And do.

Grinning, I took Daun's hand and let him pull me out of line.

As for what happened next...well, let's just say that I was a very sated succubus. Once again, Daunuan was right: I forgot all about my troubles during the five days we were together. It almost made going to the back of the line worth it. Almost.

Ah, who am I kidding? Of course it was worth it. Sinfully, delightfully worth it.

I'd just never admit that to Daunuan. He'd never let me live it down.

Jackie Kessler lives in upstate New York. She is the author of the "Hell on Earth" series, co-author (with Caitlin Kittredge) of *Black and White* and its upcoming sequel *Shades of Gray*, and, writing as Jackie Morse Kessler, the author of the upcoming young adult novel *Hunger*. She has a web presence at **www.jackiekessler.com**

The succubus **Jezebel** has turned her back on her Hellish past (sort of) and now lives as the human **Jesse Harris**, working as an exotic dancer in New York City. *Note: this story takes place before Hell's Belles.*

IMPOSSIBLE LOVE

— A Piers Knight Story —

by C. J. Henderson

"Whoso loves believes the impossible."—Elizabeth Barrett Browning

"Piers, what a surprise. Do come in—uh, both of you."

Having Professor Piers Knight show up unannounced on his front doorstep surprised Albert Harper. It was an unusual thing for the professor—Knight was not known to risk wasting time by dropping in on people who might not be where he presumed they should be. He liked things confirmed. He liked his routine neat. And part of his routine for some time had been visiting Albert Harper.

"I could say something inane about just being in the neighborhood," Knight said, "with someone in tow whom you've never met, but that would be what we in the business call 'a lie.' So I hope you'll forgive the unscheduled visit."

Knight had dropped in on the younger man numerous times since their initial contact in one of the professor's classes. Harper was a young man to whom Piers had taken a shine. The pair shared much, including liberal political views, a keen appreciation for Asian cuisine, and a taste for mystery novels. They were comfortable in each other's company, and their degree of similarity had kept them in irregular touch for several years.

It was a relationship Knight wanted to maintain.

He worked as a curate at the rightly famous Brooklyn Museum. As such, Knight had access to both religious and blasphemous articles of historical significance from throughout human history. On occasion, he had found it practical to borrow certain of those items for the purpose of self-sponsored experiments and investigations. In his time he had seen horrors and wonders. And, every time he narrowly survived one of the things he had found, he realized that he wished to spend time with the Harpers.

After a while, the thirty-four year old Harper thought he knew why; he had become, for the professor, a case study. Or, if he had not himself, his family had.

The Harper clan consisted of but two souls—Albert Harper and his daughter Debbie. Both were victims, in their own way. Debbie, of the ravages of Down syndrome. Albert, of the train wreck known as divorce. When Debbie had been born, it had only been a matter of days before her condition was diagnosed. She was afflicted not only with the disease, but with its severest strand.

Many children with the same handicap led nearly normal lives. The training was grueling for the parents and teachers, but it was possible. Working harder than regular students, many Down kids could learn to communicate with their parents, after a fashion. They could go to school, ride bikes, play with others, watch and understand television programs. In adulthood they could move about town on their own, hold down simple jobs, even marry and grow old with someone.

The high-end performance children, that is. Not those like Debbie.

Debbie was not high-end. Debbie Harper would never be able to communicate with others in any fashion. She would never go to school, ride a bike, play with others. She did watch television programs, but she did so without understanding. Her eyes were simply drawn to color and movement. In adulthood she would almost certainly never go anywhere on her own, hold down any kind of job, or marry anyone. It was not even certain she would grow old.

"So," asked Harper, as his visitors entered his living room, "what's the reason I'm unexpectedly playing host to a man who never drops in out of the blue, and a mysterious lady I don't know?"

Albert had raised Debbie for the last seven years on his own. Her mother, Linda, had stayed for almost eight months, after which she could not take it anymore.

It.

"It" was her word for what their lives—her life—had become. She had wanted a daughter who gurgled and cooed, whose eyes shone with recognition of shapes and faces, who delighted in new sounds, who turned her head with interest and excitement at each new experience. Linda had wanted a normal, regular, healthy daughter whom she could dress in pink and take inordinate pride in as the new arrival learned all the simple things babies learn every day.

Once it had become obvious that Linda was never going to have her long-dreamed-of perfect, bright-eyed child, that her baby would not be an accessory to her life, but that she would be one of her baby's—a constant care giver, the rest of her days devoted to a child who could barely respond to the simplest stimuli—she had begun talking with Albert about placing their daughter in a home. Such was not an option as far as he was concerned. And so it was, after a year and five months of marriage, and twenty-two weeks of parenthood, that Albert had been left alone with his speechless daughter to stare at the numbing future ahead of them.

"This is a friend of mine," Knight said. Giving his companion a moment, he seemed to be allowing the wrinkled black woman time to regain her strength. It had been a long walk, up the front walk from the curb to the car, and she was old, very old. It was obvious to Albert that the woman had been beautiful in her time. Indeed, her black eyes held a shine that seemed to belie the deep wrinkles.

"Madame Sarna Raniella, meet Albert Harper." The old woman nodded in a friendly enough fashion, but did not offer her hand.

Pointing toward the child sitting motionless in the living room beyond, Knight said to Harper, "Madame Raniella is going to sit with Debbie for a few minutes, while we take a walk outside." Knight turned to the old woman, and, seemingly responding to an unspoken question, she said, "As we discussed, I shall talk to her, Piers. Constantly. Fear not—I will keep her engaged."

"Good. As long as she doesn't answer, everything should be fine."

Without a further word, she made her slow way toward the sofa. Sitting down near Debbie, she began a seemingly endless stream of conversation. She spoke with the girl about cartoons she remembered, the snack cakes her mother had baked her, how fascinating it was that leaves changed colors in the fall— apparently anything that came to mind. Albert noticed that her gaze seemed intently focused on Debbie.

On her eyes, he thought. *She's watching her eyes.*

And then he finally responded to the gentle pressure on his arm, allowing Knight to maneuver him out onto his front porch and down the steps. As the two men headed for the sidewalk, Albert said, "Going to tell me what this is all about now?"

"Yes, I am. And I'm not certain how you're going to react. I have something very disturbing...well, not to me, but to you...

Knight stopped speaking, obviously at a complete loss as to how to proceed. It was clear something of great importance was clawing at him, demanding release. Suddenly, as if struck by inspiration, he said, "Albert, you once told me the story of the first time you held Debbie. Tell it again, won't you?" Harper looked at his friend through hard eyes. He started to protest, but Knight cut him off gently.

"I understand your reluctance, my boy. Truly. But I promise you, I have a purpose. *I do.*" Harper turned his head away, his shoulders shaking slightly. After a moment's silence, however, he closed his eyes and began to speak.

"It was in the delivery room. Debbie'd just been born. I was standing there a little stunned. They'd cut Linda; I wasn't expecting, no one had warned me...blood had just flown through the air. 'Normal,' they said. 'Nothing to worry about'—but I wish someone had prepared me for...anyway, let's just say I was in a state, you know?"

Knight nodded, listening patiently.

"So, while I'm still reeling from it all, out of nowhere the nurse brings Debbie over to me." Harper's face softened, the approaching memory so gladdening his heart the air seemed to freshen about him.

"She was so tiny, so fragile, I took her from the nurse, and I was staring at her. Of course, her eyes weren't open, but I could feel this, this need, you know, spilling out of her, looking for something to grab onto, and before I knew it, I'd raised her up to where I could press my forehead against hers, and when I did that, I swear I felt her *inside my mind.* I..."

Knight waited, but Harper stopped his thought, choking it back, as if suddenly spent. After a moment's silence, he muttered, "Anyway, you know all that."

"I wanted to hear you tell it again. I wanted to see if you still believed it."

"Why wouldn't I believe it? I was *there*. I *know* it happened."

"Yes, of course," Knight responded, "but after all these years, with Debbie's reversal, with no further contact with that mind you swear you felt, it is possible you might start to believe you imagined the whole thing."

Knight let the fall breeze blow about them for a moment, then interrupted its soft whisper. "Have you, Albert? Have you ever been tempted to think you were wrong about that day?"

Harper's eyes narrowed. When he finally spoke, his voice came out low and growling, bitter with sarcasm. "Sure, all the time. That's why I let my wife walk out. That's why I still won't put Debbie in a home. And that's why I'm working double shifts, driving my mother and aunts half-crazy baby sitting! How can you ask me that? How, Goddamnit? You know what Debbie means to me!"

"I do, Albert—"

"I'm telling you..." Harper paused, his voice choking, eyes threatening to betray him, "I *know*—I know she's in there somewhere. I *felt* it. I goddamn well *felt* it, do you understand? You're not taking that away from me. *Nobody's* taking that away from me!"

"I'm not trying to," Knight told him softly. "And I apologize for upsetting you. But it had to be done." Knight tilted his head down for a moment, running a hand through his hair and then down the back of his neck.

"You see, I'm going to tell you something. Something incredible. Something you may not be able to comprehend. But you must trust me about one thing. I believe what you just said. I don't just believe that you believe it, I think it happened *just as you said*.

"And after that," Knight added, his voice going dark and stiff, "I think something monstrous happened. Something I don't quite know if I will be able to explain or prove to you."

Harper turned to stare at him. The two had reached the end of his neighborhood, and were on the edge of the local business district. After surveying the block for a moment, Knight said, "Over there, I think. Come on."

Knight moved them close to a wall between two storefronts, their large neon signs buzzing "Sarah Jane's Boutique" and "Hobbies & Crafts" on either side of them. When he looked at Harper again, his expression was grim.

"Albert, I'm going to simply say this as bluntly as possible—I do not believe your daughter has Down syndrome. I believe she is possessed."

Harper gaped, as if his mind could not choose between the hundreds of possible responses that were all occurring to him at once. Before he could speak, Knight went on.

"You must understand, I came across the general idea the first time years ago. It's an ancient notion, and in older times people were more prone to recognize the signs. But, simply put, oftentimes what we think of today as Alzheimer's, or Parkinson's or DS, cancer, all manner of ailments—they're really cases of demonic possession." Harper shook his head several times, as if trying to drive the idea out of his brain.

"We've known each other a long time," answered the younger man, "and a joke this sick is completely out of character for you. So, all right. Let's say you're not deranged." Throwing his hands up helplessly, Albert demanded;

"If you're not, then just what am I supposed to do? Call the church? Get a witch doctor? Bring in the *Enquirer*—what? *What*?"

"Calm yourself, Albert." As Harper turned away, Knight put up a hand and gently stopped him. "And, please trust me when I say you don't want to leave this spot, just yet."

Harper made a gesture that took in the wall, the neon, the sidewalk—everything. "Why? What's so damn special?"

"My research has led me to a number of references to priests and shamans, across cultures and throughout history, waiting for thunderstorms, so they could prepare their defenses against such creatures." Pointing to all the pulsing lights behind them, the professor said;

"Apparently these 'entities' dare not approach a barrier of charged electrons. No one knows why, although many mythologies posit lightning as a weapon of the gods, not their infernal counterparts. In any case, if there is a demon involved here, and it is trying to listen to us, it shouldn't be able to make anything out through all the interference these signs are putting out."

"You're serious; you're really serious. Aren't you?" Harper snapped, teetering between rage and tears.

"Yes, Albert, I am. And if after all the years you've devoted to your daughter, if you're ready to risk throwing away what time you have left on this Earth in a desperate gamble of freeing her from this thing's clutches, I may be able to help you."

Harper tried to stop thinking like a protective father and strove instead to actually listen to his friend. Part of his mind had instantly rejected what he was hearing out of hand. Such ludicrous jabber was, obviously, insanity.

New Age grasping at straws. Superstition.

Nonsense.

On the other hand, a different section of his mind added, knee-jerk reactions were often born from fear. Applying only a tiny bit of rationality to the subject, Albert had to admit the professor had travelled the world to seek out the occult in a thousand dark and terrible places. The older man had told him incredible stories over the years, swearing they were true. And because it was Knight relating the accounts, the younger man had believed them.

Harper knew with utter certainty that the professor would not have come to him that night if they were not friends. Looking into Knight's eyes, he understood it was time for him to make a decision. The younger man admitted he was not certain what he believed, but he could not think of any reason why the professor would lie about such a thing. Glancing left, then right, Harper looked at the electrical signs supposedly protecting his thoughts, then said;

"All right, let's not waste all this fine wattage. Tell me what you know."

"Demons," said Knight, "in these deceptive cases of possession, are not torturing the souls they possess. Their purpose is far more devious. They torture the care-givers; crippling their lives, disrupting possible futures by diminishing those it was deemed good to distract. Reshaping fate, the monsters terrorize with guilt and duty, forcing those they feared to bleed rather than build. Holy men in every century have been attacked thus, their families set upon by afflictions brought, we have been told, by minions of Satan."

"You're saying I'm supposed to be some sort of holy man?"

"I'm saying that some thing has taken an interest in you for reasons the two of us will never be able to interpret. The motivations of demons are their own, and a distraction from what is important at this moment."

Knight was careful to look about from time to time. He felt safe from supernatural spies between the glaring neon displays, but he did not relish the notion of their conversation being interrupted by human agents, whether unduly optimistic muggers or an unusually curious police officer.

"Albert, understand—demonic possession is real, and it's terrible. Then again, so are scorpions. So is bubonic plague. We can get used to anything we can comprehend. But moreover, we can stand up to it, as well."

Having gotten Albert to the point where he was willing to accept the possibility of Debbie's possession, Knight then explained what he might be able to do about it.

"That day in the hospital, when you placed your head to hers, felt her mind, new and fresh and searching, touching yours, melding with yours—all you need do this time is go further. Go all the way inside..."

Knight paused for a moment, taking a deep breath. His eyes locked with his friend's, he said, "Once there, you'll have to find this thing, drag it out of Debbie, and kick its literally Goddamned ass until it leaves her for good."

"I just go into her mind and stop this thing, just like that?" Harper's tone was a mix of incredulity and near-hysteria. "I mean, saying this is all real, this *demon* I'm going to go after, it's been doing this kind of thing for thousands of years. How am I supposed to, I mean...shouldn't I, I don't know—what? I..."

The professor made to speak, but Harper cut him off, racing forward with his thoughts.

"I'm not afraid, not of dying—that's not it. It's Debbie. If something goes wrong, if I screw this up, I could be destroyed, wind up brain dead, or completely dead—right?" When Knight nodded, Harper went on. "Okay, say it happens. I'm not good enough. I go down. I'm dead. What happens to Debbie then? Who takes care of her?"

"You're being straightforward," Knight said, "so I'll return the courtesy. The way Debbie is now, it really doesn't matter who cares for her—does it? If you die, she becomes a ward of the state. She lives out her vegetable existence and then follows you into oblivion. End of the Harpers."

Albert swallowed hard. Knight darted his head from side to side, checking the air around them, adding, "Madame Raniella has travelled the dreamplane before. She is one of the most reliable dreamwalkers to be found." As his young companion simply stared, the professor added:

"She'll take you inside, help best she can. You'll find her far more vigorous in that realm than our own. No matter what she and I can do, however, the thing you *must* concentrate on is that, if you can catch this thing by surprise, you could give Debbie the rest of her life. If you can't, then really..." Knight paused for a moment, then in a voice filled with nothing but cold practicality, he asked, "Is it actually going to matter to her how much time she has left...or if you're there or not?"

The inside of Harper's head fizzled with an anger tempered by practicality. Knight was correct, of course. He hated to admit it, but at present there was no connection between himself and his daughter. She was a lump of breathing meat that he cleaned and fed and dressed and put to bed. She could not button buttons, take herself to the bathroom, brush her teeth—none of it. She did not know who he was. If he was dead, she would not care.

She did not know how.

A tear on the verge of breaking free from his left eye, Harper growled, "Tell me one thing. If you've known all this for so long, why'd you wait? Why'd you *fucking* wait?"

"I'll be honest," answered Knight, his voice low, "yes, I did need to find someone like Raniella to assist, but also...I got distracted...and...please understand—" The professor coughed, excused himself, then went on.

"Listen, I'm certain if I were to go from hospital to hospital, I could find hundreds, thousands of cases like yours. I don't go looking for horrors to combat. I'm not some supernatural policeman. Or demon hunter. I'm just a man. But you're my friend, and once I was certain I was correct about Debbie, then I had to pull my courage together and act like your friend."

"Yeah." Harper spat the single word, his mind still reeling from all it had been asked to accept. Finally, after several seconds that dragged on for hours, he said, "I'd call you a bastard, but you'd still be right. So, okay, since you've got me in the mood where I'd like to kill something, let's go see if I can."

Twenty minutes later, it began. Upon returning to his home, Harper took Madame Raniella into the master bedroom while Knight remained with Debbie. Knight had started in with the same kind of distracting chatter the old woman had thrown at her, keeping the girl's attention while the assault was prepared in the next room.

Giving Harper an opened bottle, Raniella told him, "Hold it under your nose. Breathe the fumes deeply."

The pungent vapors began to relax him immediately. Then, while Harper stretched out on his bed, the old woman sat in a chair next to it, cautioning him not to wander off into his own dreams.

"You must stay focused. Wait for me to arrive. Once we find each other, we will then search for your quarry." Harper nodded. Then, just as he was sinking into unconsciousness, Raniella added;

"And remember, dear boy, this is the dreamplane where we go. If you can imagine something, you can *will* it to be—as real as anything around you."

"Meaning what?" Harper asked groggily.

"Meaning," Raniella told him, "Whatever this *thing* throws at you, you just throw it right back..."

Everything worked as Knight had said it would. In seconds Harper was asleep. Remembering what he was supposed to do, he searched his memory, bringing the image of Madame Raniella clearly into his mind. The drawn face, silvered hair, delicate hands, stiff, slender body—

And then, suddenly the two were together, the scenery within Albert's mind taking on a disturbingly real substance. The two stood on a vast and open plane, a red and purple expanse stretching in all directions. As vague bits of crimson dust swirled about them, she said;

"Concentrate, Albert. Return yourself to that first moment you saw your daughter, back in the delivery room—remember it, take yourself back to it—*be* there..."

Time shattered into millionths of a second. In each passing fraction Harper saw pieces of his most cherished memory reconstructed. Bit by bit, it fell into place—the unexpected cut, the gushing blood, his shock, the assurances, and then the nurse, walking forward—

"Would you like to hold your daughter, Mr. Harper?"

He took the bundle without hesitation. Held her for the briefest of instants, then raised the tiny, fragile body upward, touched his head to hers—

—flash—

Albert Harper fell to his knees, screaming. Bolts of pain shattered his chest and ricocheted off his nerves, blasting his senses, spinning him around, slamming him onto his back—

"Look at the maggot come to hold his little freak."

Harper tried to drag himself away from the assault. Molten metal poured over him, searing flesh from bone, evaporating his skin, boiling his blood, dissolving him—

"I just knew I was going to meet you in here some day."

The taunting voice did not issue from a mouth of any kind. It rode the electric jolts pummeling Albert, crawling into his organs and ripping them open one after another. It had a female lilt to it that somehow managed to be both familiar and frightening.

"I wish I could say it was good to see you again."

That voice was one he knew. Recognizing notes, Harper began to identify its pattern. Despite the furious pain lashing every fiber of his essence, still he began to pull a face together within his mind.

"Linda?"

"Very good." The voice chuckled. "Now I suppose you're going to pull yourself back together and, how did he put it...kick my damned ass until I leave for good. Is that next, Albert, dear?"

Harper strained to open his eyes. Madame Raniella was nowhere to be seen. He was no longer in the delivery room, but further back in the past, sitting in a movie theater, the voice of the creature snarling behind him.

"This is where we met, isn't it, darling? This is where you fell in love with me."

Exactly as he remembered it.

"Is it all coming back to you, sweetheart? Is it?"

Harper remembered it all—being in a bad mood, going to a movie alone, not caring what he saw. He remembered throwing himself into the middle of the emptiest section of the theater. Remembered two women coming in and sitting directly behind him. The two talked throughout the film, but having his theater-going experience interrupted by the pair did not bother Harper for long. He was too busy falling in love with one of them.

"It never did dawn on you, did it, Al? A beautiful woman, with an interest in mystery novels, and gaming, and comics...a beautiful woman who voted the same way you did, who couldn't wait to leave the theater and go to that new Vietnamese restaurant...how vain *are* you?"

Harper turned in his seat.

"Do you think I'm going to believe anything you tell me?"

"Baby," the form of his wife said sweetly, lifting a hand to point a single finger at him, "do you think I care?"

An arc of blue-white flame erupted from her hand, cascading over Albert, roasting his skin, boiling his eyes. Remembering himself whole, inside his shower, he drenched himself, regenerating his body as he screamed:

"I don't give a rat's ass what you care about, what you think, or what you have to say. Just get out of my daughter's head!"

"Al, sweetie," the familiar thing smiled. "What makes you think I'm *in* her head anymore?"

The Linda-like thing waved its hand and boils flooded forth from every pore of Harper's body. Hundreds, thousands of them, they burst open, pus and blood bubbling up from each of them. Harper endured the torment for a moment, then rejected the plague, throwing it off as he had the earlier torments. As he did, the ever-changing landscape settled once more into the red and purple wasteland he first encountered. As Harper steadied himself, the Linda thing strode purposely into his field of vision.

"Very slow, sweetheart," it told him. Hands on its knees, body bent to show all its parts off to their best advantage, the thing told him, "Too slow, really. I mean, seriously, what do you think can really come of all this?"

Before Albert could answer, the ground opened and swallowed him. He tried to leap away, but he could not compensate for the slam of crushing gravity sent to shovel him into the latest torment. As he fell below the surface of the dreamplane, the ground rushed in, sand and gravel and choking dust, not just piling atop him, but grinding against him, digging its way into his skin—tearing it from his body, shredding it. First one layer, then the second, hair torn away, scalp bloody, nails being etched, eye brows and lashes ripped out by the roots—

"*No!*"

Albert clawed his way to the surface, breaking the ground open with his back and shoulders. His head felt cracked; blood sluiced over his ears, down his forehead. His hands ached from clawing his way free. The Linda thing cackled as he gasped for air.

"You can't do it, you know."

"Do what?" Albert's voice was a ragged, panting thing, weak and feeble.

"Beat me. Can't be done."

"Bullshit," Harper said weakly. "Human beings been...kicking the ass of your, your kind for centuries."

"True, perhaps." Sitting on a large violet rock seemingly carved to resemble a great, rolling tongue, the Linda thing added, "But that takes actual faith."

With a snap of its fingers, the thing unleashed a ravenous horde of insects to devour Albert. As quickly as he could shield himself, regenerate his flesh, the overwhelming waves of chittering creatures would find their way to him once more, begin chewing again, ripping again, tearing, slicing, stinging, gnawing—

"The moment Linda first sat down behind you," the thing snickered, "you had no faith in your chances with her."

Albert cleared his mind enough to summon a great wind to carry the horde away from him. He had nearly a full second's respite before the Linda thing turned his body to glass and began tossing shards of rock at him.

"When she started to talk," the thing laughed, shattering Albert's left arm at the elbow, "you wanted her so badly. But you never *believed* you could actually have her."

Concentrating, Albert was able to reform his body, but only for as long as his opponent allowed it. While he wiped at the sweat running down his forehead, half of it water, half of it tiny glass beads, the Linda thing took the moment to finish its thought.

"You don't have the belief in you to get rid of me, sweetheart, and that's what's going to make this so much fun."

"Fun?" asked Albert, confused. "What's going to be so much fun?"

"Why, *us*—darling."

Before he could react, the thing was behind him, its all-too-familiar arms encircling his chest. The touch jarred too many memories, splitting him, rending him—making him ache for his ex-wife the way a starving man yearns for food. The feel of her was fire; crisping skin, sweat that tasted like bacon—alluring, forbidden, salty—delicious. Her breasts came against his back in exactly the way he remembered; the heat of her breath curled across his neck, into his ear. He had been so long without female contact—any female contact—let alone hers, that his body surrendered to the touch involuntarily. Craving it; luxuriating against it—simply, pitifully, longing for it to never end.

"You're my dog, Albert," the thing whispered. "You may fight against me, but I've got you." The young man struggled against the all-too-pleasant hold binding him. The arms held him securely while their owner whispered; "Poor boy—you just don't understand yet, do you? You can't resist me. No matter how many pains you endure, how many trials you turn back, I can always think up more. You don't have any way to resist me. You don't have any faith in anything, sweetheart. And, without faith, I can't be driven away."

Chuckling, its voice a mad titter swirling the dust about his head in never-ending spirals, the creature shifted its grip and suddenly drove its hands into Albert's sides. Pulling organs free from his body, it tossed them casually over its shoulder, saying;

"And, even if you could ever drive me out of your head, what would it gain you? You sad, stupid man..."

Albert sagged, tiring from the pain, the endlessness of it—the futility of it—hurt too much, so terribly *much* he simply had to rest. As he gasped, struggling desperately to marshal his thoughts, the red-handed thing above him sighed, dribbling spittle into Albert's face as it said;

"After all, if you ever get me to run from you, where do you think I'll go?" The demon let him go then did a little dance, spinning itself madly as it screeched, "I'll just go back into Debbie."

The taunting voice grew louder as Albert pushed himself toward his scattered bits. Beside itself with laughter, the Linda thing watched with amusement as its victim labored to reconstitute himself. Stretching its body out to its fullest, the creature cooed;

"Face it, sweetie, you've got no chance. Not you or your little bitch."

Albert glowered, summoning every bit of resentment he had ever felt toward his ex-wife. Every hurt, every scorn, every bit of meanness that festered within him. If his enemy wanted to play those rules, he told himself—okay, fine—he could accommodate it.

"You whore..."

He muttered the words, staring for a moment, taking in once more the face that haunted him. Then he spun away and used the image to focus, shielding himself in familiar armor. Without warning, Albert threw himself upward, flashing backward across the dusty plane at the Linda thing. The creature dodged his efforts, but he turned in mid-air and followed its path. His life over, shattered by despair, he approached the monster's taunts with all he had.

Wrapping all the hurt he had within him around his fists, Albert burst with a dark brilliance which collapsed its way through all barriers and knocked the demon onto its back. His eyes wild with the flash of a thousand moments in time racing forward to a single instance, he slammed the laughing monstrosity across the jaw repeatedly; split open its mouth, broke its nose—closed one eye. The creature tittered as it said, "I bet you've wanted to do this for a long time."

"Not as much as I do..."

Both Albert and the Linda thing turned toward the new voice. Hands made of lightning and fire grabbed up the creature, squeezing its insides into jelly.

"You made my mommy leave me!"

The shape of Linda Harper disappeared, replaced by a noxious form, a repulsive creature comprised of a squat, flaccid body animated by long, angular hind legs. Its eyes were a frightened yellow hue, bulbous sacs filled with a red liquid which sloshed freely inside them. As the monstrous thing bellowed, its voice echoing raggedly across the dreamplane, the blazing hands tore it into smaller and smaller shreds, finally incinerating the bits when they were too tiny to grasp.

Albert Harper watched as his daughter dispatched the last scraps of their foe. Smiling, he attempted to rise to his feet. Finding he could not, he tried to speak. No words came forth, however, and he collapsed in a broken heap, all the fight gone from him.

Silent, but content.

"Well, look who's awake."

Albert blinked. The room was only dimly lit, but even the single, shaded bulb was more than he could take. Feebly placing a hand over his eyes, he croaked:

"Wha—what, what happened?"

"Shhhhhhhhh," answered Knight. "Don't try to talk. You rest. I'll explain." Albert nodded weakly. He could just make out the figure of Madame Raniella somewhere in the background behind the professor. His body hurt so fiercely, he felt that the only thing keeping him from screaming was the simple fact his voice could barely work.

"If you're thinking you were sent into something all the facts, it's true," Knight said. "Why this thing chose to bring you suffering, as I said before, there's no way for us to know. But, once you stepped onto the dreamplane, I was certain it would leave Debbie's mind to get at you."

"So...what'd that accomplish?"

"After Raniella led you to it, she abandoned you to face the demon alone. While you held it off, we repeated the same procedure with Debbie."

"I, I don't ..."

"Albert, please, don't try to talk. You'll only injure yourself further. Anyway, the rest is simple. Remember, with the demon no longer blocking Debbie's higher functions, she could think as clearly as anyone else."

"Your Debbie," Madame Raniella said, "once that horror left your mind for hers, she could think as clearly as anyone. It took me but a few minutes to inform her as to what was happening. She knows who you are, Albert Harper, and all that you have done for her."

"You have to understand, Al," Knight said softly. "She's always known what you were doing for her, or at least, half her mind has. The demon sat at the juncture between those sections of the mind where knowledge's stored and where it's utilized. The block removed, she could suddenly make sense of all she's learned over the years."

Albert blinked, the pain from the effort nearly unbearable. Although his encounter had left him with no actual physical damage, his nerve endings were afire, all his muscles bruised. As he pieced together what Knight had told him, he whispered.

"You mean..."

"I mean, there's someone here who wants to say 'hello.'"

And then, the professor and his companion stepped away from each other to allow Debbie access to the room. Heading for her father's bed at a run, she threw herself through the air, arms outstretched, hair flying wildly, eyes ablaze with happiness as she screamed:

"Daddy!"

With some 60 books under his belt, author **C. J. Henderson**, creator of supernatural detective Teddy London and, now occult investigator Piers Knight, welcomes all to come to **www.cjhenderson.com,** to comment on his story here, and to read others which he posts for the enjoyment of all.

Museum curator **Piers Knight** is a quiet fellow who likes good food, quiet evenings with a pot of tea and a good book, and being left alone by all the world. While usually well fed and well read, he rarely gets more that a week or two to himself before Fate, Destiny, or some other joker comes knocking at his door, bringing him all manner of bothers.

Running Wild

— An Outcast Season Story —

by Rachel Caine

As mountains go, Albuquerque's Sandia Peak was not especially tall; the great mountain ranges of the world were not much intimidated by it, I would imagine. Still, it had a certain austere, ragged beauty. Time and friction hadn't yet smoothed the jagged edges of its peaks and ridges, although the desert had clothed them in green, tough scrub brush to blur the raw cutting surfaces. It had been a long, difficult climb to the summit, even for someone as agile, strong and long-limbed as me, and with as little fear of death or injury.

I had not been born human. It was still difficult to truly understand fragility, after so many millennia spent as a Djinn, a spirit of fire and power, immortal and untouchable. But oddly, being Djinn had proved to be the ultimate vulnerability. It takes only a stronger, more determined Djinn to rip away all your power, your fire, your existence, and trap you in a form like this.

A human form.

It had not been my choice to become human, but I have made my peace with it, in most ways. I no longer flinch when touched, or experience uncontrollable flares of fury when I clash with others. Perhaps that is all I can ask from this experience—a teaching, finally, of patience.

I might have wished for a less direct method of instruction.

I had come up here, to this deserted and quiet place, to listen to the earth around me. Connected as I was to Luis Rocha, a Warden who wielded power through the rock, the living things grounded in it, I could feel the slow, steady heartbeat of the world as clearly as I sensed the smaller, faster pumping of the heart within my body.

And I could feel where shadows had fallen, in this sunlit and unforgiving place.

I reached in my pack and brought out the news stories I'd printed from Luis's computer. There'd been a string of odd disappearances in this part of the mountains—three female hikers over the past few months, yet no bodies found. Traces of them had been discovered in the form of torn clothing, along with abandoned tents and gear. Added to that, there had been two undeniable deaths, but not of women—of men, lone male hikers torn to pieces by some savage animal. Mountain lion, it had been speculated. Possibly a bear. The corpses had been too deteriorated to be certain, or so the official stories claimed.

I wondered.

It was, in fact, no affair of mine at all, and it had merely been an excuse to indulge my wish for solitude. I was more than prepared to forget the dead and missing hikers and spend the rest of the day—and the night—admiring the hush and whisper of the wilderness.

I did not get that chance.

The first warning came as a scrabbling fall of stones far down the trail, then a muttered curse in Spanish that carried clearly in the thin air. Then more rattling rocks, thumps, more cursing.

Eventually Luis, my Warden partner, came into view, puffing and sweating up the steep, treacherous trail. Reaching the ledge where I sat, he heaved in a deep breath, and collapsed in a heap at my side. "Holy crap," he said, and took out a bottle of water, most of which he downed in a desperate gulp, then dumped the rest over his sweat-soaked head. He wiped his lips with the back of his hand, and blotted his face with the sleeveless shirt he wore. I cast him a quick look, then went back to my contemplation of the view. Not that Luis was unpleasant to look at; he was, in fact, quite lovely, for a human. Tall, strong, with black hair and skin the color of caramel. Flame tattoos licked up both arms in still-life flickers. "*Madre*, woman, I'm an Earth Warden and even with all that connection to the Earth this is a crazy hard climb. You could slow down a little."

"I didn't ask you to follow," I told him. I was, however, not surprised that he had. Luis didn't like to let me stray too far, claiming that I was a magnet for trouble. That might have had some credence, actually; I *did* seem to draw attention to myself far too much for safety. Djinn arrogance. I couldn't seem to shake it, even in human form.

"Too damn bad," he said. "You don't get to go off roaming by yourself anymore. Where you go, I go. Just...not so fast. And maybe not so graceful."

I raised my eyebrows, but said nothing. The truth was, it pleased me in an obscure way that he had followed. There was a kind of solid peace that radiated from him, a sense of controlled and focused power.

In a Djinn, that would have been *very* attractive. I was not quite yet ready to believe there was anything that could make a mere human—even a Warden—attractive.

And yet.

Luis finished his water and stowed the bottle. He was still breathing hard and shining with sweat. I took out a bottle from my own pack and handed it over. Luis made a moan of indecent longing and reached for it, which made me smile. "I really love you right now," he said, and then thought about it for a second. "Evil bitch."

That made me smile more. I rested my chin on my crossed arms and looked out across the world, bathed in clean fresh sunlight. Below us, humans toiled and polluted, loved and created, hated and destroyed. Up here, it was almost like being a Djinn again, a creature above the earth, yet completely a part of it. I could feel the slow, sure heartbeat of the Mother herself.

"Energy bar?" Luis, ever practical, was rooting in his backpack for food. I held out my hand, and he passed one of the wrapped bars over. It tasted like flavored sawdust, but it would serve. I was not overly concerned with the needs of my body just now. "So, why'd we haul our asses all the way up here, anyway?"

I hadn't asked him to come along, and I wasn't feeling particularly cooperative. "Perhaps I like the view."

He gave me a filthy look. "You'd better not go with that one. There's a tram, *chica*. You know, you get in it, it hauls ass up the mountain all on its own without all the sweating and muscle cramps."

I couldn't explain it to him at first, and then I slowly said, "I needed to feel my feet on the ground. I needed to sense the earth around me. I needed—order, in all of the chaos."

That made him pause. He squinted, wiped sweat from his forehead, and took another drink of water before nodding. "Yeah, okay," he said. "I got that. Hate it, but I got it. So. Better now?"

"In time," I said.

"Because it's going to take us about the same number of hours getting down off this rock, and I don't want to try it in the dark. Going to get cold, too." He eyed me at an oblique angle. "Cass. Half an hour, then we got to go, okay?"

"If you're that worried, maybe we should start back now," I said, and stood up. He held up his hands in surrender.

"Okay, okay, I confess, I'm done in, Survival Girl. Give me half an hour. I need to rehydrate, or you'll be watching my body as it bounces down the side of the mountain."

I snorted, but sank back down into a crouch. It was a very still day, little breeze. He was right; as the sun drifted toward its western horizon, I could feel the heat leaving the air. It would stay in the rocks a while longer, but by full night, it would be cold and clear.

"You ready to tell me why we're really out here?" he asked me. I gazed at him a long moment, and a random whisper of wind came out of the chasm below us and blew pale hair back from my face. I'd taken the pink highlights out of it, leaving it puffball white. My skin remained pale, as pale as any human I had ever seen. I was—exotic.

Luis called me beautiful, but I did not feel beautiful. I felt... lost. Better, in the wilderness, but still disconnected. Drifting.

"There were reports of something out here," I said. "Some—thing that comes out at dusk. There have been disappearances, a few deaths."

"Accidents?"

"Perhaps. Or animals." Or something else. There was an old, unusual feel to this place, a wildness I had not felt in many places—not since the humans had civilized the world so thoroughly. "I don't know."

Luis frowned and looked around, at the scrub brush, and the deeper shadows of the pine forest just below us. "Maybe a mountain lion," he said. "We're in their territory."

"Maybe."

"But you don't think so."

I shrugged. I had no evidence; in fact, I had nothing more than instinct, a whisper of something that could not even be defined as suspicion.

Restlessness, likely enough. Our lives had been difficult lately. My first Warden partner, Manny Rocha, had been shot down in a senseless act of violence, along with his wife, and neither I nor Luis had reconciled our emotions. Luis had blamed me, and I had blamed myself; neither of us was right, or wrong. But trust was, at times, a thin shadow between us. I preferred not to shine a bright light on it.

"Okay," Luis said, sounding equal parts disappointed and annoyed. "Give me another fifteen minutes. I've got to work some of these damn cramps out."

I sat silent as he rubbed his calf muscles—which were indeed cramping, I could see the muscles jumping under his skin—and watched the wind whip through the trees below, bending them first one way, then another. If I listened carefully I could hear the voices of tourists brought up from the tram; they never ventured far from the safe, patrolled paths, so there was no danger of them making this final, perilous ascent and disturbing us. They'd buy their cheap souvenirs, take photographs, and leave as they had come.

"It's the journey," I whispered to myself.

"What?"

"Your age seems to value the destination so highly. All this fast travel, transporting from one spot to the next, rushing without experiencing. Recording to see later, at a distance. I don't understand it. Why do you choose to live so—disconnected?"

It was Luis's turn to be silent. He shrugged and kept working on his muscles. After a moment, I reached over and placed a hand over his leg, feeling the tense jump of the tissues beneath, and he took in a startled breath.

I took power from him. It felt like hot, golden sunlight moving through my body, and then I directed it out again, through my pale fingertips. Refined by the core of me, the part that was still and would always be Djinn, the power sank in deep, healing, soothing, restoring. "So odd that human Wardens can't heal themselves," I said. "That must be annoying."

"Not really," he said. Luis was now bracing himself, both hands rigid on the stone behind him, and his voice came out strained and soft. "I'd rather give than receive, anyway." His face was flushed now, and his breath came shallow and quick.

I took my hand away. He flopped back full length on the stone and put a forearm over his eyes to block out the sun, and to prevent me from seeing his expression. I didn't need to. There were certain...complications to this arrangement between us.

Healing, whether applied from him to me, or from me to him, still touched on human nerves in a way that was either painful or extraordinarily sexual.

I suspected the latter, in this case. Which meant that it was better to be up and moving, quickly, before he could suspect I felt the distant echo from him. Before it could affect me, and build between us like supernatural feedback. I stood, grabbed my pack and gathered up the empty water bottles. As I did, Luis took the arm away from his eyes and looked at me, squinting into the sunlight. I offered him a hand, and he took it to pull himself upright, testing his legs carefully before dropping my hand and stepping well away. I watched him, still hyper-aware of his presence; that was the lingering effect of the healing, I knew, but there was something else in it as well.

He glanced up at me as he shrugged on his backpack, eyebrows raised in challenge.

I shook my head, and started for the trail head.

The trail down was certainly no easier than it had been on the climb up; in fact, it took considerably more care, now that I was more aware of the failing afternoon light, and Luis's presence. I did not care to see him hurt on my behalf.

We were well into the shadows and premature evening of the trees when the first howl came, rising and falling in an eerie cadence. More than one beast. A chorus of them. I stopped, panting and wiping sweat from my face, and looked at Luis, who had gone very still. The sound grew, hushing birds and normal forest noise, and then faded away.

"I freaking hate it when you're right," he said. "Just so you know."

I wasn't fond of the fact myself, at this moment. "Wolves?"

"That's no wolf pack. And bears don't howl. Isn't a mountain lion, either."

"Then what is it?"

"Something that shouldn't be here," he said, and under the bronze color of his skin he seemed pale and shaken. "Something wrong, Cass. Really wrong. Let's move it."

"But—"

"This isn't something for just the two of us to handle."

"How do you know—?"

"I know, all right?"

"You know what it is."

He took in a deep breath. "Maybe. But the point is, a couple of Wardens alone out here isn't going to cut it. Let's get moving, fast."

I was unconvinced, but Luis's concern was genuine enough. We increased our pace, though the going remained slow; the trail was rough and treacherous, growing more so as the shadows deepened. It would be full dark before we exited the woods, even barring any delays or accidents.

Within another half hour, our pace had decreased even further, and the howl sounded again—distant, but chilling. I could barely make out Luis's face in the gloom. The sun was scraping the western horizon, expiring fast, and we were still in the thick of the trees. The temperature was also dropping, bringing chilly gusts of wind to whip the limbs of the pine trees and create a whispering hiss that sounded like a warning.

"We're not going to make it out before dark," I said. "I'm sorry. I hadn't planned for two of us. I was going to stay here for the night."

"Flashlights," he said. "Keep moving."

I had packed two, and so had he—sturdy things, and bright, but the artificial light seemed to only serve to make what it illuminated seem harsh and strange. Our pace increased, but so did our pursuers.

When the howls came again, they sounded closer.

Luis clicked off his light, and after a moment, I did the same. We stood in silence, listening. I felt something echoing through his connection to the earth— something strange and as dark as the falling night.

"What is it?" I asked. "What's out here?"

"Something old," he said. "Very old. It's an avatar."

Avatars were rarely encountered in the human world; they were manifestations of old powers, very old. Eternal, but rarely emerging from their sleep to possess and drive a human. The Greeks had known of them, and the Romans. The races and tribes even older had a history of encounters with the dark at the rawest levels—a history the Djinn had observed, even if there was little written record of it in the human world.

But here? Now? *Why?*

"What kind of avatar?"

"Madness," he said. "Primal madness."

I felt a cold chill sweep over my all-too-mortal flesh. As a Djinn, I had seen the rites of Dionysius and Bacchus enacted. I'd seen the frenzy sweep through the Bacchae as they were driven to leave behind their human, civilized selves.

I had seen the destruction they left behind.

"The missing women," I said. "Bacchae. Following the avatar."

"And they're hunting," Luis said. "Tonight."

The howls sounded again, a high, wild sound that echoed from the stones. Then the howls dissolved into frenzied screaming, filled with triumph and fury, and I heard beneath it the cries of something that voiced its pain without words. An animal. Something large.

A rabbit burst from the underbrush and dashed past us, frantic and glassy-eyed. Then another. A family of raccoons crossed the path ahead of us, fleeing the same direction, and in another moment, a doe bounded in pursuit.

"Move," Luis barked, and we increased our speed as much as we dared. More animals flashed across the limited scope of our flashlights, fixed only for an instant by the bright beams. None of them paused.

The last, another doe, had long bloody scrapes down her flanks, and she was running flat out, panting, head down. Running for her life.

I remembered the male hikers, bodies torn and half-consumed by predators. They'd never understood their risks. Never had a chance.

That chorused howl again, closer now. Chilling and yet fevered.

Luis kept moving, focused on the path, taking each step deliberately, but with all possible speed. He knew, at least. He understood what little chance either of us stood against the madness of an avatar. Earth powers might allow us to fight, a little, but our chances of truly defeating one were slim, at best.

These were the nightmares of Mother Earth, thrown up in her troubled, ages-long sleep. And they shared her power, deep in their roots.

The air smelled suddenly rank and sweet around us, drowned in rotted syrup. I whirled, flashlight flaring pale against tree trunks, swallowed in dark gaps, then reflecting suddenly from a *face*. Filthy, bearded and matted with dirt and leaves. A young man's face, and a bare, tanned, nude body whipped with scars and bruises and old dried blood.

His eyes were ancient and empty and yet full of something so intoxicating that I felt myself falling...falling...I tasted honey on my lips, felt the heat of liquor firing my veins. Felt the universe shattering around me into pieces, fierce hot pieces, and my skin was burning, even my hair, too hot, *too hot*...

I heard a thump as my pack slipped off my shoulders and fell to the trail, but it seemed so far away now. There was nothing in the world but the glow and fire and dark intoxication of the woodsman's eyes. I ripped at my shirt, pulling it apart in a frenzy. *Too hot. Burning. Had to get cool.*

"Cass!" Hands grabbed me and spun me around, a confusing whirl, and my flashlight beam fell on another face, on rich dark skin and wide black eyes and strong, flame-marked arms. "Cass, stop! Stop it!"

I slashed at him with hooked fingers, and he flinched backward. I turned, flashlight stabbing darkness in nervous jerks.

The woodsman was gone. I staggered, screamed, and heard the ring of madness in my voice. The rising, disbelieving tone of loss, of need. I still felt the burning in my veins, my skin, and I ripped again at my clothes, shredding, snapping threads like spider webs.

Luis—that was his name, Luis—grabbed me from behind, twisted my arms behind me, and forced me down to my knees on the hard rock, then forward, on to my face. The pain made me whimper with pleasure, and a growl of hunger came out of my mouth. *Violence.* That would sooth the burning. If I could run, chase, rip, tear, consume...

Luis put his full weight on me to hold me face down on the path as I convulsed, trying to get up, to run, to hunt.

"No," he panted, and I was overwhelmed with the *smell* of him, the rich male animal musk of his sweat, his body, his sex.

If not the hunt, then this. *This.*

"Oh Christ," he murmured, and I felt him shudder in response. He was feeling what I felt now, too close for there to be emotional distance between us. The bond that fed his energy into me also echoed back, and he could not fail to know what I wanted. What I needed. "Cass, stay still. *Stay still.* Breathe. Come on, this isn't you. This isn't what a Djinn does."

I wasn't a Djinn. My body—my body—

It is only a body, the cold core of me whispered. *And I am a Djinn. A **Djinn**. Not an animal, driven by meat and fury.*

I shuddered and went limp under Luis's weight, a submission that made the beast within me shriek and writhe inside. He didn't move for a long moment, then whispered, "Cass?"

"Let me go," I said. My throat felt raw with fury, as if I'd breathed in superheated air. "*Off!*"

He rolled away. I rolled the other way, breathing hard, and crouched with my back against the rough bark of a pine tree. I felt hot, still, and the fury pounding through my veins was maddening, trembling on the edge of uncontrollable. My shirt hung in rags around me, and the fluttering pieces annoyed me; I pulled it free and threw it away, snarling, and glared down at the thin sports bra that I still wore beneath it. I had ripped it in places, but it was mostly intact.

My denim shorts had survived my frenzy, though they were fraying at the hems in untidy strings. I struggled with an urge to strip them off, rip at them with teeth and nails, and closed my eyes to focus on slowing my hot, panting breaths.

The howls sounded again, a longing chorus that pulled at the desire inside me.

"Cassiel." Luis's voice. He'd ventured closer, but he was keeping a safe distance between us. "What happened?"

"The avatar," I said. "I saw him."

"*Him?*"

"The Bacchae are followers. They have no mind, only hungers. I saw the avatar. He *thinks*. We have to stop him if we want to stop them."

But the Bacchae were his guard, his army of teeth and flesh and claws. There was no avoiding a confrontation with them, if we hunted him. Just as there was no avoiding the fact that I remained perilously close to becoming one of them. I had to push aside the memory of the avatar's eyes, of the furiously empty hunger in them, of the sweet, hot intoxication of honey on my lips and in my blood. I *had to.* Or I would turn on Luis in an instant, and the first drop of blood I drew would trigger the final frenzy, reduce me to a naked, clawing, biting animal made of hunger and lust. I would not stop. I would take everything from him, down to the marrow of his bones, and then I would be lost.

"Can you handle this?" Luis asked me. He sounded tense, cautious, ready to move back at a single tremor from me. "Because I need to know. I can't turn my back on you if you're not in control."

"I'm fine," I lied. I had to make it true by sheer will; Luis couldn't defend himself from other threats if he had to watch me as well. "We have to find the avatar *now*, if we want to survive the night." Because the Bacchae would have caught Luis's scent by now, that rich male musk that had drenched me in frenzy. They'd chase him down and rip, rape, consume. It was what the avatar had infused in them. Individually, they were normal human women, probably mild and gentle creatures. But here, in the wild, with the honey and wine in their veins, they were Furies.

I rose smoothly and loped off into the dark. Luis cursed and stumbled in pursuit. I did not need a flashlight, now; my eyes pulled in light in new ways, new colors, painting the world in flashes of red and gold and white. The eyes of the avatar, shared with his hunters.

I could feel him out in the darkness, moving through the forest. Wandering. Seeking...whatever fathomless thing avatars sought. It was nothing humans could understand, and the human body it was using at present would be destroyed in the process, either from hunger or thirst or sheer overdriven exhaustion. It would leap to another male body if it could, unless there was nothing to receive its spirit. Then it would sink back into the earth, back into sleep.

Luis. Luis would be here to receive it. I couldn't permit that to happen.

In the next second, I realized that I couldn't worry about that; I had to think of myself first. The avatar's presence pulled me like a tide, drawing me closer, and I heard him now, padding through the forest, plunging through brush and thorns, leaving bare, bloody footprints on the ground and rocks. I smelled his rotted-honey stench.

I ran, loping like a lion giving chase, feeling the frenzy inside me mount and boil.

I burst out of the trees into a clearing. Overhead, the stars were white cold chips set in an onyx sky. A crescent moon had cleared the eastern horizon, bathing the small meadow in icy light.

The avatar stood in the center of it, staring up at the moon, arms raised. His back was to me, and I saw the claw marks scoring his back, his buttocks. The scratches and cuts. The trickling black blood.

Ecstasy was a deadly dangerous, shockingly beautiful thing.

I dropped into a crouch, teeth bared, made all animal in his presence. The pounding of sweet, hot fire inside me rose up, burning all my control to ashes.

All except that ice-cold core that had been mine since the beginning of time. *I am Djinn,* it whispered. *I am not his meat. I will not be turned.*

His back remained to me. His worship was aimed at the moon, and I could see the shudders running through him—sexual, most surely. I could feel the pulses from here, booming inside me like a drum.

I could not approach him, not without losing what little control remained. If I did, I would end up pinned beneath his rampant body, screaming, biting, giving and receiving violence and sex.

I reached instead for the rich warm glow of power, grounded through Luis, and brought it up around the avatar's feet.

The grasses whipped up, knotting into ropes, growing at a staggering pace. They tied his ankles, then wrapped his legs, his torso...and a thick, meaty vine whipped around his neck and began to tighten.

Behind me, I heard the hollow shriek of the Bacchae. They had found Luis's trail now, and I sensed the hot burst of his fear through the link between us. He couldn't outrun them. Not in the dark. He'd have to turn and fight—a battle he was sure to lose.

The howls and shrieks burst out of the night, and I thought I heard Luis call my name, but my world had narrowed to the avatar, and the vine around his neck. I poured all the power I could muster into it, commanding the living green rope to tighten, to squeeze, to crush the life out of the avatar before his minions tore the life out of Luis.

It wasn't going to work .

The vine was withering fast. The earth didn't wish to kill him; the creature was part of it, part of *her*. A memory, a nightmare, a dream. Something lost and almost pitiable in its hunger and loneliness. I couldn't fight him with the tools of the earth. Iron wouldn't kill him. Neither would stone. I could batter at him, and the life inside him would heal all I inflicted, because he was raw, bloody power, and nothing else.

I lunged, hit the avatar in the back, and slammed him face down to the grass. The bonds I'd put around him withered, blackened, and turned to ash, and his slick naked body writhed, bucked, tried to turn to face me. I couldn't risk that. I put a hand on the back of his head and slammed it deeper into the dirt, snarling, but somehow he slipped free, and his body moved beneath me, and then his eyes...

...his *eyes*...

I felt sanity pour out of me like water from a broken jar, and the moonlight burned cold and empty, blinding me, and suddenly I wanted...I felt...I was...

No.

I am Djinn.

The thing inside me, the thing in the core of me, that tiny spark of ice and rage that would never be human, seized control of my hands, grabbed the avatar's jaw in my left hand, the back of his head in my right, and pulled power out of Luis in a blinding flood, a scorching wave that burned my muscles with its force.

I don't remember twisting his head, but I remember the springy, tough resistance of his neck, his body trying to fight me, and I remember the exact instant that the fight was lost, and his bones snapped with sudden, muffled clicks. I kept twisting as the body went limp beneath me. Kept twisting, jerking his head back and forth as if I would wrench his head off his shoulders like a bloody triumph.

His eyes...

His eyes faded into confusion, and then into silent darkness.

I felt, then saw, the black flood pour out of the corpse like mist, creeping over the meadow in all directions, searching for a host. It couldn't take me. The ice inside me wouldn't thaw.

Luis. It would take him first.

I stumbled away from the avatar's body and raced ahead of the mist.

I fell over the first of the Bacchae less than a hundred yards out from the clearing; her naked, battered body lay shuddering on the side of the narrow path. She was curled into a ball, shut away from the horror of what had taken hold of her. Without the avatar's power fueling them, the Bacchae were just...lost.

I picked her up and carried her. I couldn't leave her. The mist might reject a female avatar, but it might not. I had to keep all of them away from it.

I found Luis lying another hundred yards out, with the other two Bacchae. He was dirty and scored with cuts, but he'd avoided any serious injury. The Bacchae were, like the one I carried, naked, bloody, and pathetically bruised by their time of insanity; the bottoms of their feet were raw wounds, sliced and torn by their rampage through the forest. They had been knocked unconscious. Luis had collapsed, his breath ragged, felled most likely by the raw power I'd pulled from him to destroy the avatar's body.

I dumped the third Bacchae, and turned to face the black mist. It was mere threads now, spread too wide and too thinly.

The last whisper of the nightmare, creeping over the ground, crawling, searching blindly for rescue.

I dragged Luis another twenty yards, as a precaution.

The mist reached the Bacchae, and they twitched and whimpered and whined, even in their deep trauma.

It couldn't touch them. It had wounded them too deeply already. That was one small blessing.

I took hold of Luis's limp form beneath the arms and hauled, gritting my teeth, pulling him one torturous inch after another down the treacherous path until finally, I looked up to see that there was no black mist flowing toward me.

It had pooled on the ground, exhausted, and as I watched, it sank slowly into the ground from which it had come.

Gone like the nightmare it had been.

I collapsed next to Luis, my eyes full of the moon, and like the other Bacchae I curled in on myself, cold and empty and sick with what I had felt.

Luis stirred enough to gather me into his arms, and we lay together in the cold with the whisper of pines around us, as Mother Earth dreamed her insane, cold dreams of hunger and fear and loneliness and need.

After a long few minutes, Luis rolled to his feet and went back up the hill. I didn't have the strength to protest, curling back into my traumatized ball. The world seemed so cold. So quiet.

One after another, he carried the naked women down the path. He'd retrieved our packs, and he spread out a thin insulating ground cover, then bundled the three together under a blanket. He fed them some water, a little food, and gave them gentle touches on their hair, their faces.

They needed gentleness. I knew, because I was myself starved for it, and I hadn't sunk so deeply into the violence as the others.

As Luis worked on building a campfire, I managed to pull myself to a sitting position. He was shaking with exhaustion and weariness as he tried to set match to tinder. I took it from him and lit the fire, watched it catch with dull eyes, and took the bottle of water he passed me without much enthusiasm. The first mouthful tasted like filth, and I gagged and spat it out. My mouth still remembered the taste of honey and blood.

The second mouthful was better, and I swallowed and kept swallowing until the foreign taste was gone.

Luis settled back against a tree, stretching out his legs, and I sank down next to him. Not touching, not quite, until he reached out and pulled me closer. My head fell against his shoulder, and I felt his lips brush the dirty, sweating skin of my forehead.

"You're safe now," he said, and the heat of his body—a gentle warmth, not the burn of the avatar—crept into me in slow waves. Animal comfort, but a very different kind. I felt trembling muscles slowly begin to relax, and my breathing slowed to a deeper, slower rhythm. "Did he—did you—are you all right?"

I knew what he wanted to ask, and looked up into his face. He had dark eyes, shifting and gleaming in the firelight, but they were not empty. What was in them was gentle and warm and sweet, and it too came from the earth, from human kindness and compassion and...love.

"He didn't take me," I said, in all the ways it could be meant. "He couldn't. I'm not human, Luis. Not fully. You understand that?"

He did, and it made him sad. He touched my hair, stroked it, and the pleasure of that echoed inside us both. I relaxed and let my head rest once more against his chest, listening to the hollow rush of his breathing, the solid, steady beat of his heart.

"Don't worry about it. Being human ain't what it's cracked up to be," he said, and I knew he was looking at the women, who might never be able to face what they had done. What had been done to them, by forces they couldn't possibly comprehend or resist. "I'm glad you're who you are, Cassiel."

In that moment, that oddly gentle, oddly sweet moment that I closed my eyes and let the night steal over me...I was glad, too.

Rachel Caine is a fictional person who writes many, many novels, including the "Weather Warden" series (8 novels to date, and one more in 2010), the "Morganville Vampires" series (8 novels, with 12 planned), and the "Outcast Season" series (3 novels so far, with 1 more to come). She lives in the Dallas, Texas area. Her website is at **www.rachelcaine.com**

Cassiel was once a Djinn (genie), and is now, thanks to a disagreement with a higher ranking Djinn, trapped in human form as a punishment. Her only hope for long-term survival is partnership with a supernaturally-gifted Warden, Luis Rocha, who controls the elements of the earth. Cassiel and Luis both reside in Albuquerque, New Mexico, when not battling supernatural forces elsewhere.

Our titles are available at major book stores and local independent resellers who support Science Fiction and Fantasy readers like you.

EDGE Science Fiction
and Fantasy Publishing

Tesseract Books

www.edgewebsite.com

Our titles are available at major book stores and local independent resellers who support Science Fiction and Fantasy readers like you.

Alphanauts by J. Brian Clarke (tp) - ISBN: 978-1-894063-14-2
Apparition Trail, The by Lisa Smedman (tp) - ISBN: 978-1-894063-22-7
As Fate Decrees by Denysé Bridger (tp) - ISBN: 978-1-894063-41-8
Avim's Oath (Part Six of the Okal Rel Saga) by Lynda Williams (pb)
 - ISBN: 978-1-894063-35-7

Black Chalice, The by Marie Jakober (hb) - ISBN: 978-1-894063-00-7
Blue Apes by Phyllis Gotlieb (pb) - ISBN: 978-1-895836-13-4
Blue Apes by Phyllis Gotlieb (hb) - ISBN: 978-1-895836-14-1

Captives by Barbara Galler-Smith and Josh Langston (pb)
 - ISBN: 978-1-894063-53-1
Children of Atwar, The by Heather Spears (pb) - ISBN: 978-0-88878-335-6
Chilling Tales: Evil Did I Dwell - Lewd I Did Live dited by Michael Kelly (pb)
 - ISBN: 978-1-894063-52-4
Cinco de Mayo by Michael J. Martineck (pb) - ISBN: 978-1-894063-39-5
Cinkarion - The Heart of Fire (Part Two of The Chronicles of the Karionin)
 by J. A. Cullum - (tp) - ISBN: 978-1-894063-21-0
Clan of the Dung-Sniffers by Lee Danielle Hubbard (pb) - ISBN: 978-1-894063-05-0
Claus Effect, The by David Nickle & Karl Schroeder (pb) - ISBN: 978-1-895836-34-9
Claus Effect, The by David Nickle & Karl Schroeder (hb) - ISBN: 978-1-895836-35-6
Courtesan Prince, The (Part One of the Okal Rel Saga) by Lynda Williams (tp)
 - ISBN: 978-1-894063-28-9

Dark Earth Dreams by Candas Dorsey & Roger Deegan (comes with a CD)
 - ISBN: 978-1-895836-05-9
Darkness of the God (Children of the Panther Part Two)
 by Amber Hayward (tp) - ISBN: 978-1-894063-44-9
Demon Left Behind, The by Marie Jakober (pb) - ISBN: 978-1-894063-49-4
Distant Signals by Andrew Weiner (tp) - ISBN: 978-0-88878-284-7
Dreams of an Unseen Planet by Teresa Plowright (tp) - ISBN: 978-0-88878-282-3
Dreams of the Sea (Part 1 of Tyranaël) by Élisabeth Vonarburg (tp)
 - ISBN: 978-1-895836-96-7
Dreams of the Sea (Part 1 of Tyranaël) by Élisabeth Vonarburg (hb)
 - ISBN: 978-1-895836-98-1
Druids by Barbara Galler-Smith and Josh Langston (tp)
 - ISBN: 978-1-894063-29-6

Eclipse by K. A. Bedford (tp) - ISBN: 978-1-894063-30-2
Even The Stones by Marie Jakober (tp) - ISBN: 978-1-894063-18-0
Evolve: Vampire Stories of the New Undead edited by Nancy Kilpatrick (tp)
 - ISBN: 978-1-894063-33-3

Far Arena (Part Five of the Okal Rel Saga) by Lynda Williams (tp)
 - ISBN: 978-1-894063-45-6
Fires of the Kindred by Robin Skelton (tp) - ISBN: 978-0-88878-271-7
Forbidden Cargo by Rebecca Rowe (tp) - ISBN: 978-1-894063-16-6

Petrified World (Determine Your Destiny #1) by Piotr Brynczka (pb)
- ISBN: 978-1-894063-11-1
Plague Saint by Rita Donovan, The (tp) - ISBN: 978-1-895836-28-8
Plague Saint by Rita Donovan, The (hb) - ISBN: 978-1-895836-29-5
Pock's World by Dave Duncan (tp) - ISBN: 978-1-894063-47-0
Pretenders (Part Three of the Okal Rel Saga) by Lynda Williams (pb)
- ISBN: 978-1-894063-13-5

Reluctant Voyagers by Élisabeth Vonarburg (pb) - ISBN: 978-1-895836-09-7
Reluctant Voyagers by Élisabeth Vonarburg (hb) - ISBN: 978-1-895836-15-8
Resisting Adonis by Timothy J. Anderson (tp) - ISBN: 978-1-895836-84-4
Resisting Adonis by Timothy J. Anderson (hb) - ISBN: 978-1-895836-83-7
Righteous Anger (Part Two of the Okal Rel Saga) by Lynda Williams (tp)
- ISBN: 897-1-894063-38-8

Silent City, The by Élisabeth Vonarburg (tp) - ISBN: 978-1-894063-07-4
Slow Engines of Time, The by Élisabeth Vonarburg (tp)
- ISBN: 978-1-895836-30-1
Slow Engines of Time, The by Élisabeth Vonarburg (hb)
- ISBN: 978-1-895836-31-8
Stealing Magic by Tanya Huff (tp) - ISBN: 978-1-894063-34-0
Strange Attractors by Tom Henighan (pb) - ISBN: 978-0-88878-312-7

Taming, The by Heather Spears (pb) - ISBN: 978-1-895836-23-3
Taming, The by Heather Spears (hb) - ISBN: 978-1-895836-24-0
Ten Monkeys, Ten Minutes by Peter Watts (tp) - ISBN: 978-1-895836-74-5
Ten Monkeys, Ten Minutes by Peter Watts (hb) - ISBN: 978-1-895836-76-9
Tesseracts 1 edited by Judith Merril (pb) - ISBN: 978-0-88878-279-3
Tesseracts 2 edited by Phyllis Gotlieb & Douglas Barbour (pb)
- ISBN: 978-0-88878-270-0
Tesseracts 3 edited by Candas Jane Dorsey & Gerry Truscott (pb)
- ISBN: 978-0-88878-290-8
Tesseracts 4 edited by Lorna Toolis & Michael Skeet (pb)
- ISBN: 978-0-88878-322-6
Tesseracts 5 edited by Robert Runté & Yves Maynard (pb)
- ISBN: 978-1-895836-25-7
Tesseracts 5 edited by Robert Runté & Yves Maynard (hb)
- ISBN: 978-1-895836-26-4
Tesseracts 6 edited by Robert J. Sawyer & Carolyn Clink (pb)
- ISBN: 978-1-895836-32-5
Tesseracts 6 edited by Robert J. Sawyer & Carolyn Clink (hb)
- ISBN: 978-1-895836-33-2
Tesseracts 7 edited by Paula Johanson & Jean-Louis Trudel (tp)
- ISBN: 978-1-895836-58-5
Tesseracts 7 edited by Paula Johanson & Jean-Louis Trudel (hb)
- ISBN: 978-1-895836-59-2
Tesseracts 8 edited by John Clute & Candas Jane Dorsey (tp)
- ISBN: 978-1-895836-61-5
Tesseracts 8 edited by John Clute & Candas Jane Dorsey (hb)
- ISBN: 978-1-895836-62-2
Tesseracts Nine edited by Nalo Hopkinson and Geoff Ryman (tp)
- ISBN: 978-1-894063-26-5
Tesseracts Ten: A Celebration of New Canadian Specuative Fiction
edited by Robert Charles Wilson and Edo van Belkom (tp)
- ISBN: 978-1-894063-36-4

Tesseracts Eleven: Amazing Canadian Speulative Fiction
  edited by Cory Doctorow and Holly Phillips (tp)
  - ISBN: 978-1-894063-03-6

Tesseracts Twelve: New Novellas of Canadian Fantastic Fiction
  edited by Claude Lalumière (pb)
  - ISBN: 978-1-894063-15-9

Tesseracts Thirteen: Chilling Tales from the Great White North
  edited by Nancy Kilpatrick and David Morrell (tp)
  - ISBN: 978-1-894063-25-8

Tesseracts 14: Strange Canadian Stories
  edited by John Robert Colombo and Brett Alexander Savory (tp)
  - ISBN: 978-1-894063-37-1

Tesseracts Q edited by Élisabeth Vonarburg & Jane Brierley (pb)
  - ISBN: 978-1-895836-21-9

Tesseracts Q edited by Élisabeth Vonarburg & Jane Brierley (hb)
  - ISBN: 978-1-895836-22-6

Those Who Fight Monsters: Tales of Occult Detectives
  edited by Justin Gustainis (pb) - ISBN: 978-1-894063-48-7

Throne Price by Lynda Williams and Alison Sinclair (tp)
  - ISBN: 978-1-894063-06-7

Time Machines Repaired Whie-U-Wait by K. A. Bedford (tp)
  - ISBN: 978-1-894063-42-5